S0-AVY-793

"When we get it up, I'll try to twist it to my side, and you lift on yours, and between us maybe we can roll it over."

"And if there's an alligator under there?" Dodee asked again.

"Anything moves down there, drop it."

"You don't have to tell me twice."

They heaved the aft end out of the water. And Dodee screamed. Something like a giant turtle swirled from under.

Except, it wasn't a turtle, not unless turtles wore a green shirt and green cargo pants with zippers above the knees for turning them into shorts.

"I told you this was a crime scene," Harold the Hound said in a flat voice.

Then Phyllis screamed as the body of the Natural Resources agent rolled on its side.

Jim stared down at what was left of Hank Davis's bearded face after it had reverted to a lower position on the food chain.

★

"...a good plot, good characterizations, an unusual setting, and a smooth, easy-to-read writing style..."

—*Mystery News*

"...fans will find plenty to enjoy...a surprise ending; the outdoor scenes are vivid; and the story is well-paced."

—*Booklist*

Previously published Worldwide Mystery titles by
PETER ABRESCH

BLOODY BONSAI
KILLING THYME

TIP
A
CANOE

Peter
Abresch

WORLDWIDE.

TORONTO • NEW YORK • LONDON
AMSTERDAM • PARIS • SYDNEY • HAMBURG
STOCKHOLM • ATHENS • TOKYO • MILAN
MADRID • WARSAW • BUDAPEST • AUCKLAND

If you purchased this book without a cover you should be aware
that this book is stolen property. It was reported as "unsold and
destroyed" to the publisher, and neither the author nor the
publisher has received any payment for this "stripped book."

For my brother Robert J. Abresch
who is and always will be uglier than me,
and his wonderful wife, Nellie; my sister Lorraine Killen
who is and always will be more beautiful than me;
and my brother Ralph E. Rice who tells
and always will tell a better story than me.
I love you all.

TIP A CANOE

A Worldwide Mystery/February 2002

First published by Write Way Publishing, Inc.

ISBN 0-373-26412-7

Copyright © 2001 by Peter Abresch.
Pfwriter@olg.com
http://www.olg.com/pfwriter
All rights reserved. No part of this book may be reproduced
or transmitted in any form or by any means, electronic or
mechanical, including photocopying, recording or by any
information storage and retrieval system, without permission
in writing from the publisher. For information, contact:
Write Way Publishing, Inc., P.O. Box 441278, Aurora, CO
80044 U.S.A.

All characters in this book are fictitious, and any resemblance to
actual persons, living or dead, is purely coincidental.

® and TM are trademarks of Harlequin Enterprises Limited.
Trademarks indicated with ® are registered in the United States
Patent and Trademark Office, the Canadian Trade Marks Office
and in other countries.

Printed in U.S.A.

To all the folks at Elderhostel Inc.
who have treated me so generously.
On all the Elderhostels I have attended
I have found nothing but fun, camaraderie
and adventurous spirits and nary a body...yet.

Acknowledgments

To my editor

Dorrie O'Brien
whose $50,000 advance to me got lost in the mail
—oh, yeah.

Dewey Pleake and Annemarie Abresch
who pre-editing helped me dot the *i*'s and cross the *t*'s

John Lindsay and Don A. Campbell
who helped me brainstorm this sucker

Russel Bonner
who shared his bereavement with me

Robin Drain Duguid of Weyerhaeuser Co.
and
John Williams of Mountain Lumber Co.
for sharing their knowledge of trees and woods

Lex Glover
S.C. Dept. of Natural Resources
for sharing his knowledge of South Carolina birds

Pam Ardern
Clemson University
for on-site knowledge and a great Elderhostel

Carl & Joan Middaugh and Helen & Morton Sternheim
for letting me use their Elderhostel reports

Cinderella Ages

She wears
The charm of years,
And beauty shines from eyes
Alive with ageless tales of love's
Magic.
—James W. Olson
Editor, *Elderhostel Notebook*
Ehnotebook@aol.com

ONE

BRING BUG SPRAY.

Does that sound like a fun week?

Jim Dandy powered his blue Lincoln down Interstate 95.

"Bring bug spray?" he said aloud.

He glanced at his passenger, but Dodee Swisher kept her head of full soft curls, about the color of ripened wheat, buried in the information sheet on her lap.

"What is bug spray, anyway?" he asked.

She wore a light-blue jean shirt with red plaid showing at the collar and cuffs, cream-colored denim pants, and soft loafers on her feet, her trim body a testament to leading senior citizen aerobics classes.

"Like window spray to make the bugs clean? Hair spray to make them stiff?" He turned down his lips and nodded. "Now stiff might work. If you wanted to conjure up a really fun Elderhostel week, you'd say, 'bring genital spray.'" He glanced at her again. "Right?"

"I'm not touching that."

"The trouble with spray is it covers everything. Pan spray to make pans slick. House spray to make rooms smell nice. WD-40 spray to loosen nuts." He grinned. "Probably not something you want in a genital spray."

"Repellent."

"Damn right it would be repellent."

"Bug"—she let it hang in the air a moment—"repellent."

"Oh, that sounds a whole lot better. Bring bug repellent. Does that sound like more fun?"

She lifted her head and her cornflower blue eyes riveted him with points of steel. "How does 'single rooms' sound?"

He turned back to the black-ribbon road, cut between leafless trees, as the flat South Carolina countryside rolled by. The air conditioner purred away against an unseasonable mid-afternoon sun that belied the lateness of October.

Had he pushed one button too many?

How did single rooms sound?

About as welcome as an Arab terrorist at a bar mitzvah.

"Forget about the bug spray," he said. "As long as we're here together I know it will be a fun week."

"Are those words from your heart or farther down?"

No answer to that.

He hadn't seen Dodee in three months, and meeting her at the Columbia airport—five foot two with a smile that lit up her lightly tanned face—had made his heart jump. Made everything jump for that matter.

"We will have fun," Dodee said, and reached over to pat his knee. "You were the one who wanted to do something more active this Elderhostel."

He chewed on the inside of his lip.

This was their third Elderhostel. Adventures in Learning for those over fifty-five. They had studied Bonsai in New Jersey, when he had first met her, and then were together again in Baltimore where they learned Mediterranean cooking. But Adventures in Learning didn't capture the flavor of fun and camaraderie these things engendered.

He frowned.

Of course, in their case it had been much more. What could be more benign than studying bonsai and cooking? And yet bodies kept popping up at both places. They nearly ended up in jail on the first one. In fact, on the second as well.

So, now they were off into the woods. Canoeing and

hiking through swamps. Not much chance of finding bodies mucking about in the muck, which was just as well considering Dodee's double predilection for nosing into police matters and getting him hip deep in horse shit.

"We're minding our own business this trip."

The big blues turned to him again. "What do you mean?"

"I mean we're staying out of police stuff. That's not a question, Dodee. That's an ord—that's a statement," he said, switching at the last moment as he remembered her remark about separate bedrooms.

She smiled and pointed at him. "If it hadn't been for that police stuff, sweetheart, we might never have gotten into—to put it delicately—the other stuff."

He pressed his lips together and glared at the road.

Now was not the time to be contrary.

"Besides," she said, "I doubt if we'll find many police officers running around the swamp." She tapped the papers in her lap. "You want me to read the rest of this list or not? If you'd read your own list at home—"

"Why?" He held out his hand. "You told me everything over the phone. Bring shorts; I brought shorts. Bring layered clothing in case it gets cold; I brought layered clothing in case it gets cold. See how it all fits?"

Dodee folded up the papers in her lap and stuffed them into a large envelope. "Suppose I hadn't been there to read all the things to bring?"

"If you had not been there, I would not be here in South Carolina. If all I wanted to do was tramp through a swamp, I'd have stayed home in Maryland."

"You have a swamp? With cypress trees?"

"As a matter of fact, yes. The cypress swamp in Calvert County is the northernmost stand of natural cypress in the country."

"Then why did you want to come on this Elderhostel?"

He turned to her and grinned. "What was that other stuff you mentioned?"

TWO

THEY TURNED OFF Interstate 95 at Exit 115.

"We're supposed to be heading away from Manning," Dodee said.

"I'm heading away from Manning, wherever the hell that is."

"And look for a sign for Rev. J.W. Carter Road."

"That's a strange name for a road. Why not Carter Road? Or Rev. Road? Even J.W. Road?"

"You don't seem to be too happy about coming on this Elderhostel."

"Oh, I am." He reached across and took her hand. "I'm just grousing because of the long trip down. Still, it's a funny name for a road, don't you think?"

"I don't know, but we don't want to miss it."

"Reminds me of a road back home called Ball's Graveyard Road." He stepped down on the gas, plowing the Lincoln down the state road, glancing to the left as they passed a road without a sign. "Actually that made more sense because Ball's Graveyard Road went by Ball's Graveyard."

"We passed a road back there."

"I know. Can't be it. There was no sign." He rolled his shoulders a couple of times, trying to loosen them up from the long drive. "The problem came when a county commissioner died and there was a movement afoot to rename the road after him."

He pointed up ahead to a car pulled over to the side of

the road, a tan SUV with a pontoon boat on an attached trailer.

"Shall we ask?"

"Just keep going, we'll come to it."

"No, we could go on for miles," he said, pulling over.

"I thought men didn't like to stop and ask directions."

He got out and strode alongside the pontoon boat on the trailer, *Two For the Road* painted in red on its side, fishing rods sticking up from built-in holders. A man stood at the back door of the tan Mercedes SUV with Missouri license plates, manhandling what looked like oxygen bottles and scuba gear.

"Hi," Jim called.

The man spun around to confront him. Two small eyes peered out from under the heavy brow of a bulldog face, accentuated by fleshy jowls. The meatiness of his face echoed in his body, a camo shirt with the sleeves cut off at the shoulders covered a mid-forties spread, but it had a hardness to it, like an overweight truck driver who could toss beer barrels around all day long. He stood with his hands on the hips of cut-off jeans.

"I wonder if you could tell me where Rev. J.W. Carter Road is?"

A head popped up on the other side of the pontoon boat, a younger man, early thirties with a flat crew cut that complemented his straight jaw to give him a squarish face. Black hair partially covered his scrawny, bare chest. "We ain't from around here. Just fishing."

"Wait a minute," the first man said, features softening, "I got some maps might show it." He reached into the back of his Mercedes and came out with a roll of maps that he spread on a seat of the pontoon boat. "What was the name again?"

"Rev. J.W. Carter Road." He turned and called to Dodee. "What's the name of the place?"

She stuck her head out the window. "The Robert M. Cooper Leadership Center."

He took his reading glasses and slipped them on as he turned to the man. "We're actually looking for the Robert M. Cooper Leadership Center. Supposed to be on a lake."

"Well, if it's on the Santee Lake, we got it here."

"Sarg," said his square-faced companion, raising his eyebrows.

"Yeah, Bill."

"That's the 4-H center."

"Huh?" Sarg glanced at Bill. "Oh, yeah, we got that." He shifted through three well-detailed maps of Lake Marion. "Here it is," he said, coming upon the R. M. Cooper 4-H Leadership Center on the fourth. He placed his hands on a point of land, then traced backward with his finger and found the road. "It looks like you passed it. I'd say go back a mile or two and it should be off to your right."

"Thanks. Sarg, is it?" Jim shook the man's hand. "What kind of fish you catching?"

"Whatever will bite," said the square-faced Bill from the other side of the trailer.

"We've been doing pretty good with wide-mouth bass," Sarg said.

"Well, thanks again," Jim said, storing his glasses back in his shirt pocket.

He hurried back and climbed into the driver's seat, swung the car around, gave a last wave to the crew of *Two For The Road,* and headed out.

"See," he said, "if we followed your philosophy, 'keep going and we'll find it,' we'd have ended up in Florida."

"Then we could have camped out in the sun and forgotten about the bug spray." She pointed ahead. "There's a road up here. And a bent-over sign. Can you see…? This is it. Rev. J.W. Carter Road."

He turned onto it and barreled along through wooded flat land, deserted of traffic except for a lone lumber truck coming the other way. "Still a dumb name for a road."

"What about your county commissioner?"

"My county commissioner? Oh, you mean about Ball's

Graveyard Road? Well, when the commissioner dropped dead of a heart attack, they wanted to rename it H. Gordon Truman Road, which is as bad as Rev. J.W. Carter Road. Others, those who didn't politically agree with H. Gordon Truman, wanted to keep it Ball's Graveyard. After much debate, a woman proposed a compromise to call it Truman's Ball's Road, and that ended the discussion."

"You're making this up."

"Would I lie to you? Today it's simply called Ball Road."

After a million miles they came to a spot of civilization called Davis Station. It reminded Jim of something he might find in the Australian outback, only wetter. A drinkery called the Bronco Club perched on one corner, a gas station on another, and a cotton gin farther on.

They followed the directions around the gas station to Rickenbaker Road and charged through some more flats for another two million miles to the entrance of Robert M. Cooper 4-H Leadership Center, woods and fields on the right, a parking lot and buildings on the left with a big lake on the other side of them. A "Welcome Elderhostelers" sign greeted them with an arrow pointing straight ahead, farther into the boonies.

Bring bug spray? Great, just great. Why had he wanted to come on an *active* Elderhostel?

He should have chosen an easier learning adventure. Like basket weaving. Or music appreciation. Or the art of gazing at the inside of your eyelids while stretching out between food breaks in the sun.

He followed the road, now a dirt track at the end of the world, running alongside the large lake—Lake Marion, Dodee said—and winding to an end in a small parking area littered with tall pine trees and bordered by railroad ties. Jim parked the Lincoln in front of a U-shaped building elongated on the left to form a large glassed-in room with a hip roof. They had arrived at what the map called the Conference Center, but it looked more like an Aztec motif motel, single story, beige stucco, with a grass courtyard in the center, their bring-bug-spray home-away-from-home.

He climbed out and slowly straightened muscles that had been cramped too long in a sitting position, first on the trip down from Maryland to Columbia Airport, where he had picked up Dodee, and then here. He went through a stretching routine he did everyday before exercising, an abbreviated one that helped limber him up. Dodee came around the car and put her arm under his and he allowed himself to be led down a hundred feet to the lake's edge. He gazed out at homes on the other side, maybe a mile away; the mid-afternoon sun cast a sheen on the water until a pontoon boat sped by and stirred its surface.

''Pretty, isn't it?''

He breathed in warm air, nodded, and turned to her. She had her little smug smile pasted on her upturned face and he bent and kissed her lips.

It was a wicked kiss.

It erased any lingering doubt why, bug spay or no, he came on this Elderhostel.

Yeah, buddy.

THREE

THEY ENTERED THE LARGE glassed-in extension to the motel-like building through a door onto a small hallway. Two restrooms led off it and Dodee slipped into the ladies' room. He cut left into the main room; two other couples looked up and nodded as he came in. Bowls of goodies—fruit, miniature candy bars, cheese cubes, mixed nuts—sat on end tables between easy chairs and settees placed around the glass wall perimeter. Two tables, each with four straight chairs, occupied the middle-land. A pass-through window and a door farther on led into a small kitchen where a coffeepot rested on a coffeemaker. He poured himself a cup and came back out to scoop up a handful of mixed nuts and stare out at the lake.

A few moments later Dodee came in. "Hi," she said. "Are we all here to go canoeing?"

"I hope so," said one of the women, wearing glasses and short gray hair in a style made famous by Dorothy Hamill, and gold pandas for earrings. She had the tan complexion of someone who worked a lot in a garden.

"That's what the program says," added the man sitting with her, looking up from a newspaper. He spread a warm smile on a long face with a bulbous nose and thin brown hair. "And that's what it better be."

"Yes, sir, it is canoeing," said the male half of the other couple, standing up from one of the tables. He had a round face, a bald head, a short, bantam-cock body, and spoke with a southern, no-nonsense voice. "The coordinator just drove down to the office to get her list. My name is Doctor Clyde Porter," he said, pronouncing it "Parter," "and this is my wife, Becky."

Becky gave them a no-nonsense smile, brief, pinched, and to the point. She was taller than the bantam Clyde, carried more weight as well, but edging up on the slim side of heavy. The mousy hair swept back in a severe bun, on a head held stiffly erect, lent an air of sternness to her pinched face.

"And we're the Gramms," said the woman with Hamill-cut hair, "Dorothy and Dave.'

"I'm the Dave," the bulbous-nosed husband said.

"I'm Dodee Swisher and this is my friend, Jim—James P. Dandy," she said, turning to give him a smile that said, *See, I didn't call you Jim Dandy.*

He nodded to the others, but in studying their faces he realized he hadn't been paying attention to the names.

Dodee would remember.

Anyway, that's what nametags were for.

Any Elderhosteler who didn't wear his nametag should be shot at dawn. That was his credo. It would humble those who thought they were so well known they didn't need a nametag, and be a major example for those left behind.

"I just hope everyone is up to this," Doctor Porter said. "Canoeing can be strenuous for those not used to activity."

"Yes," his wife Becky said, "the brochure said it was an active Elderhostel. We don't want anyone holding us back."

The Doctor nodded. "Had a drowning on this lake just yesterday."

"Where did you read that?" Dave Gramm asked, flipping through the newspaper. "I didn't see that."

"I heard it when we stopped for gas at Davis Station. Just happened yesterday; it's under investigation."

Dave nodded. "I guess that's why I didn't see it. I've been reading about that Spanish galleon they found off the coast near Georgetown."

"In the Bahamas?" Jim asked.

"No, right here in South Carolina."

Jim turned as the sun glinted off the windshield of a dusty red Ford SUV pulling into the rustic parking lot. A late-twenties woman hopped out dressed in a short-sleeved khaki shirt and shorts. Firm breasts, thin waist, and young legs.

He shook his head.

He exercised seven hours a week, but even so, he couldn't keep up with someone at that age doing absolutely nothing.

She bounced into the room with a bright smile on a round, lightly freckled face, blond hair swinging in a ponytail. "Okay—oh, we have two more. Hi, I'm Jody Sundance," she said, sticking out her hand to Dodee. "I'm the Elderhosteler coordinator for the week."

"Hi," Dodee answered. "I'm Dodee Swisher and this is my friend, James P. Dandy."

"Hello," Jim said and took the woman's firm, strong handshake. He showed her the Styrofoam cup. "I hope it was okay to pour some coffee."

"Oh, yes. Help yourself." Jody smiled again, squinting her eyes, and motioned with her hand to take the others into the conversation. "The Hospitality Room is set up for you all. So, please enjoy. Okay, let me put out my stuff and I'll give you your room assignments." She took over one of the tables and set out a list, Elderhostel packets, and nametags. "Since Elderhostel started collecting all money up front, it's made my life easier."

"There's been other Elderhostels here before?" Doctor Clyde Porter asked.

"We've had Elderhostels here for the last seven years, about four of them a quarter." She set about handing out nametags and packets and checking people off the list, starting out with Dorothy and Dave Gramm.

"Pardon me," Clyde Porter said as the Gramms started to leave. "Mind if I look at your newspaper?"

"It's not mine. It belongs here."

Jim picked up his and Dodee's packets and headed outside.

"Wait a minute," Dodee said as they reached the door, "I forgot my pocketbook."

He stepped outside and stood in the fresh air as a man lugged a suitcase in from the parking lot.

"Harold Rucker?" the man asked, his dark brown eyes set deep in a thin, lined face, his black hair under a straw hat, all placed on a lean, six-foot-plus body like a stock picture of a midwest farmer. All he needed was a piece of hay between his teeth.

"Excuse me?"

"Are you Harold Rucker?"

"I'm James P. Dandy."

"Leopold Kohl," he said, sticking out a surprisingly soft hand. "I'm supposed to be paired up with a Harold Rucker for a roommate. I saw you alone and thought you might be—"

Dodee came through the door. "Ready."

The small eyes turned to her. "My mistake. I see you already have a roommate, and far prettier than mine will be for sure."

"This is my friend, Dodee Swisher. Leopold Kohl."

"Leo. Less formal and austere." He tipped his straw hat to her, adding to his farmer posture. "Leo Kohl. Glad to know you, Dodee. Guess I better get in there and register."

They found their bring-bug-spray home-away-from-home two doors down the open walkway from the Hospitality Room, a motel-like accommodation with closet and sink immediately to the left, forming a small hallway to the bathroom beyond. Dresser with mirror and desk with lamps and chair lined the wall on the right. Two queen-sized beds occupied the majority of the floor space, with a night table in between. A picture window with a shelf looked out onto a few scrubby pine trees.

"See," he said, spreading his arms, "we each have a bed to ourselves."

She folded her arms and glanced sideways at him through long lashes. "I can live with that."

Jim rubbed his nose. "On the other hand, why muss up two beds and make more work for the cleaning women?"

"That's very generous of you, sweetheart, but they only come in to change the sheets on Wednesday."

He nodded. "Think I'll get the bags."

"I'll help."

They hiked out to the car and he folded up all his maps, unplugged his cell phone from the cigarette lighter—replacement for the cell phone that got smashed the last time they had been together—and stuffed them all in the glove compartment. Then he hefted his and Dodee's bags, while she brought her flat sketchbook case and her camera slung over one shoulder. He locked the Lincoln and they carried everything toward their room as two more cars arrived, kicking up a small dust cloud.

"We should have stopped off and picked up snacks," she said.

"Kidding me? Didn't you see all the candy and nuts they have laid out in the Hospitality Room?"

He hung up some of his clothes, put underwear in one of the drawers, left the rest in his bag on the spare bed, and stretched out on the other, watching her put things away in shelves and drawers and on hangers, taking up the lion's portion of storage space in spite of coming in on a plane.

She shut the dresser drawers and turned, hands on her hips, as if looking around for anything she had missed. She had a mature body, but trim, muscular, no doubt able to handle a canoe paddle without a lot of trouble.

"You want to take a walk?" she asked, then shook her head as she gazed down at him. "No, you're tired from the long drive down. In fact," she kicked off her shoes, "I could use a rest."

He put out his arm and she stretched out beside him, scrunching up close and putting an arm around his neck.

"Now aren't you glad we came on this Elderhostel?" she asked.

"There's still the matter of the bug spray."

"Start on that again, sweetheart, and—"

He turned slightly, wrapped his arms around her and snuggled her in, running his hand down her back, feeling the muscles on either side of her spine.

"You still teaching aerobics?"

"What brought that on?"

"You look terrific and feel better."

She lifted her head and the blue eyes gazed down at him. "Are we taking a nap or what?"

"A nap. The flesh is willing, but the spirit's weak."

She kissed him lightly on the lips. "It was a nice thing to say, anyway." She laid her head on his shoulder. "Actually I only assist the teacher. It allows me to work out without paying for it. Something for the chronologically-challenged." She ran her hand down his chest and patted his stomach. "You're still working out."

"Have to. Ever see a fat physical therapist? It's like an astronaut afraid of heights."

He closed his eyes, breathed in her perfume, a mix of vanilla and herbs, and pushed the afternoon away. *Carpe diem.* Seize the day. Except he wanted to cease the day, at least for a bit, and tried to think of the Latin equivalent, but all he could come up with was *caveat emptor,* and like a mad shopper being bashed in a fire sale, he went down for the count.

FOUR

WHEN HE POPPED open his eyes it took a minute to zoom back from the end of the world into the strange room. The sun sent long shadows through the scrubby pines outside the window to splash on the opposite wall. Dodee no longer lay by his side.

So where was she?

He hopped out of bed, washed his face, and hurried out the door, almost bumping into her on the way in.

"Oh," Dodee said, "I was just coming to get you. We should get going down to dinner." She carried her sketchbook and propped it against the spare bed. "The dining hall is at the other end of the 4-H camp. About a half a mile." She walked into the bathroom, calling back to him. "It looked like everyone was walking. We can ride if you want."

"No, let's walk." He picked up the sketchbook and flipped back the cover. Bold black pencil strokes captured a pier hanging out into the lake, the rough shoreline on the far side, and a pontoon boat speeding by. "Nice work," he called in to her, but she had already come out, drying her hands on a towel.

"Thank you, but it's just a rough sketch. Ready?"

They grabbed light jackets and slipped them on; the still-warm October afternoon carried the promise of a night chill. They left the room and started down the open walkway when a short, rotund man popped out of the Hospitality Room.

A red baseball cap sat backward on his head, stubble on a swarthy face, bright multi-colored shirt with two buttons opened at the collar, showing a gold chain resting among chest hairs. Thick, hairy arms stuck out of the short-sleeved shirt. "Hey, yez going down to the chow hall?"

Dodee nodded. "Uh-huh, want to come along?"

"Jeez, yeah. I don't know where it is. The wife's just in the toilet," he said, pronouncing it "terlet." "Just got in from New York. Longer drive than I thought, ya know." He turned as the door to the ladies' room opened on the other side of the glass wall. "Ah, here she is. C'mon, Bernice, we're waitin' for yez. We gonna walk with these guys."

Bernice fussed with the waist of an oversized pair of slacks as she came through the outer door, her embroidered blouse covering a large bosom, her small eyes studying them from under bleached blond hair, her fleshy face dour until she gave them a smile that lit up the world. "Hi. Ya here with the Elderhostel, right?"

"I think everyone is," Dodee said, as they started down the dirt road.

"I think this is marvelous. We just drove in from New York."

"I already told 'em."

"And it's so marvelous. The lake and everything. We live in Brooklyn. I'm Bernice and this is my husband, Barry."

"Barry Rhodenbarr, that's me. This is our first Elderhostel. How about you guys?"

"This is our third," Jim answered.

Dodee took Jim's hand. "We met on our first."

"Well, ain't that romantic. Ain't that romantic, Barry?"

"Yeah, it's romantic," Barry said, rolling his eyes.

They crossed over onto a grassy strip and headed toward a clump of buildings by the lake. Eventide came on and the afternoon chilled with a small breeze coming in off the water. Birds squabbled in the trees and a great blue heron wading along the shore suddenly spread its wings wide, as if spooked by something, and took off trailing its long legs behind.

"Jeez, how far is this place?"

"You know where we're going?" Jim asked Dodee.

She pulled out a small rough-drawn map and handed it to him. "It's near the entrance of the camp, across from a parking area. About a half a mile walk."

"Fagedaboudit. I'm goin' back and get the Cadillac."

"We're over halfway there," Dodee said.

Bernice motioned with a fleshy hand, big diamond on her finger, and bracelets clinking on her wrist. "I'm walking."

Barry threw up his hairy arms and followed along.

Jim checked the map as they passed two long buildings, the first listed as a dormitory, the second a lodge, then the administration building on the left, and to the right, at the water's edge with a swimming area fenced off, something called Rast Hall. Straight ahead, the dining hall. "You follow the smell of the food from here."

THEY HAD TO WALK around the building to the entrance. A sign above the door announced it as being Lazar Hall, one large room about sixty by one hundred feet, big round tables and chairs scattered about, all empty except for four in the middle of the room occupied by Elderhostelers, already eating away. Barry bee-lined it for a buffet table set up to their right—like metal to magnet—with Bernice right behind.

"Shall we find seats first?" Dodee asked Jim.

He shrugged. "Might as well get our plates."

They followed the Rhodenbarrs to a line of stainless steel pans, kept warm with hot water underneath. Jim picked up a salad, two chicken thighs, a baked potato, and string beans, and followed Dodee, setting their plates down at the last two free seats at one of the tables. Drinks were set up on a moveable counter, tall soda bottles and coffee carafes.

Dodee got a glass of iced tea and Jim poured himself a Coke.

"Hi," said the man next to Dodee as she sat down. He had a round milk-chocolate face with bright dark-brown eyes, black tight curls to his hair. "I'm Simon Cinnamon, like the spice," he said, with a voice so deep it came up from the floor. He sat tall in his chair and Jim figured him at six-two standing, two hundred plus pounds. "And this is my wife"—he gestured to the much shorter woman sitting next to him—"Phyllis."

Phyllis gave them a warm smile. She was a honey-blond with gray highlights, fair skin usually associated with redheads, and blue eyes that gave the impression of a joke lurking somewhere behind. "How do you do," she said in a cultured New England voice.

"And I am Oxra Farhang," said a diminutive woman next to Phyllis. She had the body of a child, long black hair streaked with gray, an oval face with light olive skin, and strong white teeth shining in an easy smile. "And this is my husband, Farouk Farhang."

Farouk turned to give them a curt nod, not smiling from a gaunt face the color of well-worn leather, a full head of black hair, sharp blue eyes that had a wild cast about them, like the man had just come in from the desert or off the Steppes. He wore a rough, gray wool shirt, and looked to be in his early sixties, which gave him twenty years on his younger wife.

"And we met this afternoon," Doctor Clyde Porter said. His wife, Becky, sat sternly erect next to him, staring across the round table.

"I'm James P. Dandy, Jim, and this is my friend, Dodee Swisher."

"Well, sir, we're quite a crowd," Simon said in his deep-bass voice, well modulated, as if addressing an assembly. He glanced at the other tables. "I wonder how many more there'll be of us?"

"I reckon we're just about all here," Clyde said, surgically slicing off a piece of chicken and stuffing it in his mouth.

Jim ate a small potato and then tried the chicken, juicy with a trace of herbs and spices. It brought back a memory of what his wife, Penny, had always said: "I like anything I don't have to cook myself." That was before she got so sick she couldn't keep down the best he had to offer. Lately he noticed his daughter, Cee Cee, using the same saying, picked up from her mother.

He glanced around the big room.

Penny would have loved Elderhostels.

"We're supposed to canoe through the swamps?" Dodee asked, throwing the question on the table.

Phyllis gave a shivering motion. "I hope there aren't any snakes."

"My wife has a thing about snakes," Simon said.

"Me too." Oxra Farhang turned her lips down and nodded. "It might be irrational, but I still cannot help it. We canoe in Illinois. We have a rack on our van and just go, and sometimes when I see a snake, I just want to turn around and go home. But we don't have snakes in the water like the cottonmouths down here. I hope we don't run into one."

Simon shook his head. "As cool as it is, you won't have to worry about snakes."

"I don't know," Jim said, taking another bite of chicken, "if it's not going to be so warm, why tell us to bring bug spray?" Dodee gave him a sidelong glance and he smiled. "Of course, that's probably just a precaution."

"We're from Alabama," Clyde Porter said, "and here in the South, despite it being the end of October, we can get some hot days where the mosquitoes will swarm." He turned to his wife and pushed his cup and saucer toward her. "I believe I'll have some coffee now."

Becky Porter blinked, then she stood and picked up his cup, moving off to the drinks table.

Jim realized Becky had been staring across at Phyllis,

and turned to study her, but saw nothing that would demand so much attention. But then, he wasn't a woman. Perhaps Becky, with her mousy hair in a severe bun, was intrigued by Phyllis's soft honey-blond do.

A lady in a white apron brought out a tray of pies and puddings and set them at the drinks table.

Dodee leaned over close. "You're eyeing those desserts like you're lusting after them."

"Is that apple pie over there?" Clyde asked as Becky set his coffee down. "I believe I'll have a piece."

"How is everybody making out?" asked the ponytailed coordinator, Jody Sundance, coming up to their table. "Enjoy your dinner?"

"It is delicious," Oxra said, turning to her husband, "is it not?" But Farouk only made a quick nod and kept on eating.

Simon gave a white-toothed smile and brought his voice up from the basement. "I think the dessert will just about do it."

"One piece, darling," Phyllis said with a touch of New England accent, then looked at Dodee. "The doctor said he has to lose fifteen pounds."

"I'll burn it up canoeing."

"Wait a minute," Jody Sundance said, a smile spreading up her lightly freckled face, "before we get into a domestic discussion, I just want to announce that we'll meet at seven in the Walter Cox auditorium, that's the building next to the Conference Center where you have your rooms. We'll go over some of the things we'll be doing during the week, and Hank Davis, a Natural Resources agent, will give us a quick rundown on the lakes. Everyone wear your nametags. I see most of you have them."

Jim reached up to his chest and realized he was the only one not wearing one.

Sonofabitch.

He would be the one shot at sunrise as an example to the others.

FIVE

WHEN JIM USHERED Dodee into the auditorium of the Walter Cox Building, a beige concrete block structure with a concrete floor, a semi-circle of chairs focused on a lone table where Jody Sundance stood talking to a man in his late forties, with a full beard, thinning brown hair, and brown eyes behind large aviator glasses. He wore a khaki shirt, and green cargo pants from Cabela's. Jim knew that because he just bought a pair for himself and another as a present for Dodee, convertibles, zippers above the knees for switching between long pants and shorts.

He led Dodee to a seat on one side of the semi-circle next to the Rhodenbarrs. Barry, despite the chill of the evening, still wore his short-sleeved sport shirt, gold chain peeking through the open collar.

Latecomers hurried in to claim the remaining seats.

Jody Sundance set an insulated cup on the table and clapped her hands for attention. "Okay, everybody." She clapped again, a Take Charge expression on her freckled face. "This is Hank Davis everyone. Hank's our Natural Resources agent. Since he hasn't been home for his supper yet, I'm going to let him tell you a little bit about the lakes before we talk about our 4-H Center and our schedule for this week. Hank."

"Thank you, Jody," Hank Davis said, talking with a southern accent like he had a mouthful of spit. "I'll be giving you all a full lecture on Tuesday afternoon"—he turned to Jody—"Tuesday?" She nodded and he turned back to the group. "On Tuesday afternoon and we'll get into more depth then. And maybe take a bird walk. I know that's one of the things you all are supposed to be studying, the birds in the area."

He took some maps, of the Santee-Cooper area put out by the state of South Carolina, from his briefcase and started handing them out, one to a couple.

"Lake Marion, which you see out here"—he motioned toward the water—"and Lake Moultrie, the next lake down, are part of the Santee-Cooper Water Management System, which includes the Jefferies Hydroelectric Plant, a state owned utility you'll be visiting sometime this week. Both lakes combined cover one hundred and ninety-four thousand acres of outdoor sports and boating recreation with over four hundred and fifty miles of shoreline. The main reason I'm here tonight is to emphasize that when you all are out on the lake and in the Santee-Cooper waters, always wear your PFDs, personal flotation devices. I know Jody and the 4-H staff will instruct you all on that before you all set out on your canoe trips, but it doesn't hurt for me to come by and move the awareness up a notch."

Doctor Clyde Porter stood. "I heard someone drowned here yesterday."

"Not here," Jody said, "not at the center—"

"The 4-H center has an exemplary safety record," Hank Davis cut in. "The death yesterday should still be a warning to us that you can never be too careful. It happened up near Pack's Landing, above Santee State Park, eight or ten miles from here, to an experienced boater I might add, one who spent many hours out on the lake."

"I heard the police suspect foul play?"

A chubby-faced man across the room shifted to the edge of his seat. "They think he was murdered?"

"Wait a minute," Hank Davis held up his hands. "We don't want to speculate on what may or may not have happened. The man was a friend of mine, and while it's hard for me to understand how one with his water smarts could end up drowned, sometimes it happens. We get careless. This should be a big heads up for all of us. As far as speculation on how it happened, let's leave that up to Sheriff Darby."

Hank ran his hand over his full beard, smoothing it down.

"The second thing to be aware of is the Santee Dam's spillway across the lake. It's not all that close, but not that far either. I doubt if you all will be going there, but it's a restricted area and can have swift moving water, so I caution you all to stay away from it."

He stroked his full beard again, this time with both hands.

"The last thing I'd like to mention is that we've had a few fish kills on the lake in the last few days, mostly up by Santee State Park, but we're not sure what the cause is. I can't say you all won't find them down here. If you all do come across fish floating in the water, I ask you not to touch the fish, but to call Jody's attention to it as soon as you can. She'll get in touch with me and maybe we can track this thing down."

Gray-haired Hamill-haircut Dorothy Gramm raised her hand. "Is there any talk about taking down the dam?"

Hank Davis' bushy eyebrows rose and his jaw dropped. He glanced at Jody Sundance before coming back to Dorothy.

"Tear down the dam?"

"Yes, to restore the river to its natural state."

"I can't envision why we would ever want to do that. The plant provides electric power to half the state and lake recreation is the major economic resource in the area."

"I'm an environmentalist and surely you've heard about other dams being torn down to provide habitats for fish and wildlife, dams that have caused the decline and near extinction of everything from salmon to sea otters."

"That might be in areas where the dams are marginal,

but I can't see them tearing down the Santee any more than Hoover or the Grand Coulee—''

"Well, they ought to, from an environmental standpoint. We no longer have naturally spawning salmon, and if the government were to stop the federally funded hatcheries, salmon would become extinct. And that's just the start of it."

Hank Davis turned his lips down and ran his fingers over his beard. "No, to answer your question, no one has considered tearing down the Santee Dam. To my knowledge we've never had salmon in this area."

Another hand went up, from across the room, from the chubby-faced man with a belly that overloaded his belt, like too many German pastries had been stored in there.

"Yes, sir," Hank Davis asked, looking like he welcomed a change in subject.

"Any idea what's caused the fish kill?"

He shook his head and scratched at his beard. "They obviously suffered from some trauma, but we haven't pinpointed it yet. It's only happened in the last couple of days. There's no sign of disease, but until we check it out, I'd rather err on the safe side. We have found some fish parts, but we don't know if it's a correlation or the result of predators."

The chubby-faced man gave his eyebrows a couple of flicks. "Well, I'm retired FBI. If I can give you a hand in your investigation, or with the drowning death of your friend, feel free to call on my expertise."

Jody stepped beside Hank Davis. "If we have more questions, let's save them for Tuesday afternoon when Hank will be back to give us an in-depth lecture on Santee-Cooper." She turned to the Natural Resources agent. "Thanks for coming, Hank. We'll let you get to your supper." She turned back to the Elderhostel group and clapped her hands and everyone joined in.

"Okay," she said as Hank Davis left, "what we want to

do now is get acquainted with one another. Remember to always wear your nametag.''

Jim covered his chest with his hand, like maybe nobody would notice his was missing.

''Your nametag will be your admittance to a lot of the places we will be visiting. I'm the program coordinator. We are part of Clemson University, the Extension School, and we have programs going pretty much twelve months out of the year. Did you notice how empty the dining hall was? Normally we have a couple of hundred kids running through here every week of the summer, climbing the obstacle course, swimming, canoeing. There's so much noise you can hardly hear yourself think. Since no one else is here right now, those of you who wish to drive to the dining hall can park across the street in the parking lot. We started having Elderhostels here seven years ago, I think, and we run them about four a quarter. We have a lot of repeaters to the center, and we have one now''—she held out her hand to indicate a thin man with a wrinkled face in the middle of the semi-circle—''Leopold Kohl. You were with us in the spring?''

''Early summer,'' Leo said. ''I had to leave in the middle because of business, so I thought I'd come back now when it's not so buggy and finish what I missed.''

Jody gave him one of the smiles that lit up her round face and squinted her eyes. ''Well it's nice to have you back, and I hope the week lives up to your expectations.''

She took a drink from her insulated cup.

''I like doing Elderhostels. First of all I don't have to worry about making bed checks. If you stay out late I don't have to call your parents and report you. I don't have to worry about you falling off something on the obstacle course and breaking your neck. And—''

''Wait,'' said the chubby-faced man whose belly overloaded his belt, ''you mean we can't use the obstacle course?''

Which brought laughter from the group and a big, toothy

smile to Jody's face. "Be my guest. I'll turn on the lights so you can hop right on it tonight." She clapped her hands. "Okay. Where was I? Oh, yes, it's just a lot of fun having you Elderhostelers here. I find you stimulate me more than I stimulate you."

She took another sip from her cup.

"Tomorrow we'll be going on our first canoe trip, not a long one, something to give the beginners some experience. And like Hank says, we'll be birding the whole week, so if you have binoculars, you'll probably want to bring them."

Jim turned to Dodee and raised his eyebrows.

"My camera has a telephoto lens," she whispered.

"The Hospitality Room—oh, the rooms where you're staying, even though it looks like a motel, is called the Conference Center. Don't ask me why. The Hospitality Room is open twenty-four hours a day. You are free to use it whenever you like. We just ask that the last one out in the evening turns off the lights to help us save a little on electricity, and clean the coffeepot so it's set up for the morning. For the first one up, the coffee is pre-measured in packets, one packet for each pot. It's there for whenever you want it."

She held her hand to her chin, looking to the ceiling.

"I think I'm missing—oh, yes. We do have a television in the Hospitality Room so you can keep up with the news. We don't get the *New York Times* or the *Washington Post* down here, but in the mornings I'll bring one of the local papers and sometimes one from Charleston."

She picked up a stack of sheets and riffled through them.

"Okay, what we want to do now is get to know one another. I have some questions here I'd like you all to answer. They are really simple questions to help us get acquainted. We want you to only put down what you feel comfortable with answering. I promise you no one will see them but you. No one will check your spelling. There will be no grade score at the end of the evening."

Jim took one of the sheets, slipped on his reading glasses, and looked at the questions.

Where is home? What work do/did you do? What are your hobbies? What is your greatest quality?

Oh yeah, this sounded like fun.

Home was easy, Calvert County, Maryland. And so was work, a physical therapist, part-time now that he was retired, just enough to keep his hand in and use all their strength machines a couple of times a week.

Hobbies—what? He bowled once a week. Was that a hobby? He went away fishing with some old cronies to Chincoteague once a year, but mostly he rode his bike rather than fish. Was that a hobby? Building model boats, that was a hobby more than anything else, something he did on a regular basis. Cooking. He liked to make soup, especially on a Sunday when he babysat for his grandchildren, Courtney, Joseph, and Wendy. And he sort of fooled around with bonsai, although occasionally he wished all his plants would die so he didn't have to water them all the time.

Sometimes you have no luck.

Greatest quality? Kind? Thrifty?

How about, brave, clean, and reverent, the Boy Scouts' solemn creed?

He peeked over Dodee's shoulder and she turned her cornflower blues on him. "What are you doing?" she whispered.

"Just wondering what question you're on."

"The last one."

"What have you got?"

She smiled. "This is not an English test. You can't cheat."

"I'm not cheating."

"You're trying to steal my best quality."

"That's because without you, I'm nothing."

She leaned in close, lips against his ear. "Your best quality is your bedside manner.'' And she went back to her paper.

Oh, yeah, that would work.

Then Penny crept unbidden back into his mind, the last year of her life, especially near the end, handling bed pans and trying to coax her to eat. For better or worse, but does anyone really stop to think what they are committing to when they take that oath? The best that could be said was that he had been there for her. Maybe that had been enough. Maybe that was his best quality.

He wrote down ''loyalty.''

''Okay,'' Jody clapped her hands together. ''What we want to do now is choose a partner, someone other than your spouse or the one you came with, and introduce yourself.''

He turned to Dodee. ''Hi, my name is James P.—''

''Oh, no you don't. You have to choose someone you don't know.''

''I never saw you before in my life.''

She stood up. ''Meet someone. It'll be fun.''

''Bullshit.''

She batted her eyelids at him. ''You'll have a Jim Dandy time.'' And she walked off across the room.

Great. Just great.

Who would he partner up with now?

He turned to the person next to him, a slight woman in a heather sweater, oval face, a poodle-cut head of auburn hair, hazel eyes behind small oval glasses.

She gave him a small smile. ''Do you have a partner?'' she asked in a low, tentative voice.

Just absolutely great.

But as he let the question hang, he saw there was more than shyness in her eyes. Loneliness, yes, and something familiar, something he had seen before, but couldn't recall.

Unless it was sadness. Yes, sadness lurked there, and something more.

"Hi," he said, giving her a big smile, "my name is Jim Dandy, and if you make a joke of it I'll have to punch you in the nose."

And her return smile came full on, warm and sincere.

SIX

"I PROMISE NOT to make a joke, Jim." She held out her hand. "I'm Topsy Horwitz."

He took the handshake, strong and firm for a slight woman.

"We're supposed to share our best quality?" she asked.

"That's what Jody Sundance said."

"That's an odd name isn't it, Sundance. Like a Native American name."

Jim turned toward the ponytailed blond. "She doesn't look Native American."

"No, she doesn't. I suppose I'm beating about the bush because I'm not sure what my best quality is. I was talked into coming on this Elderhostel by my friend, Elaine"— she motioned to the plump redheaded woman sitting next to her—"but I don't think I'm going to be much company this week. Oh, my, I shouldn't have said that. Don't you tell her."

He looked into the hazel eyes behind the round glasses. What was he seeing there?

"Tell you what," he said, "I don't know what my best qualities are either. Suppose we just name a bunch and pick something out?"

Topsy gave him another tentative smile. "We could do that. Like bravery?"

"Brave, clean, and reverent is the Boy Scouts' solemn creed."

"Considerate. Gentle. Strong. Oh, Lord, I have to stop doing this."

"I'm sorry, I don't—"

"It's not you. I just realized I'm naming off all my husband's qualities. He passed away last year."

He nodded. Yes, that's what he saw in Topsy's eyes. And now he remembered where he had seen it last, in his own mirror, staring back at him a year or so ago. "You were married long?"

"Thirty-five years. Everyone tells me I'm supposed to be adjusted now, but I'm having a hard time. Here I go again, talking about it."

"I'd been married the same, almost thirty-five years, when my wife died. Two, almost three years ago. I don't think you ever get over it. The memories are always there. They just become less painful, and life becomes more tolerable. Tell those guys who think you should be over it that they don't know what they're talking about."

Topsy turned to him, squaring her shoulders. "Was it a long illness?"

He nodded. "Long. Two years that felt like eternity. You?"

She pressed her lips together. "Not quite that long. It was tough though, seeing this giant of a man slowly crumble away. I cared for him, bathed him, tried to make dishes he enjoyed eating to keep his strength up, but there was nothing I could do to stop it. When he finally left me it was almost a blessing."

"No, it *was* a blessing, no *almost* about it."

"You seem to have recovered."

"Yeah, well, I needed some pushing. Like you I went on my first Elderhostel under duress, but I ended up having a great time. This is my third Elderhostel and I've come to the conclusion that you always meet neat people on them, and if you give yourself half a chance, you'll have a great time."

"I suppose." Her brow wrinkled. "If I don't try to com-

pare it to the Elderhostel we took together before he died.''
She pressed her lips together for a moment. ''I used to
canoe when I was younger.''

''Don't worry about younger; you look in good shape
now. I work out all the time, but one thing I've found is
that I can't do things as easily as I could when I was
twenty-five. Exercise helps, it may take some extra stretching and warming up, and I can still do most things. I still
enjoy them. The only trouble comes when I'm foolish
enough to try to compete with a twenty-five-year-old.''

''I suppose.'' She sighed. ''I know I have to get on with
my life.''

He chewed on the side of his lip.

What could he say to that?

If she had a muscle ache, he would know how to massage it, give her exercises to strengthen it, but what exercises strengthen the mind?

''You know,'' he said, ''getting on with your life is such
heavy business. Why don't you take a little vacation first?
Not only from getting on with your life, but also from the
bereaving process. Take this week as a vacation. You de-
serve it. Every time you find yourself thinking about how
things were, or what might have been, or the heavy things
you'll face in the future, stop and say to yourself, no, I'll
think about them later. This week I'm on vacation. It's not
forever. It's not saying I will never worry about these things
again. It's just managing this one short week to say, I de-
serve a little bit of relaxation, a little bit of fun. For this
one week I'm on vacation. Think you can shove all the
memories and worries aside for one week?''

Topsy raised her chin and pressed her lips together again,
and nodded slowly. ''I think I could try.'' Her hazel eyes
sought his. ''Is that what you did?''

He shrugged. ''I wish I had been that smart, or that
brave. Everyone finds wonderful friends on these Elderhostels, but I found myself thrust into a relationship that
takes up all my worry time just to keep up with her.''

"Oh, you mean your friend. I could see there was something between you. So you fell in love again?"

Wow, he wasn't ready for that.

He sought out the soft curls of wheaten hair and found Dodee across the room. She stared back at him, but she was listening intently to the chubby-faced, retired FBI guy.

How did he feel about Dodee? He mulled it over occasionally, holding it delicately on edge like a photograph, but Topsy's question brought it full on, naked as a drunken streaker at a meeting of the Women's Temperance League.

"Okay, everyone." Jody Sundance clapped her hands. "What we want now is for everyone to think of an animal that starts with the same letter as your first name, something you can relate to, or that at least starts with the same letter. For instance, my name is Jody the Jaguar, because it's muscular and strong and I'd like to be like that. You see?"

"It's also a fun car to drive," Simon Cinnamon said, a white-toothed grin on his milk-chocolate face.

Jody pointed at him. "Yes, that too. I'll give you a couple of minutes to think about it, and then what we'll do is, the first person will give his name and animal, like I'm Jody the Jaguar, and the next will give the name and animal of all the people who went before and then add his or her own, and so forth until the last person ends up reciting all the names and animals. You see?"

"I want to go first," said Elaine, the woman sitting next to Topsy.

"No," Topsy answered, "then I'll have to name everybody."

"Ready?" Jody asked.

"Fagedaboudit," Barry Rhodenbarr said, holding out his bare, hairy arms. "ya gotta gimme a minute to think."

"You can think as we go along. I'll start."

Jim waved her off. "Wait a minute. That gets you off the hook."

Jody smiled. "I was wondering if someone would catch that."

"Just because we are mellowing into fine wine, Jody," the honey-blond Phyllis Cinnamon said, "doesn't mean our minds are fermenting."

"Yeah," Barry added, "like what she said."

"Okay, I'll start it off and then I'll go again at the end, and name all of you animals, all you fine wine animals. I'm Jody the Jaguar." She turned to her left, looking into the wild eyes of Farouk Farhang.

"Me next? You are Jody the Jaguar, and I am Farouk the Famous Hero."

"No, darling," Oxra said, sitting on the other side of him, "an animal. It has to be an animal."

His lean face turned to her, studying for a moment. "All right. I am Farouk the Salamander, because I can change colors."

"No, darling, it has to start with the same letter. Like Farouk the Falcon."

"Yes." His eyes opened wide, a grin slit his lean face, and he held up a fist. "I am Farouk the Falcon, because I am fierce."

Jim nodded.

One look in the guy's eyes had convinced him of that.

"And I am Oxra—oh, I have to name the others first." She brushed her long, gray-streaked black hair out of her face. "Jody the Jaguar and Farouk the Falcon, and I am Oxra the Otter who likes to swim and play in the water."

Dorothy Gramm followed with Dorothy the Dove because she wanted to bring green peace to the world, and her husband chose Dave the Donkey because he tended to be stubborn, to which Dorothy agreed.

Barry Rhodenbarr chose Barry the Bear because he was strong like a bear, to which Bernice Rhodenbarr said it was also because he was hairy and hibernated whenever work was to be done. Bernice picked the Bat because she was a night person.

When it got around to Jim he struggled through naming

those who had gone before him, managing to make it with only one slip up. Ha. Not bad.

"And I'm Jim the Jackrabbit for reasons—it's all I can think of."

"Yeah," Barry said, "gimme a break. I can think of a Jackrabbit reason, but ya gotta get Dodee to verify ya not braggin'."

Which brought out a lot of smiles and a blush to Dodee's face.

Topsy came next, naming all the animals. "And I'm Topsy the Turtle, because I feel like a stick-in-the-mud."

Jim waited until the naming moved around to the Smiths, the couple from Arkansas, and leaned close to Topsy. "You know those qualities you mentioned. Brave, strong, gentle, considerate. They're your qualities. You named them yourself. And something else, loyalty." She turned to him, hazel eyes studying him, and he nodded. "Another thing about a turtle. The only way it can get ahead is by sticking its neck out."

She smiled and nodded back. "Don't bother me, I'm on vacation."

Phyllis chose the Panda because she liked to cuddle with her husband and he picked Simon the Seal because he liked to fish and finally had the time to do so since retiring from the Army.

The tall, thin, Leopold Kohl went next. "I am Leo the Lion because I always wanted to be king."

When it came to Dodee, she zipped through everyone who had gone before her. "And I'm Dodee the Dolphin because"—she turned and raised her eyebrow at Jim—"they are much smarter than jackrabbits."

"Fagedaboudit, Jim, she put it to ya."

The pudgy man next to her turned out to be Harold Rucker. "Harold the Hound," he said, "because when I worked for the FBI, once I got the scent of a criminal I never gave up 'til he was behind bars."

After a couple from Iowa, the Jacksons, and the Porters

took turns, it finally came back to Jody the Jaguar. She took a deep breath. "Okay, it's up to me." And she started with Farouk the Falcon and wound through all the Elder-hostelers to finish up with Doctor Clyde Porter's "Clyde the Coyote," and the mousy Becky Porter's "Becky the Beaver who was always busy," completing the circle to everyone's applause.

"See," she said, "I'm like Doctor Doolittle, because I can talk to all you animals and you can talk to me."

SEVEN

AFTER THE MEETING, Jim and Dodee headed back to their room in the light of a nearly full moon.

"You seemed to be in deep conversation with Topsy the Turtle," Dodee said.

"Um."

"Um? That's not saying very much."

"She lost her husband awhile back and she's still suffering through it." He ran the conversation back in his mind, and his advice to take a vacation, like he knew what he was talking about, especially since the last Elderhostel had been with her husband. He took a breath and let it out. "I tried to be sympathetic to her. I know what she's going through."

Dodee put her arm around his waist. "You're a nice guy, Jim Dandy."

"Hell yes." He put his arm around her shoulder, pulling her close, huddling against the night chill. "And humble."

"And humble."

"How about you and that FBI guy?"

"Whose name is?"

"Whose name is…FBI guy."

"No. Didn't any of this animal stuff rub off? I'll give you a hint. Dog."

"Okay, David the Dog."

"Harold the Hound."

He opened the door for her. The room felt warm and

cozy. "Are you going to tell me what you were talking about or not?"

"He has a theory on the fish-kill business."

"Don't get involved with that," he said, shutting the door on the cold world.

"I am not involved." She took off her jacket and hung it in the open closet. "You asked me a question, I answered it."

Jim slipped off his jacket and she hung it up for him. "So what's his theory?"

"He thinks that whatever's killing the fish has to do with the power plant."

"How can he say that? The power plant has been there for fifty years and suddenly it starts killing fish?"

She got a black nightgown from a dresser drawer. "He didn't say the power plant killed the fish. He said it had something to do with it. You want the bathroom first?"

"What do you think?"

"It was his theory, not mine. There could be something to it if he works for the FBI. I'll take the bathroom first."

He sat down on the bed and took off his shoes and socks, then flopped back and stared up at the ceiling.

How could there be a connection between dying fish and the hydroelectric plant?

He shook his head.

If there was, he didn't want to know.

Dodee came out of the bathroom a few minutes later dressed in the black nightgown that came to mid-thigh.

"Why did you call yourself a jackrabbit?"

He stood up and shrugged. "I told you. It was all I could think of."

She came up to him, rubbing lotion into her hands. "You realize that we could be in for a lot of ribbing."

"How come you called yourself a dolphin?"

"Because the only other thing I could think of was a dromedary."

"Duck, dog, dragonfly. Besides, what's wrong with dromedary?"

"Because, sweetheart"—she put her arms around his neck—"after you chose jackrabbit, I was afraid Barry would ask, 'one hump or two.'"

He gave her a phony frown. "You have an earthy streak in you that slips out once in awhile."

"It's the artist in me." She ran her hands through his hair, then bent his head to her and kissed him.

He smelled soap and her vanilla-spice perfume, and tasted peppermint toothpaste. He put his arms around her, running his hands down the muscles lining her spine to her round bottom, and found only the silky nightgown between hands and bare skin, and the feel of it zapped him to attention like a bolt of lightning.

She broke the kiss. "I thought you might have chosen jackrabbit for other reasons." Her lips brushed against his as she spoke. "Like maybe you were thinking of acting like a jackrabbit."

"That has possibilities."

She gave him another quick kiss. "I'd say probabilities from the way something seems to be jacking up."

"You're being earthy again."

Another kiss, a smooth hand caressing his ear. "But hopefully not a speedy young jackrabbit." This time she pushed up against him, their tongues caressing. "I think I'd like an old and slow jackrabbit."

"Old and slow I got plenty of."

"If you're going to the bathroom, make it fast."

"I thought you like old and slow."

"Um." She pulled her head back from him, half smile on her lips. "Oh, my." She gave an exaggerated yawn. "I think I'm suddenly too tired—"

"Be out in a minute."

He hurried into the bathroom, gave his teeth a cursory brush, threw some Paul Sabastian cologne on his face, peeled off all his clothes, and realized he hadn't unpacked his pajamas.

Screw it. He cut off the light and opened the door. The room was dark except for the moonglow from outside the window. He climbed into bed, the sheets cool against his skin, moved over to where her body heat had warmed them up, and took her in his arms, slipping the nightgown slowly up her body, cuddling her next to him with smooth caresses and soft kisses.

And Dodee the Dolphin took him for a ride to the bottom of the sea, racing down sandy slopes and back up on the other side, in and out and around coral reefs, bursting with color, in and out watery caves and down into the depths with the air sucked from his lungs, then a rocket ride to the surface and bursting into a white-hot light, groaning and gasping and calling out, engaging one another in a primordial conversation, before finally falling back to the surface in a crumpled heap, hearts pounding, blood coursing to oxygen-starved muscles, and slowly, slowly settling down in a long sigh that floated on the air.

She kissed him on the nipple. "Thank you, Jackrabbit."

"There's no jack left in this rabbit." He kissed her on the top of her head, and she raised up so he could kiss her on the lips. "Thank you, Dolphin. I missed being with you these last three months."

She rested her head on his chest again. "And getting a little horny? You seemed a little testy on the way down." She kissed him on the nipple again. "Never mind, I was also looking forward to being here with you." She raised a leg over his. "It's nice finding all the familiar humps and bumps of your body again."

He cradled her head with one arm and gently stroked the small of her back with his free hand.

"You have some nice humps and bumps of your own."

He held her close and stared at the moonlight giving an undefined shape to the bushes outside. Even after Dodee's breathing stretched out into the long, even gait of sleep,

Topsy Horwitz's nagging question kept running around in his mind.

So you fell in love again?

Two Elderhostels they had spent together, three counting this one, and a million telephone calls in between, but they had never mentioned feelings. Only a desire to see one another.

Why was that? Was it time to express something now? Except, what? How deep did his feelings go? And, still wrestling with the question, he slipped off the edge and followed her down into the depths of the sea.

EIGHT

THE DAY HAD NOT YET bloomed when he oozed out of a delicious sleep. He lay there for a few moments, luxuriating in the warmth of Dodee's snuggling body, until the call of his bladder won out. He disentangled himself and headed into the bathroom. When he came out, shaved, showered, face splashed with Sabastian aftershave, dressed in jeans and plaid cotton shirt, loafers on his feet, he slipped out of the room in search of coffee.

The cold morning air chilled him and he thought of going back for a jacket, but the warmth of the open Hospitality Room dispelled it. No one there. He sauntered around to the small kitchen, found instructions for the coffeemaker, and started it up. He came back out to the main room, found a bite-sized Heath bar in one of the goody bowls, and popped it into his mouth. He stood looking out the windows, seeing mostly his reflection as the night fought back the dawn.

A movement caught his eye and he spun around to see Dorothy the Dove Gramm steal into the room. Hamill-haircut neatly in place, arms wrapped around herself as if to ward off the cold in spite of the heavy brown sweater.

"Good morning," she said.

"Hi. Coffee's making."

She slipped off her glasses, which had fogged up, wiped them off and went into the kitchen. "I wonder if they have any herbal tea," she said, opening and closing cabinets.

He picked up another bite-sized Heath bar and popped it into his mouth. An early sugar burst to get him going.

"No," came the voice of the Dove in the kitchen. "No tea of any kind." She came back into the Hospitality Room and sat on one of the sofas by the window. The gold panda earrings of the evening before had given way to silver bears. "I think your coffee might be done."

It was. He added two packets of powdered cream to a Styrofoam cup, poured in the coffee, and peeked through the pass-through. "Can I get you one?"

"No, thank you."

He took a sip. Not bad. Thank you, God, for the first sip of the first cup of coffee on a cold morning.

"You're up early," he said, coming back into the room and sitting across from her at one of the tables.

"I don't sleep well away from home. I don't sleep very well there either."

"This your first Elderhostel?"

"Twelfth. I try to go on those that have an environmental focus."

"Doesn't seem like this is an environmental Elderhostel. Except last night you were talking about the dam. I don't think they'll tear it down."

"I know, but they should. They should just blow it the hell up." She jumped up and strode for the kitchen. "I think I will have some coffee after all."

He watched her go.

If she was that wired naturally, what would happen after a jolt of caffeine?

"Dams are just one more assault on the environment. They not only destroy the natural landscape, they screw up fish spawning and bird egg laying and completely change the habitat. A lot of the animals on the endangered list are there because of dams. A good deal of forests have been turned into mud flats because of dams. That's why they are starting to tear them down in a lot of places."

"They're tearing down hydroelectric plants?"

She came back into the room. "In some places."

The door opened and the FBI guy came in, Harold the Hound Rucker, his heavy body gathered about his middle like a jelly roll.

"Coffee's made," Jim said.

"Thanks," Harold said in a grunt.

"In some places they've torn them down," Dorothy the Dove continued. "Not like here where so many people use electric power, but places where the power is marginal. But even here it would help. Just blow the dam up and let the river seek its natural level."

He glanced over her shoulder at Harold the Hound.

"I know it seems drastic, but sometimes we have to take drastic action to get people's attention."

The man had poured himself a cup of coffee and now stood sipping it, barely visible, on the kitchen side of the pass-through.

"How many years have you heard about global warming?"

Jim shifted back to her as he realized she was waiting for an answer. He shrugged. "Fifteen or twenty years?"

She peered at him through her glasses. "More like thirty years, and all that time scientists have been warning that if we don't change things around, the polar icecaps will melt and we'll end up with shrunken land masses and an overheated environment. And all during that same time, we have had other scientists, those connected with industry, telling us there is no definite proof it's happening, even with holes in the ozone layer. Does that sound familiar?"

He shrugged again.

"It's the cigarette companies all over again, telling us for years that it was okay to smoke, when all the time they had proof that it was not only bumping people off left and right, but it was also addictive. So now we have Big Auto telling us it would cost too much to reduce car emissions when it's really not necessary. But big chunks of the icecap like the size of Rhode Island are melting. And we're still saying it costs too much to reduce emissions? Eventually we'll reach a crisis point and everyone will be screaming to do something. The only trouble is, by then we could have passed the point of no return." She nodded. "Blow up the dam."

Jim finished his coffee and stood up. "Think I'll take some of this stuff back to the room and see if Dodee's awake."

He started into the kitchen and met the FBI guy, Harold the Hound, who gave him a smile and a flick of his eyebrows on the way out. Jim poured another coffee, fingered a second Styrofoam cup for Dodee, then shook his head. Doubtful if she would be awake yet.

"Look, look," Harold the Hound said.

Jim hurried to the doorway.

The dawn had broken now, pushing back the night, and two deer skulked across the dewy lawn, their dun-colored bodies back-dropped by a mist rising off the water.

"See them?"

Dorothy nodded. "This is their home. It's natural for them to be here. You must live in the city."

Something suddenly spooked them and they bounded off into the woods.

Jim headed for his room, catching a glimpse of the bantam Clyde the Coyote and his mousy wife, Becky the Beaver, heading down the dirt road, elbows bent, arms pumping, swift steps, probably the ones who had spooked the deer.

He eased open the door to the room and peered across at the bed. Empty. He heard the shower start up and retreated to the Hospitality Room. Bernice the Bat Rhodenbarr, dressed in a quilted robe and slippers, finished off the coffee and set the empty pot back on the hot plate. She spread a smile on her fleshy face as she left the kitchen. He shrugged and made a fresh pot, coming out to gaze through the windows as it dripped.

Simon the Seal Cinnamon, dressed in a camouflaged

khaki jacket, put a small box into the trunk of a big bur-gundy Mercedes and marched around to enter the Hospi-tality Room.

A white-toothed grin lit up his milk-chocolate face. "How's that coffee coming, Jackrabbit Jim?" he asked, his voice out-basementing James Earl Jones.

"A few minutes to go. It seems this animal thing works, except I remember the animals more than the names."

"It's one of the tricks," he said, yawning and scratching his head of tight curly hair. "When I was younger I had to train myself in remembering names. I'm career military and I was always in a mix of people. If you wanted to get ahead, you had better remember the name of a superior even if you hadn't seen him for five years."

"You're retired now?"

"Uh-huh." He straightened up, square shoulders and barrel chest, as if standing on a parade ground. "I retired from the army as a lieutenant general."

"Wow, that's impressive."

"For a kid growing up on the wrong side of the tracks, it is. I do some consulting work for a defense firm now, and I'm on a committee with Phyllis for the renovation of an historic mansion. Eventually it will become a museum. And I run a volunteer mentoring program for inner city kids. Keeps me out of trouble."

Jim refilled his cup and poured two more, handing one to Simon. "I'm taking one to Dodee," he said, adding pow-dered cream and Equal to hers.

Simon's lips turned down. "I'd take one to Phyllis but she'll wait for the breakfast bell before she gets up." He smiled. "But you can bet she'll be at breakfast."

Jim carried the coffee to his room, nodding to the Jack-sons from Iowa on the other side of the grassy courtyard, and with both hands occupied, kicked at the bottom of the door. A moment later it cracked and her big blues peeked out at him, wheaten hair combed in place, a warm smile spreading on her lips.

Damn Topsy and damn her question. *So you fell in love again?* Maybe she was right.

NINE

"YOU WEARING A JACKET?" Dodee asked when they had returned from breakfast—two eggs, bacon, home fries, and sweet roll for him, a bagel with cream cheese for her.

"Yep," he said, pulling on a light windbreaker for the first canoe trip. "You should too. You can always take it off." He turned to see her holding her flat, black sketch-book case. "You bringing that?"

"What do you think?"

"You're the artist. Whatever you want."

She replaced it on the floor, leaning it against the wall. "It will get in the way." She lifted her face up to him. "Somehow I don't think you want to be paddling me all over while I'm sketching."

"I don't know. Paddling you all over sounds like it might be fun."

She gave him a smile and he kissed her, wrapping his arms around and giving her a little paddle on the butt.

"I'll just take my camera," she said, breaking the kiss. She placed it in a backpack. "I'm taking two water bottles along, as recommended by that pre-check-in list which you never read."

"I brought binocs." He showed them to her before stuffing them into the backpack. "So I guess I read something." He smiled and rapidly blinked his eyes at her.

She added two apples snatched from the mess hall. "In case we get hungry." She slipped on the blue-jean shirt with plaid underlining, using it as a jacket over a blue and yellow long-sleeved shirt, complimenting denim pants, and sneaks on her feet, and handed him the backpack. "Ready to go."

He sighed, shook his head, and took it. "I have to do everything."

The morning turned out clear and sunny, and pleasant for October, but chilly enough to be glad for long sleeves. They ran into Harold the Hound coming out of the Hospitality Room, stuffing his pockets with miniature candy bars.

"Gotta keep my strength up." From the paunch overloading his belt it looked like he had been keeping his strength up for some time. "You see anything that inspires you to paint, Dodee?"

"Everything's inspiring." She waved her hand to take in the lake and the tall pines about them. "It's a matter of just searching for a kernel of truth that speaks out to be captured."

They passed the Walter Cox Building, catching sight of the Cinnamons farther down, Leopold Kohl in his straw hat, and the Rhodenbarrs with something on their heads, all turning from the dirt road toward the water near the dining hall.

"You artist people fascinate me," Harold said, puffing slightly to keep up. "How you start out with nothing but a blank canvas and build a picture to show us a scene. On the other hand, I guess you could say that about me. Not painting. But coming into a crime scene, seeing things that everyone else sees, but through the trained eye, being able to pick out from amongst the litter those clues that build into a picture, if you will, of what happened, and who did it, and why." He turned to Jim. "I guess Dodee told you I'm retired FBI."

"I heard you offer your help to the Natural Resources agent last night."

"Oh, right." He shook one finger in the air. "Well, you know, I feel it's my duty. Thirty-eight years I worked for the FBI. Had thirty agents under me. Pick up a lot of expertise over the years.'' The chubby face turned to him. ''You used to be a physical therapist?''

They turned off the rutty road where the others had and followed the path.

''Still am. Part-time now, just to help out and keep my skills.''

''Yes, sir, you look in great shape. I'm writing a book on my FBI experiences, the main reason I've put off getting into an exercise program. In fact, why I came on this canoeing trip. That was before the fish-kill business. Now I got other things on my mind.''

Jim pressed his lips together, afraid that with a pinch of prompting Harold would go on forever.

''Yep,'' the man said a few moments later, apparently needing no prompting, ''got this case of the fish-kill on my mind. Hear what that Gramm woman up there said this morning, Jim?''

''About global warming?'' he asked. Oh shit. He had given him an opening.

''Well, yes,'' Harold jumped in, ''that too. But what she said about blowing up the dam. That doesn't sound subversive to you? I mean, there are environmental extremists just like there are Arab extremists, and while I'm not accusing her of being one, some of the statements she made don't bode well.''

Jim motioned toward the lake. ''Looks like we're going to have a nice day for canoeing.''

''What statement was that?'' Dodee asked.

Oh shit again. Now, with a ready listener, the guy would go on forever.

''She said they should blow up the dam and the hydroelectric plant. I'm not sure of the connection yet, between that and the fish-kill, but I'm working on it.''

Jim pointed toward the swimming area. ''There's Jody the Jaguar. I guess we'll find out where we're going.''

''Think about it. A quiet, out of the way place like this.

Be a lot easier than New York for terrorists to come in, blow up the dam, and be gone again.''

They joined the rest of the group beside the open door to a storage room in Rast Hall, a recreation building at shoreside, opposite a swimming area made by driving pilings into the lake bottom and fencing it in, with a boardwalk that included a sunning area, a diving board, and a water polo net.

Jody handed out red life preservers. "These are personal flotation devices, PFDs for short. Some of you more experienced canoeists may feel comfortable without wearing them, like Farouk and Oxra have brought their own from home, but to keep us all on the same track, I'll ask you to put them on anyway, if only as a good example to the others. One thing about a canoe, while it does glide easily through the water, they're subject to tipping over if care is not taken.''

Jim picked up a couple of PFDs, red vest types, like flat flack jackets except with foam flotation and a zipper up the middle. He helped Dodee into hers, then pulled on his.

He was ready for the briny. Or the freshy, since there was no brine in the lake.

"Hey," Barry Rhodenbarr said, standing next to a set of double doors to another storage room, hand hanging onto a lock holding them together. "Will yez look at this, Bernice." They topped both their short, rotund bodies with big, floppy, polka-dot caps, more at home on Piccadilly Circus than out in the wilds. "Know what this is?" he asked, jiggling the lock. "An old Rabson. Can you beat it?"

Bernice looked up from trying to zipper her PFD over her large bosom, big-rock ring on one finger, bracelets clanging on her wrist. "Is that the lock nobody's supposed to be able to pick?"

"Not supposed to?" He held out his bare, hairy arms. "They can't. Only one person in the world can pick a Rabson lock.''

"Marvelous," Bernice said, rolling her eyes, and went back to working on her zipper.

Jim glanced over the crowd and stopped at Farouk and Oxra, snug in bright yellow PFDs while everyone else had red ones.

"Okay," Jody called out, clapping her hands, "if everyone has a PFD, let's go over to the canoes, but wait before you pick one out."

Jim hung back as Dodee snapped off pictures, as much at home behind a lens as behind an easel, then hurried her after the others. They gathered at the back of the dining hall where red canoes lined the shore.

"Okay, everybody," Jody said, standing next to a young, dark-haired woman with a thick braid of black hair running down her back to her waist. "This is Rebecca."

Rebecca, holding a paddle, stood five feet eight in bare feet. Oblivious to the cool air that had everyone else in light jackets, her long, strong legs stuck out of a form-fitting bathing suit that covered a flat tummy and two of her own built-in personal flotation devices.

Dodee leaned in close to his side. "Put your tongue back in your mouth," she whispered.

"Me? I was studying her paddle."

"Rebecca will be following along with us this morning helping the strays while I'll be at the head of the pack. Between the two of us we'll keep you straight." She turned to the woman. "You want to take over, Reb?"

"Yes, good morning everyone. When we pick out a paddle, we'll want one that will come up to about our nose. If it's too small we'll not get enough leverage and one too long will be awkward to handle. Both will exert extra pressure on your back. So pick out one that will come up to the tip of your nose and that should be about right. The next thing to worry about is the canoe."

She moved down the slope and straddled the end of a canoe. "Whoever's sitting in the back, you want to brace the canoe between your legs to hold it steady 'til your partner moves forward. The one in the front climbs in and keeps a low center of gravity, staying along the center line until you get to your seat. Once you are seated, place your paddle athwart the canoe—"

"That means across it," Jody said.

Rebecca gave Jody a phony grin and held the paddle horizontally in front of her ample breasts, hands gripping it rigidly. "We want to hold the paddle athwart the canoe, that's across"—she glanced at Jody—"pressing down on the gunnels, that's the canoe sides"—she gave Jody another phony grin—"keeping your hands wide apart to steady the canoe until your partner climbs aboard and is seated. Then the one in the back can gently push off and step aboard, keeping your gravity low, and sit down quickly. Never stand in a canoe, not unless you feel like going for a swim."

Smiles rippled through the crowd.

"The last thing is to decide who is going to steer, because that person sits in the back. Any questions?"

"How far are we going?" Phyllis Cinnamon asked as she rubbed sun-block onto her pink nose.

"Not far for our first trip," Jody said, taking over from Rebecca. "A couple of hours. We'll take off here and circle around the point to a small swamp and we'll pull out."

"I did that once," Barry Rhodenbarr murmured, for which Bernice poked him in the ribs.

"Vans will meet us there and we'll ride back. Did you all remember to bring your binoculars? We'll point out birds as we go along. Hopefully we'll at least see a great blue heron and maybe an egret. Any other questions? Okay, pick out your paddles, select a canoe, and shove off, but stay in this general area until we're all ready to go."

TEN

"I'LL TAKE THE BACK," Jim said to Dodee after they had picked out paddles.

"You've done this before?"

"All the time. We used to canoe a lot along Battle Creek, go up to the cypress swamp and eat lunch."

He picked out a canoe and braced it between his legs as the buxom Rebecca had demonstrated, and Dodee wobbled forward to the front seat, put her backpack under it, and sat down. She spread the paddle across the gunnels and looked over her shoulder.

"Okay, I'm ready."

He inched the canoe into the water, climbed in, and sat down. He put his shoulder into a power stroke and the canoe sliced through the water as if it had a life of its own.

"Awright," Jim said.

Dodee dipped her paddle in the water and they sped out a hundred feet from shore before he ruddered into a circle.

"This is great," Dodee said. "I haven't done this since I was a kid in summer camp." She reached underneath her, opening the backpack and extracting her camera, snapping off a few shots of the other canoeists scrabbling from shore.

Phyllis and Simon Cinnamon paddled smoothly out to them. "It's a perfect day for it, isn't it?" Phyllis called to them. "We haven't done this in years. Where were we, Simon?"

"In Washington."

"Washington State?"

"DC. Along the C-and-O canal. A group of us went out for an afternoon."

"That's right."

"Of course it's right. I just told you."

"Don't get smart, Simon. I'm not in the military."

"Oh shit," Bernice's voice floated across the water as she flailed her arms, knocking off her polka-dot cap, but grabbing it at the last minute. "You damn near tipped us over, Barry."

"Relax, Bernice, relax—"

"Relax, hell. You ain't got no idea what you're doing." And they almost ran into the canoe with Harold the Hound Rucker and Leo the Lion Kohl.

Finally they all grouped up and headed into the sunshine.

"What side do you want me on?" Dodee asked.

"It doesn't make any difference. When you switch, I'll switch."

They paddled past the Conference Center with the Hospitality Room, around the point of land on which it rested, and into virgin territory as the expansive lake opened up to them. Jody, up in front with Farouk and Oxra Farhang in their yellow PFDs, waved to them and pointed across to a great blue heron wading in the shallows, its large ungainly body moving on stilts, its curved neck shooting straight out as its long beak plunged in the water. It took off as they approached, beating its wide wings as it grabbed for air, looking like a flying dinosaur.

The canoe moved easily, like gliding along on slick ice. Pines and swamp oak lined the shore while bald cypress trees, some a hundred feet from the water's edge, sent out spreading root systems to anchor themselves to the shallow bottom, their woody knees peeking above the surface. Somewhere a woodpecker drilled for insects hidden in a tree trunk; everyone had binocs plastered to their faces, but no one called out a sighting. Occasionally fish jumped as they skimmed along, and while they appeared to be in deep water, at times Jim's oar would stir up a muddy bottom inches below the surface.

As the sun got higher, Dodee peeled off her jacket and kicked off her sneaks. She pulled a water bottle out of the backpack, took a drink. "Want some?"

He nodded and she tossed it back. He sipped at it. "This is our view from a canoe," he said, echoing the Elderhostel brochure. "Having fun?"

"Um."

He took off his jacket, watching as she focused her camera on something, but couldn't figure out what she found so interesting. Perhaps it took an artist's eye.

"It's nice, isn't it?" She swung the camera toward him. "Smile, sweetheart."

He gave her a secret hand sign.

"Oh that's nice. Now whenever anyone in Kansas asks what you look like, I'll show this picture of you advertising the length of your appendage."

"In feet?"

"Millimeters."

She picked up the paddle again and they scooted between two cypress trees, ducking under the Spanish moss hanging from bare branches, and came up to a third.

"I thought cypress trees had needles," she said.

"They do, but they drop them when they go dormant in the winter."

"Is this the truth or are—"

"Would I lie to you? It's the truth. I told you we have cypress trees back in Calvert County. In fact, there's one not more than a couple of hundred feet from my home."

"I'm glad it warmed up. We could almost sunbathe."

"Or go skinny dipping."

"You mean with Rebecca the Amazon?"

"I only noticed her paddle until you pointed out her other attributes."

"And you wouldn't lie to me? Right? You need to have your eyes checked?"

Clyde the Coyote and Becky the Beaver glided past them, the Doctor keeping cadence—"Stroke, stroke"—as if they were a two man scull team. Over close to shore, Rebecca was helping Topsy, a white cap over her poodle haircut, and her plump friend, Elaine, untangle themselves from shore. Topsy's laugh drifted across the surface, sounding like she had taken his advice about giving herself a vacation.

"Besides," he said, watching Rebecca follow behind as Topsy and Elaine got underway again, "she's not an Amazon, and that doesn't fit, anyway. It's got to start with the same letter."

"Like Rebecca the Rabbit, Jack?"

"No I was thinking more like Becca the Body. I wonder if FBI guy has got that under surveillance?"

Two hours later they pulled into a long, narrow cut in a swampy area between cypress trees, two canoes wide, where a couple of men, big bruisers from camp, were waiting for them. Jim powered hard in, getting up momentum and driving the front of the canoe over the mud to dry ground. One of the bruisers, a kid around twenty, grabbed the front and half pulled, half lifted them in. Dodee gathered her backpack and hopped out. Jim, staying low, crept to the front and followed.

"Can I give you a hand with this?"

"That would be a help, if you can handle it."

If he could handle it?

"No problem."

He dropped his paddle in the canoe, grabbed the back end, and off they went. Like in a marathon. For a hundred and fifty feet.

Sonofabitch.

No problem?

His heaving chest was sucking in gobs of air by the time he set the canoe down on top of a specially rigged trailer. Another ten feet and he'd have had a coronary.

"You okay?" Dodee asked.

"Sure," he said, trying not to show the heavy breathing, "no problem."

He turned from the trailer and stumbled toward the van. Another vehicle sat twenty-five feet in front of it, a brown SUV with a big star on its rear door. A short, wiry man in a khaki uniform with a badge on his chest stood with his back against the open passenger-side door. Dark sunglasses over his eyes gave him the face of a raccoon.

"I wonder if I can ask you all to gather up here before you head back."

He spoke with the authority of one wearing a badge. Another man sat in the driver's seat with his arm resting on the back, looking out the rear window.

"Something wrong?" Jim asked.

The man's tan face creased in a smile. "Nothing really to worry about. Just got a couple of questions I thought you all might be able to help us with."

When all the Elderhostelers had gathered in a semi-circle, the short, wiry man pulled a stiff, dark-brown cardboard box from the back of his SUV.

"Hello, folks, I'm Sheriff Ward Darby, the law in these here parts," he said sternly, then allowed them a little smile to creep in to show he was joking. "I want to welcome you all to Santee-Cooper. It's always nice to have visitors and we hope you all enjoy your stay here. But we're also hoping for you all's help." Sheriff Ward Darby raised the box high so all could see. "Have any of you seen a box like this in your travels about the vicinity?"

"Isn't that a dynamite box?" asked Harold the Hound.

Sheriff Darby's eyes couldn't be seen behind the dark glasses, but his brow wrinkled. "What makes you ask that?"

Harold's eyebrows jumped a couple of times and a smug smile spread on his chubby face. "Because I know dynamite and how it's handled."

The sheriff glanced down at the box in his hands and back up. "Have you seen one of these in the area?"

Dodee leaned against Jim, wrapping both her arms around one of his. "Is it a dynamite box?"

Sheriff Ward Darby's lips screwed over to the side of his mouth and worked a bit. "Yes, ma'am, it is," he said finally. "But it's nothing to be alarmed about. Sometimes folks chere 'bouts use a stick or two to clear a stump out of a field. The main thing is that we like to keep track of these things just as a precaution."

"In case someone's trying to blow up the dam," Harold the Hound said and nodded. "I was thinking about that."

"Now don't go jumping to conclusions. It would take a pile of dynamite to blow up a dam—"

"But it could be used as a trigger for a truckload of fertilizer, like in Oklahoma."

"Say, who are you?"

"Harold Rucker, retired FBI."

"Ah." The sheriff nodded. "Well, Mr. Rucker, there's nothing like that happening around here, but I 'preciate your insight. What we'd like, folks, knowing you all will be goin' out canoeing in the swamps and down the Edisto River, what we'd like is if you all happen across a box like this"—he held it high again for all to see—"we'd 'preciate it if you'd let it be and call us 'bout it."

Harold nodded. "We'll keep our eyes open, Sheriff. You make a connection between this and the man killed up near Pack's Landing?"

The sheriff's brow wrinkled again. "There's no connection. The man—"

"I haven't ruled it out."

"The man drowned. It was an accident. He wasn't killed."

"Not what I heard. Like maybe foul play. Heard he received a blow to his head. Doesn't that—"

"He hit his head falling out of his boat. It knocked him out and he drowned. Case closed. We don't need to start any rumors chere."

Harold extended thumbs and forefingers of both hands

and cocked them toward the sheriff. "Right you are. Well, I still have contacts back at FBI headquarters in Washington, say, if you need an analysis expedited. And if I can help out in any way on this case, I place my expertise at your disposal."

"Well, thank you, Mr. Rucker, that's warmin' to know, but there is no case chere. Nothing to be alarmed 'bout. Just a standard investigation to occupy our time and earn our taxpayers' money."

ELEVEN

"WE'RE RUNNING a little late," Jody Sundance said when they piled out of the van at the Conference Center, "so make a fast pit stop if you need to, then hightail it for the mess hall. Unless you want to skip lunch."

"If it's paid for," Barry the Bear said, heading off for his room, "we ain't missin' it."

Jim changed into a short-sleeved polo shirt and ran a comb through his white hair while Dodee switched from a long-sleeved shirt to a light yellow blouse.

"Ready?" she asked. "Or do you want to skip lunch?"

"Do you have something better in mind?"

"Do you think you're up to it?"

"We better go to lunch."

They headed out and started power-walking toward the dining hall. Up ahead waddled the overweight figure of Harold the Hound.

"Slow down," Jim said.

"No, I want to catch up to hear what Harold has to say about the dynamite box."

"That's why I want to slow down."

"Aren't you curious?"

"There is nothing to it, Dodee." He slowed his pace. "You heard the sheriff, there is no case. It's just a standard investigation. Either way, it's none of our business."

"Well," she said, slowing down to stay with him, not happy-faced about it, "that's a Jim Dandy way of putting it."

"And don't start that either." He reached and patted her on the rear to punctuate it, and got a swift fist in his side for his troubles. "Ugh. I just gave you a tap."

"That was for your patronizing remarks."

"What's patronizing? It's not our business."

"I was just wondering if the dynamite might have something to do with the man who got killed the other day."

"He drowned, Dodee. Nothing to do with dynamite. Unless a massive explosion sent a tidal wave over him."

The buffet lunch consisted of simple fare, fruit cocktail, hamburger patties and rolls, salad makings with bottled dressings. Dodee built herself a salad, picked up one of the fruit cocktails and moved off. Jim put together two hamburgers and spread them with relish since the patties looked dry, and took along a small salad with blue cheese dressing. He wound through the maze of round tables for the space beside Dodee, and hesitated.

Sonofabitch.

She had put him next to Harold the Hound. She turned and gave him a smile of revenge.

He sat down, gave her a big phony grin, and leaned close. "Paybacks are hell," he whispered.

"Ya sez ya worked for the FBI?" Barry Rhodenbarr asked, hairy arms resting on the table.

"Thirty-eight years." Harold stuffed most of a hamburger into his mouth and kept on talking, oblivious of little bits that popped out. "Had a lot of interesting cases. Put a lot of people behind bars."

"Ya mean like bank robbers and things?"

Harold shifted a wad of food into his cheek. "Remember one time when we were asked in by the local police in West Virginia. A serial killer was murdering young men. Bodies kept turning up along a river bank, but by the time they were found the crime scene had been obliterated by rain and animals. Well, my boys looked at the forensics and figured out all the blood in their bodies had collected along their backs and the back of their legs. That meant the bodies had been lying on their backs after they had been murdered. When someone dies, gravity pools all the blood at the lowest spot where it solidifies.''

Harold swallowed another hamburger.

Topsy peered around the table through her small oval glasses and smiled. ''This is a gruesome topic for lunch.''

''No, go on,'' said her roommate, Elaine. ''What happened?''

Harold placed both hands on the table. ''Since the bodies had been found helter-skelter on the river bank, and there was no water in the lungs, we deduced that either they had been killed somewhere else and dumped there, or that the killer had revisited the bodies and turned them over sometime after he killed them. But like I said, the crime scene wasn't much help because of the time lapse between death and discovery. So we decided to make a helicopter pass along the river every few days, so if another body showed up we'd have a fresh crime scene. Well, as luck would have it, we made our first pass down the river and on the way back up we came upon a car parked on a bridge and a man dumping a body. You don't get that lucky very often.''

Harold stuffed the last of his hamburgers into his mouth.

''Jeez, don't let us hang here,'' Barry said, holding out a hairy arm, ''what the hell happened?''

''We caught him.''

''You mean he just threw up his hands and surrendered?'' Dodee asked.

''Oh, no. He hopped in the car and sped off, but we were in a helicopter. No way to outrun us. We alerted all the state police in the area and eventually got him road blocked. He gave up without a fight.''

''Fagedaboudit.''

''You must have had an exciting life,'' Topsy said. ''What do you make of this dynamite business?''

Jim looked at Dodee and rolled his eyes, but she paid no attention.

Harold the Hound tapped a finger at the side of his nose

and gave his eyebrows a couple of jumps. "Too early for things to fall into place," he said, his voice a whisper, "but I have a hunch it has to do with the dam and the hydro-electric plant."

Jim grimaced. Oh, great. Something to stir up Dodee's juices.

"That's bullshit," Leo the Lion said, knitting his brows to rearrange the furrows in his face. "It has nothing to do with the plant. You heard the sheriff. Probably a farmer using it to clear a field of tree stumps."

"What do you do, Topsy?" Jim asked, trying to change the subject.

"Me? Oh, nothing so exciting, Jim. I teach music in the Ohio school system." She turned to her roommate. "But Elaine's got an exciting job. Tell them about that."

"It's unusual, but not exciting," the plump Elaine said, then giggled. "Well, maybe it is. I take care of baby gorillas."

"Fagedaboudit!"

"You're kidding?" Dodee asked.

"Uh-uh. If for some reason the mother rejects them, or she has trouble with her milk, I get them to raise."

"They must be so cute. I'd love to paint them."

"They are cute," she nodded and smiled. "So ugly they're cute. And cuddly, like real children, reaching up to play with my hair. Just like real babies."

"See," Topsy said, "I told you she had an exciting job."

"How long have you been doing it?" Jim asked.

"Oh, about twenty years."

"What does your husband think of them?" Dodee asked.

"He's not especially happy about it. He tolerates them as long as he doesn't have to get involved. Just like I tolerate that he likes to come home from work and pretty much veg out."

"Are you retired, Dodee?" Topsy asked.

Jim shook his head. "She's an artist and has her own art gallery." He turned to her. "Sorry."

She shrugged. "That's okay."

Topsy's green eyes took her in from behind her oval glasses. "You're an artist?"

Dodee gave her a shy smile and nodded. "I've been doing more and more of my own work as my daughter's been taking over the gallery."

"Barry's in antiques" Bernice said. "This is an antique ring he bought me," she said, holding out the large diamond on her fat finger. "I guess we're both in antiques since I help out at the store sometimes."

"That's interesting," Harold said. "I'm interested in antique furniture. Do you go to auctions and things?"

"Yeah," Barry answered, scratching his stubbled neck and fingering his gold chain, "sometimes I gotta."

"He gets most things from his cousin, Bernie," Bernice said.

"Okay, everybody," Jody Sundance called out, clapping her hands as she walked to a spot where everyone could see her. "This afternoon we're going to the Carolina bays. We're running a bit late. We have the vans out here and we'll take you back to your rooms for a quick pit stop and then we'll head out. We'll be hiking around in the swamp, on dry land, if you want to change shoes. Let's go. Move 'em out."

"I want to change out of these sneakers," Dodee said, carrying her tray to the kitchen. "And I want to get my sketchbook."

"I want to take a nap," Jim said, following along. "I want to lie flat on my back and let all the blood pool to the bottom of my body."

She placed her tray of dishes on the kitchen pass-through. "You're not going?"

He put his arm around her. "Oh, I better go. In case someone tries to blow off a box of dynamite to drown you."

And she gave him another fist in the ribs.

Sonofabitch.

He had to stop making these wise-ass remarks.

TWELVE

THEY DROVE THROUGH a lonely wood, passed a sign for Woods Bay State Park and pulled into a small parking lot just past the ranger station. Jim climbed out of the van's side door and helped Dodee down.

"Here," he said, "let me take the backpack for you."

She handed it over and they started for the ranger station. He pointed to two trees with trunks five inches in diameter. "Those are bald cypress."

"Are they?" Topsy commented, coming up behind them. "I thought they only grew in water."

"No, they can grow on land. If you ever go up to Long Wood Gardens in Pennsylvania, you'll see some great ones growing on a stretch of lawn nowhere near water."

"You know a lot about trees?"

"Not a lot. I know about cypress because we have some near where I live. Also, I know of a man killed by one, stabbed through the chest."

Dodee, who had been snapping pictures, spun around. "That's right, it was a cypress. I forgot about that."

"You both saw it?" Topsy asked as they strolled.

"It was on our first Elderhostel. Where we met. It wasn't a pleasant sight."

"No, but it's nice that you two found each other, after losing your partners. That had to be special."

Jim held his breath. Was she also going to ask Dodee the "L" question?

But it was Dodee who spoke. "Oh, it was just Jim Dandy."

A tall, lean man in a green uniform and peaked hat stood on the porch of the rustic ranger station, one foot on the railing. His watery blue eyes looked out of a furrowed, leathery face, ancient enough to be in his late nineties or early zeros.

"Welcome to Woods Bay State Park." The ranger turned his leathery face to Jody Sundance. "Understand you're running a bit late. Want the ten-or twelve-cent tour?"

"I think we're caught up now. We can go for the long version."

The ranger opened the door and led the way into the station.

Jim followed to see a raised platform in the middle of the room with a long alligator in the middle of it. Stuffed. On a bed of sand along with some artificial swamp flowers around it. But nothing phony about the alligator; probably a mean critter when it was alive.

Outside it was rustic logs, but inside the walls were white wallboard, with pictures all around, and four fish tanks with snakes in them.

"Hello, everybody, I'm Ranger Spuds Darby, nicknamed that as a child because I loved potatoes. Fact is, I still do. The critter you see on the sand pile is called George, a fifteen foot alligator that used to live out here until one day he got into an altercation with an Oldsmobile. We believe George's grandfather is still out in the swamp, although we haven't seen him in five years. Perhaps we'll see him on our hike today."

"Fagedaboudit," Barry the Bear said. "Count me out. I'm a city guy."

"Shut up, Barry," Bernice said. "Let him finish."

"Thank you, ma'am. I'll be out front so if we run into granddaddy he'll have a lot to eat before he gets to you."

"Which if it got to Barry is only gonna give it indigestion," Bernice said.

"I kid about alligators, but they don't eat humans. At least as far as we know. They're not critters to mess with in any case. There are crocodiles in the United States, farther down in Florida—"

"If they're not extinct," Dorothy the Dove threw in.

"Yes, ma'am, but if you run into them they'd be interested in inviting you to dinner. Fortunately, they're not around here."

Ranger Darby stepped over to the fish tanks. "We have some interesting snakes here. When we get back I'll tell you about them. For now, if you see any along the trail, leave them be. This is their home, not ours. But I'll be sure to point them out to you. Especially if we see any cottonmouth moccasins. Normally this time of year we wouldn't have to worry about them, but this has been an especially warm Fall, although I hear that'll change shortly. I'll also try to point out some birds as we go along, but I 'spect Jody can do a better job of that."

She nodded. "Between Ranger Darby and myself, we'll try to call your attention if we spot anything."

"If there are any questions?"

"Are you any relation to Sheriff Darby?" Simon Cinnamon asked.

"Ward's my nephew. How did you meet him?"

"He came by the camp this morning," Jody said.

"Looking for a box of dynamite," Harold said.

The wrinkles on the ranger's leathery face rearranged themselves as his lips turned down. "Someone must be fixing to blow up some stumps. I guess we're 'bout ready to head out. May I be so indelicate as to suggest you may want to use the facilities; we're in for a decent walk and there are no outhouses along the way. We'll gather outside and when everyone is ready, we'll give it a start."

Old Ranger Darby led them on a fifteen-minute chase that belied his age, down a raised trail through the swamp until he shunted them off onto a small boardwalk, leading them over black water to a fenced-in area with some benches at the end.

"We're 'bout in the middle of the Carolina bays now, so called for the bay bushes and bay-like trees that inhabit them. We're not sure what formed the bays, but we believe it goes back to the last ice age when the rise in the water tables slowed swiftly flowing streams to a 'possum's crawl. Vegetation built up and was submerged on a layer of mud to form something akin to peat bogs. All Carolina bays have certain similar characteristics. All are oval in shape and all orientated northwest to southeast. They have a mat of vegetation and soil, and below that a deeper layer of black peat which holds in the water, with brown peat below that, a plug of clay, and finally sandy soil. They are dependent upon rainfall to maintain the water level."

Jim glanced over to see Dodee with her sketchbook out, making bold strokes as the man talked.

"In the city of Sumpter is a big Carolina bay that fills in the wet years and dries up in the dry years to become a sea of grass. Some years ago, during one of the dry spells, a developer put a shopping center in one portion of that bay and the last couple of years the parking lot and buildings have been flooded out. The business leaders have been screaming to the city to pump it out and do something about all the frogs. So you want to be careful how you all treat a Carolina bay."

Dodee continued to work, rapidly capturing the man's furrowed countenance.

"If you'll look over the side," he said, bending over the railing, "you'll see knobby wooden knees belonging to this chere cypress tree, which we reckon to be five hundred years old. Funny thing about the cypress knees, we don't really know what purpose they serve. We believe it has to do with aeration of the submerged roots, but we're not really sure. Also notice how black the water is. That's caused by tannic acid leaching from the cypress trees and from the peat underneath the mat. It turns the water black and helps keep down the mosquito and insect population. If you all are rested up, we'll strike out on an old trail that leads through the swamp, part of an old canal that was once used to pipe logs through.''

And off they went.

Jim sidled up next to Dodee. "How did it turn out?"

She showed him. "He's got a beautiful face, full of life's journey, like he's a million years old."

"He walks like he's twenty-one."

Simon Cinnamon leaned in close. "Amen to that, brother. I keep fit, but I'm having a hard time keeping up."

"You keep fit, ha," Phyllis said, her five-foot-one glaring up at his six-foot-two, "you come walking every morning with me, then you can say you keep fit."

Simon glanced at Jim, raised his dark eyebrows and screwed his lips to one side. "Every morning when I went into the office, I was a general at the top of the heap, and every evening when I came home I was a private in charge of the garbage. Sometimes I think I should have retired from the marriage and stayed in the military."

Phyllis, ten feet ahead of them now, turned and cocked her honey-blond head toward him. "Did you say something, Simon?"

"I said we're having so much fun together, I'm glad I retired from the military."

She raised her head and wrinkled her nose at him before turning back to the trail.

"Did you ever handle explosives?" Dodee asked.

"Yes, ma'am," Simon answered, using his deep military voice. "I had training in demolition."

"How about dynamite?"

Jim shook his head. "Oh, boy, here we go."

"Well, I'm just asking, sweetheart."

"Am I missing something?" Simon asked.

"Dodee is ready to solve a crime even when one doesn't exist."

"No, it's just the opposite. I was just thinking about the ranger's casual reaction when he heard the sheriff was looking for a box of dynamite."

"The explosives I handled were plastic. They're stable, easy to mold and shape, and fairly easy to use."

"If you were going to blow up something, like the dam—"

Jim held out his hand. "See what I mean?"

"—would you use dynamite?"

An ivory grin split Simon's milk-chocolate face. "You've been talking to Harold Rucker. Now there's a man ready to solve a case before there is one. Good thing he's rooming with Leo or he'd be following the sheriff so close the man wouldn't be able to turn around."

"How's that?"

"If Leo didn't laugh down Ricker's theories we'd all be suspects."

Suddenly the ruckus of something banging away at a tree stump cut across the quiet of the swamp. Everyone bunched together and fell silent. Heads swung toward the noise, binoculars raised to their eyes. A large bird flitted into sight, landed on a dead tree, and started pounding away, like it was time to shout "Tim-m-m-mber!"

A murmur of "pileated woodpecker," spread through the group, to which Dorothy the Dove added *"Dryocopus pileatus."* A large bird, about the size of a crow, it had a flaming red crest on its head that could be seen whenever it paused long enough from banging away to get a look.

"Reminds me of my grandchildren's joke," Simon whispered. "A woodpecker walks into a cocktail lounge and asks, 'Is the bartender here?' "

The bird got tired of the show and flew off with a "kik-kik" in search of a better tree.

"We have quite a few in the park and will probably come across some more," the ranger said, then pointed down a new path. "Notice how straight and how much higher the ground is chere?"

Jim stared down the trail that cut a swath through the forest. Water hickory and cypress trees grew right up to it on the right. A deep path of black water twenty feet wide followed on the left, before bay bushes and clumps of bog took over again, like little islands where wildflowers grew. Three mud turtles eyed them suspiciously from a fallen tree branch that dipped into the water.

"Back in the days of slavery, they made this a road running along chere and piled the dirt high so that this became a horse path to pull floated logs to market. Notice also some rusty metal bands down here."

The ranger moved to the other side of the trail and pointed down to a few chunks of metal interspersed among tree trunks and roots.

"That's all that's left of a still that operated back chere in the twenties to keep it hidden from the revenuers. They floated skiffs of corn and sugar up the canal and returned with it in liquid form. This was an ideal spot, not only in the way of secrecy, but because there was plenty of wood to fuel their kettles, and there is a fresh-water spring down there with sweet water. One more thing of interest, up here 'bout fifty feet."

Ranger Spuds Darby led them forward and Jody pointed out a northern parula warbler, a blue-black bird with a yellow throat, and closer by, a flame-red bird with black wings.

"That's a scarlet tanager," Jody said.

"Piranga olivacea," Dorothy said, giving its Latin name.

When they came to their next halt, the ranger pointed to a spot of high ground full of moss and flowers. A rotted stump and the barest remains of what could have been a log now provided a home for whatever vegetation could find purchase.

"What you're seeing there is all that's left of a giant American chestnut, killed by the blight that ripped through the eastern United Stated. It started in the twenties, in the thirties by the time it got down this far, and wiped out the major hardwood of our virgin forests. Every once in a while a sprout will still pop up from that stump, grow to 'bout twenty feet I reckon, even produce nuts occasionally, before the blight brings her down again. It's almost rotted away chere, but had that log rested down in the peat, not exposed to the air, it would still be in the same condition as when it fell. Okay," he raised a hand in the air and signaled like a cavalry officer of old, "as Jackie Gleason used to say, 'and away we go.'"

The tall, gaunt figure of Farouk Farhang remained rooted to the spot as the crowd of Elderhostelers flowed around him, his wild blue eyes staring up at the stump.

"See something?" Jim asked.

The wild eyes turned on him, as if a bright light had just snapped on. He said nothing for a moment, then blinked. "Yes, I am looking at the rotted log. I am thinking of what the ranger said, yes, about if it had been sunk in the peat. I would like very much to have that log."

Jim looked at the rotted remains and back at him.

"What would you do with it?"

"Chestnut's not a good wood," said a voice behind him, and Jim turned to see Leo the Lion's small eyes peering out from under his farmer's hat, but when Jim turned back he saw Farouk's eyes blazing at the man.

"Even a good log by the side of the road wouldn't be worth cutting up," Leo said and moved on.

Farouk's gaze followed him.

"What would you do with the log?" Jim asked again.

Farouk turned back to him, turning his whole body as if his neck was frozen in place. "He knows nothing of wood. American chestnut in a bog and hardened over years, worth big dollars for special furniture and paneling for old homes."

Jim glanced up ahead to see Dodee and Harold the Hound talking as they followed the ranger, then she turned and motioned to him, forming her fingers into a rectangle in front of her face to indicate the camera he carried in the backpack. He hurried forward to where everyone stood in a semi-circle, gazing out over the water at a hump of marsh, cameras snapping around him. A shaft of sunlight shined through the canopy onto a fallen log, like a stage spotlight with shadows surrounding it. Then he suddenly realized it wasn't a log.

"My, my," Ranger Spuds Darby said, "there's George's grandfather."

Jim stared at it. The alligator had to be twenty feet.

"Tell you the truth," Spuds Darby said, "I heard others say they had seen him, but I didn't believe it. Now here he is. I want to tell you this chere critter has made my day."

THIRTEEN

"Could i ask you to do something for me?"

After dinner they had gone to the showing of *Path of the Paddle,* a video about various paddle strokes to get a canoe to do everything except stand on end, but ravaged by exercise, fresh air, and lack of an afternoon nap, he kept falling asleep. Afterward, washed up and in pajamas, he had revived enough to study Dodee's sketches while she had gone into the bathroom.

The door opened and she came out. "Could I ask you to do something for me?"

He turned to see her standing in a nightshirt with two teddy bears and the announcement Born to Hug.

"What did you have in mind?" he asked.

She moved her shoulder around. "I might have overdone it a bit. It feels okay, but I don't want to be sore when we go down the river tomorrow. I was wondering—"

"Oh, now you need me. This afternoon you were poking me in the ribs, but now I'm a nice guy."

"You are a nice guy."

"Sweet and generous?"

"Double sweet and generous."

"Handsome and strong?"

"Not only handsome and strong, but humble."

He sat on the bottom of the bed, spread his legs, and patted the space in between. "Sit down and I'll massage it for you. Because, sweetheart," he said, trying to imitate

Humphrey Bogart, "I'm a sucker for a good-looking dame."

She sat down and he started working on her neck, breathing in the cinnamon-spice of her perfumes as he slowly worked his fingers into the complexus muscles right at the base of her skull and slowly moving down. It wasn't what she had complained about, but he felt some tautness there, and he wanted to relax the whole muscle chain.

She moaned. "I could kill for this."

"You say that every time."

"Do I?"

He gave a little laugh. "Yes, you do."

"I can't remember, but I would kill for it."

He started on trapeziuses, connecting the base of the neck to the shoulders, moving gently at first, then digging in more deeply.

"What were you and Harold the Hound talking about today?"

"When?"

"Out on the trail, before we saw the alligator."

She wagged her head back and forth. "He thinks there's a connection between the man who was killed—"

"You mean the man who drowned?"

"—and the dynamite that was found—"

"Empty dynamite box."

"—and has something to do with the lake. Like the power plant."

"Oh, boy." He took her left arm with one hand and applied pressure against the back with the other, slowly stretching and relaxing to ease the tension. "And you supplied him with eager ears."

"What do you mean by that?" she asked, an edge to her voice.

He kissed the back of her neck. "I didn't mean it to sound so negative. I just don't want us needlessly involved in police matters like our last two Elderhostels."

She half-turned to stare at him, face inches from his.

"And wasn't there something there? Didn't someone end up in jail before it was all over?"

He took hold of her head, turned it around, and started stretching the right shoulder.

"You didn't answer me, sweetheart." He kept working on her shoulder. "Besides, it's not me. It's Harold Rucker."

He finished on the shoulder. "How's that?"

"Ummm," she moaned.

"I take that to mean it's better." He scrunched back, bringing his leg from around her and standing at the side of the bed. "Lie down flat and let me get your back while I'm at it."

"But you have to admit," she said, doing as he commanded, folding her arms under her head, "he is a retired FBI agent and there does seem to be something going on."

He started working on her back muscles. "If he really thinks that, why doesn't he do something about it, like tell the sheriff?"

"He is doing something about it. He's sent the names of everyone on the Elderhostel to Washington to get background checks."

"You're kidding."

"S'what he said. But he doesn't want to get the sheriff involved until he has some proof."

He continued kneading her back muscles and when the hem of the nightgown hiked up, he started on her gluteus maximus.

"This is helping my shoulder?" she asked.

"You never know." He slapped her softly on the bare rump. "Roll over and raise your knees while I get the light."

"This is going to make me feel better?"

"I hope so," he said, snapping off the light, "I know it certainly will me."

He crawled into her arms, kissing her, tasting her toothpaste, feeling the smoothness of her legs coming up to encircle his, the smell of soap and perfume and her body. And they did the old and slow jackrabbit trick again, a lot older and slower this time with yesterday's hunger now only a whimper, warm and tender, and just a little mad at the end, breaking up into gasps and soft cries in the night.

She snuggled close, the nightgown lost somewhere in the fray. "Two nights in a row?"

"I've been saving up."

"So you have." She raised her head. "You asked me about Harold, what were you talking about down at the end of the line?"

"Go to sleep." He listened to the quiet of the night, the sound of an owl somewhere outside the window, voices approaching the front door, then passing and receding in the distance. "End of what line?"

"When you and Farouk were talking."

"Oh, it turns out he's a woodworker and wished he could have had the chestnut log before it rotted. Leo said chestnut wasn't good for anything, but Farouk seemed to think it was."

"What did you say?"

"I said, there's Dodee up there waving for me and if I want to get any tonight I better get my ass in gear." She slapped him on the stomach. "Ugh. You're getting very physical this trip. I didn't know I was getting tangled up with a sadist."

"You're tangled up, as you put it, with an exceptionally refined lady who, at times, needs to chastise her partner for being what's known in the vernacular as a smart ass."

"Be careful what you say about that part of my anatomy. We did have beans for dinner."

She swung a leg and arm over him to scrunch up to his side. "Are we tangled up enough for you?"

"We're as tangled up as we can get."

"As a warm body you're just Jim Dandy."

"Don't start."

He felt himself drifting off, until the call of the owl

brought his eyes open, and he stared at the night patterns playing on the window, shadows cast by a waxing moon.

Were they tangled up enough for him? Had he missed something there? A call to take their relationship to another stage? And Topsy's question came back like a haunting refrain: *So you fell in love again?*

He and Dodee had only been together for a year, if he counted all the times they talked on the phone, but slightly more than two weeks face-time. Whatever he felt for her, it certainly was more than a casual friendship.

But love?

Not like with Penny. But he had been with Penny over thirty-five years. Memories glued a relationship together.

Maybe he and Dodee just needed more glue.

Even so, how deep did his feelings go?

And suppose she didn't share them?

He craned his neck and looked down at her, already deep in sleep.

One thing he did know, he loved looking at her.

As for the rest, he would give it a rest. A vacation. Time to take up the quest again in the morning. With that decision out of the way, he closed his eyes and turned off the world.

FOURTEEN

HE SLIPPED OUT OF BED as the first light of dawn gave definition to the trees outside their window, leaving Dodee in a rumpled heap. He went to the bathroom, washed up, and put on the tan pair of convertible cargo pants he had bought from Cabela's, like those of the Natural Resources agent. He laid a second pair on the bed for Dodee. Then, wondering if she would realize they were a present for her, he scribbled a note to that effect and left it on top.

If they were going for a long canoe outing down the river, changing from long pants to shorts as the day warmed up would be a plus.

He put on a mushroom-colored travel shirt, a pair of trail shoes and, feeling like a Cabela's advertisement, eased out the door into an early morning chill.

A stiff breeze off the lake hit him in the face as he hurried to the Hospitality Room, smelling coffee perking as soon as he entered. He came around the corner to see the tall, gaunt figure of Farouk Farhang. The lean, olive face turned to him, wild eyes staring, as if the man were going to pull out a scimitar and hack him to pieces on the spot.

"Good morning, Farouk," he said, breaking the silence.

The man started, as if popping out of sleep. "Oh, good morning, Jim. It is Jim, yes, Jim the Rabbit?"

"Jim the Jackrabbit. Coffee smells good."

He gave a curt nod with his lips turned down. "Yes, I make it. I make it good. Like in Afghanistan. No, not like Afghanistan. There we made it dark and thick like syrup.

Like Oxra make." He raised a fist in the air. "Strong. Not weak like here. But I make it stronger. Give more taste. You tell me you like?"

Was that a question or an order? Some pops and sputters came from the kitchen. Farouk gave him a smile that complemented the crazed eyes. Was there anyone home inside?

Farouk threw two fists in the air. "Coffee is finished."

Jim nodded. And he would like it even if it shriveled his penis.

Farouk led the way, poured a cup, and handed it to Jim. "You taste, you like."

He thought of adding a cream packet, but Farouk's wild eyes were watching his every move. Sonofabitch. It felt like his hair had been zapped. "Good coffee, Farouk."

The man beamed. "You have taste, Jim the Jackrabbit. You find welcome in my home country." He poured himself a cup and tasted it, then wiggled his hands back and forth. "Not bad. But not good like Oxra."

Jim wandered back into the main room to see that Harold the Hound had slipped in. He sat reading a magazine and munching on bite-sized candy bars from the bowl that someone had replenished.

"Coffee's ready," he said to the FBI guy.

Harold waved a hand. "Maybe later." And he popped another miniature Heath bar into his mouth.

The door slammed and they both turned as Dorothy Gramm came in, brushing back her Hamill-haircut to reveal golden earrings that looked like birds in flight.

"Stiff wind out there," she said and sniffed. "Ah, coffee. Normally I'd opt for herbal tea, but this morning I need something to open my eyes."

Jim nodded. Ha. Not only open her eyes, but every other orifice as well.

Farouk sat on one of the couches and Jim took a straight chair across from him. "You retired?"

"Me, no. I am engineer. Am engineer for the Corps of Engineers."

"Then you must be a citizen."

"Of course."

"And you do woodworking in your spare time?"

"Of course."

"Those yellow PFDs you had on yesterday, are they your own?"

"Of course."

Jim nodded. Of course.

"Oxra and I have canoe." Farouk turned and motioned to the white Toyota Sienna minivan sitting out in the parking lot with a roof rack on top. "Sometimes we canoe where I work. I look for old wood. Sometimes when I work, I take old stumps from river."

"You work for the Corps of Engineers?" Dorothy asked, coming out of the kitchen with her coffee.

"Yes, Corps of Engineers."

"You're the ones who are disturbing the natural balance of the rivers with canals no one uses and dams that are marginal."

"No, I open side channels."

"Side channels?"

"Of course."

Jim nodded. Of course.

"I don't understand," Dorothy said.

"When Corps close up oxbows and side channels, river become fast and deep, but the forest turn into mud flat. Now we go back and open side channels like before. Slow water, sandbars, many fish, ducks and longneck geese. Much better. The forests comes back."

Jim turned to the window as two figures whisked by, Clyde and Becky, quick-walking down the hill. He turned back to Farouk. "You dig them out again?"

"They are still there. Only the entrance dammed up. We take away the dam."

"Like with a bulldozer?"

"Sometimes, sometimes with dynamite."

Jim watched Harold's eyes pop open at that, the FBI guy taking it all in.

"I never heard of this," Dorothy said. "Where are you doing it?"

"Hamburg chute in Iowa. I do that." Suddenly he jumped to his feet. "Ah, Oxra." He pointed to his wife standing in the doorway of their room across the grass courtyard, her long black and gray hair reaching almost to the child-like woman's waist. "I go take Oxra coffee now." He beamed at Dorothy. "Good coffee, yes?"

She took a swallow and nodded. "Good coffee."

He strode into the kitchen, came out seconds later with two steaming mugs, and marched across the courtyard.

"You like this coffee?" Jim asked her.

She gave him a nod, then shook her head. "Actually, it's terrible."

"Right, I think he put in three packets. Come on, I'll make a fresh pot."

He dumped the remains and started fresh while Dorothy emptied both cups and rinsed them out.

"If you didn't like it," she asked, leaning against the cabinet, "why were you drinking it?"

"Because Farouk might be all right and everything, but he looks a little weird."

She nodded. "Intimidating. I think it's the eyes." She glanced sharply at him. "You think he's telling the truth about blowing up those side channels and returning the rivers to their natural state?"

A shadow slipped by the kitchen pass-through. No doubt Harold the Hound doing a little eavesdropping.

"Whatever else Farouk may be, he seems to be guileless. I believe if he told you he's blowing up dams to open side channels to rivers, that's what he's doing."

"Um. That makes him one of the good guys."

"You're really wrapped up in this environmental stuff."

She sighed and nodded. "The oceans are heating up and the polar ice caps melting. People our age need to get involved so we can leave something for our grandchildren. We have the power if we'd only use it."

The coffee perked away.

"What else do you do?"

"I act as a surrogate mother to establish new migratory routes for large birds."

He blinked at her. "You mean like in the movie, *Fly Away Home?*"

She smiled and nodded. "I lead them in an ultra-lite plane and they follow behind, thinking I'm mama. I've helped reestablish some old routes for geese and sandhill cranes. The next big adventure is to try to set up a second flock of whooping cranes."

She fingered her earrings and Jim saw that's what they were, whooping cranes.

"There are only one hundred and eight-three whooping cranes left in the wild. One oil spill in their Texas winter grounds could wipe them out. If we can establish a second wintering flock, we'd go a long way toward taking them off the endangered list."

The coffeemaker sputtered in the last throes of completion.

"How does your husband feel about all this?"

"Dave goes along with it. He's involved."

The coffeemaker finished with a last spit and Jim poured two mugs. "I wish you a lot of luck with relocating the whooping cranes."

"I've been following them since there were only sixteen left back in the forties. We need money more than luck." She went on to say that the organization was listed on the Internet, at http://fathergoose.durham.net. "We're independent and nonprofit."

"I will." He handed her one of the mugs and filled up a third. "For Dodee," he said. "I'll check out the website and make a donation. And I'll start paying more attention to the environment. How's that?"

"Join the Sierra Club. Make a difference. Blow up a dam."

He took both mugs and strode back into the Hospitality Room in time to see Harold the Hound jump away from the pass-through. "Just made a fresh pot of coffee."

"Thanks, Jim. Get one in a minute."

Outside, the chill wind rippled the surface of the lake, visible now with the morning sun filtering through broken clouds. He headed back toward his room.

Dorothy had gotten to him.

He pictured his grandchildren, Joseph Paul, Wendy, and Courtney, and Morgan, a little sweetie at nine months.

What kind of world did he want to leave them?

He kicked at the door to his room and it cracked a few moments later. Dodee looked out at him.

"Coffee man."

She let him in, dressed in a wheaten chamois shirt the color of her hair and the Cabela's two-in-one pants he had laid out for her. "Thank you, sweetheart," she said, taking the coffee, then putting an arm on his shoulder, "for both the coffee and especially the pants."

She gave him a lingering kiss.

"Careful," he said, coming up for air. Her eyebrows arched. He kissed her on the tip of her nose. "Don't make promises I can't keep."

FIFTEEN

THE COOL BREEZE had picked up by the time they started for breakfast at Lazar Hall. They ran into Harold the Hound coming out of the Hospitality Room.

"Morning, Dodee, Jim," he said and pointed toward a yellow Dodge Neon. "Can I give you ride?"

"You go ahead," Jim answered. "We'll walk."

Harold hesitated, glancing at his car, then shrugged. "Yeah, you're right." He patted his heavy stomach. "Gotta get back in shape."

Jim glanced at him. *Back* in shape? The guy had never been in shape. Except he must have if he had been an FBI agent.

Harold glanced all around, like he was checking for someone, and Jim glanced around himself, woods and grass fields buttered with dandelions on one side, the wind-mottled lake on the other, but nobody that he could see.

"Called the office this morning, Dodee," Harold said in a low voice. "Getting background info on everyone here."

Jim turned to him. "Why are you doing this?"

"You're asking that after this morning? Farouk and Dorothy talking about blowing up dams and handling dynamite?"

"You didn't tell me about that," Dodee said.

"Because there's nothing to it." They hiked past one of the lodges under a sky now swept free of clouds. "Dorothy was just making idle conversation about the environment, and Farouk's job is opening up old creek beds that have been dammed up.''

"With dynamite,'' Harold added.

He shrugged and let it go, but Harold stopped them after they rounded the dining hall to the entrance.

"If I'm wrong, doing a background check won't hurt. In the meantime, can I depend on your discretion to keep it quiet?'' He placed his index finger against the side of his nose. "I don't want to tip anyone off.''

Dodee ran two fingers across her lips in a zipping motion.

Jim stared at them both for a second, then shook his head. "I'll keep it quiet, not because there's anything to it, but because I don't want anyone getting upset.''

He entered the large dining room and caught up with the honey-blond Phyllis Cinnamon as she turned from the buffet with her tray.

"Where's the General this morning?'' he asked, loading two pancakes onto his plate.

"I ran out of sun block and he went to the store for me.'' She nodded toward the sunny day outside. "I have fair skin and sunburn easily. Now I hear we're not canoeing down the river.''

He added two sausages, three pieces of bacon. "Where are we going?''

She shrugged. "Some swamp, I think Jody said.'' And she headed off for a table.

He topped everything off with three eggs, grabbed an apple juice and followed after. "Morning, everyone.'' He took one of the last three chairs, Dodee to sit next to him, and Phyllis saving the last for her husband. He spread his breakfast booty around and got rid of his tray. "The wind has picked up.''

"Yes, it has,'' Clyde the Coyote said.

Simon Cinnamon marched up to the table in light blue poplin jacket and brown pants, white-toothed smile on his milk-chocolate face. He slipped on a pair of horn-rimmed glasses and read the label on a plastic bottle he held. "Sea-and-Ski, Sun-block Thirty-two." And he set it in front of Phyllis.

"Thank you, dear, I saved you a seat."

He nodded and boomed out in his basement voice, "Morning, Leo, Barry, Bernice, Clyde, Becky, Dodee—"

"Hey, whaddya doin'?" Barry asked, holding out hairy arms. "Takin' a memory test? Ya pass."

"Duh," Bernice said, fingering a name tag on her flowery, big-bosomed blouse, "we're all wearing tags."

"Oh, yeah."

"I see you're having a hearty breakfast, Jim," Simon said.

"I believe in having a good breakfast. It sets you right up for a good lunch. Besides, we got a long canoe trip ahead of us." He glanced at Phyllis. "Except you said we're not going on the river?"

Leo jerked up from his plate. "Who said that?"

"That's what I heard," Phyllis said.

Leo's furrowed face turned to Jody Sundance at the next table. "We're not going canoeing?"

"Yes, we are, just at a different place."

"I need some breakfast," Simon said. He put the horn-rimmed glasses in his pocket and headed for the buffet table.

"Has anyone been keeping up with the Spanish galleon they found off the coast?" Clyde the Coyote asked. He moved his cup over in front of Becky the Beaver. "I believe I'll have a second cup of coffee this morning." He turned back to them as she picked up his cup and trooped off to the coffee thermoses. "I've been reading about it in the local newspaper. Seems like they found treasure worth between two and three hundred million dollars."

Barry dropped his fork. "Two hundred mil? Faged-aboudit. That much money, gotta keep it in Fort Knox."

Becky returned with Clyde's coffee.

"Thank you, my dear." He added cream and sugar and

stirred it. "They've been storing the treasure in a local bank in Georgetown. Like to go down there and see that."

Phyllis glanced at Simon as he returned with a tray full of breakfast. "The doctor said we were to lose weight, dear."

"He didn't say *we* were to lose weight, dear. He said I could stand to lose a few pounds."

"Fifteen pounds."

"That's a few pounds. Look, I'm on vacation. Besides, I'm stoking up for the long trip on some Jim Dandy advice."

"Believe me," Dodee said, with a smile, "that's the worst kind."

Jody stood up and clapped her hands for their attention. "Okay, everybody, listen up." She clapped her hands again. "The wind has picked up and shifted on us, so we're going to change our morning schedule. We're going to Sparkleberry Swamp, where it's more protected, and we'll shift the down-river paddle to Thursday. We'll still have Hank Davis' nature lecture this afternoon. He's the Natural Resources agent we met Sunday night." She looked at her watch. "I'll give you forty-five minutes to do what you have to do and then the vans will be by to pick you up. A word to the wise, there are no bathroom facilities once we get out in the swamps at Sparkleberry. Any questions?"

"What should we wear?" Topsy asked, running her hand through her auburn, poodle-cut hair.

"It's chilly now, but they are calling for it to warm up a bit during the day, so I would wear some layered clothing that you can take off."

"When did you decide to change our plans?" Leo the Lion asked.

"This morning when we saw how the wind was blowing. Okay, I'll see you in forty-five minutes."

Jim took his and Dodee's plates, put them on his tray, and took them both back to the kitchen. They strolled back by way of the lake shoreline, holding hands and looking out at the white-capped chop kicked up by the breeze. They took Jody's advice about the bathroom, and Dodee stuffed a sweater for each of them in the backpack, just in case.

Two vans waited in the parking lot and as they boarded the second, towing a trailer stacked with red canoes, Rebecca—Becca the Body—smiled at them from the driver's seat.

"Put your tongue back in your mouth," Dodee whispered.

"I told you, sweetie, I only have eyes for you."

They watched out the window as Phyllis waited while Simon got a jacket out of his burgundy Mercedes, then both climbed into the van, taking the back seat.

Jim swung around toward them. "Well, Phyllis, we're off to the swamp to visit some of your friends."

"My friends?"

"Didn't you say you liked snakes?"

"Oh, God, don't even mention them," Simon said.

Phyllis grimaced. "I think I'll wait for you all right here."

Jody stuck her head into the van and made a head count. "We're still waiting for two people."

Barry nodded toward the window. "Here's Harold."

The overweight FBI guy came wobbling down the walk.

"Leo coming?" Jody called to him.

"Already gone," Harold said, coming up. "He said he had to go somewhere afterward and took his own car."

Her brow wrinkled. "How does he know where we're going?"

Harold shrugged. "Wasn't he here in the spring?"

"But I'm not sure we went to Sparkleberry."

Harold shrugged again. "He seemed to know. If he doesn't show up, I guess he was wrong."

"Maybe he followed the truck with the rest of the canoes. Okay, Rebecca, let's head 'em out."

SIXTEEN

THEY BOUNCED OVER humps and dips in a bucking-bronco dirt road and followed Jody's van down into Sparkleberry Swamp's parking lot, a circle of sunlight surrounded by trees. A white pickup waited for them with another trailerful of red canoes. Leo the Lion's blue Taurus was parked under a tree overhang on the far side of the lot while the only other car, a tan Mercedes SUV with Missouri license plates, sat on one side of a double-launch boat ramp.

Becca the Body parked the van next to the pickup and Jim followed Barry and Bernice out the side door, turning to help Dodee down.

"Look at that." He pointed to the Mercedes where Leo stood, straw hat hiding his eyes from the sun, talking to a man cranking a pontoon boat onto a trailer, *Two For The Road* painted in red on its side. "I think those are the guys we met Sunday," he said, strolling toward them.

Leo turned at his approach. "Hi, Jim."

"Jody didn't think you knew the way to this place."

He shrugged and grinned, rearranging his furrowed face. "I'm here."

"Right." Jim turned to the man cranking the boat, bulldog face, heavy body of a beer truck driver, dressed in a camouflage shirt with the arms ripped off. "Hi, I see you're still fishing. You must be catching something."

The man gave a last crank to the boat and cocked his head at Jim, an unspoken question on his face.

"We met. You gave us directions to the 4-H Center on Sunday."

The guy hit himself in the head. "Right. I knew your face was familiar, but I couldn't place it."

A second man, square jaw and flat crew cut, hopped out of the tan SUV. "That buttoned up, Sarg?"

"Yeah, Bill, I got it."

Jim nodded at him. "What have you been catching?"

"A cold mostly," answered Bill.

"Some largemouth bass and some black crappie," Sarg said.

Dodee came up and put her arm under Jim's. "Hi," she said to the two men.

"Looks like you made it to the 4-H Center," Sarg said.

"Thanks to your directions." Dodee turned to Jim. "They're putting the canoes in the water. I didn't know if you wanted to help."

"Yeah, I guess I should." He waved at the men. "Good fishing."

Leo followed along. "Those guys been out since early morning."

They grabbed the last canoe off the trailer and hustled it down the free side of the concrete boat ramp to the water's edge. Jody was handing out PFDs and Dodee already had one on and an extra for him. He slipped into it as Jody called for attention.

"We have one piece of open water to cover, a channel leading to the lake, before we head off into the swamp. We have a little bit of shelter here, but a couple of hundred feet out we'll come to the channel. The wind will be against us. It's only about ten knots so it's not a major problem, but we'll have to fight it 'til we get to the turnoff. On the plus side, when we're tired on the way back, it will give us a nice push. I'll go first and Rebecca will bring up the rear. If you're having trouble, call out and one of us will come and give you a hand. Any questions?"

"Yeah," Barry Rhodenbarr said, "I wanna go home."

"Don't pay attention to him," Bernice said. "We're goin'."

"We're goin'?"

"We're goin'."

"Marvelous."

Jim turned to Dodee. "How's your shoulder?"

"Fine. I had an expert massage it last night."

He braced the canoe between his legs while she moved forward, stowed the backpack, and sat down, then he climbed in and shoved off as she braced her paddle across the gunnels.

"Okay?" Dodee called.

"We're on our way," he said, giving three fast power strokes.

He steered them around a tall cypress tree and grabbed onto a drooping branch, steadying the canoe. "When we head out, let's get near the front and keep a steady pace. If you get tired, switch sides and I'll follow you. Then when we get to the turnoff we can rest while everyone else is catching up."

She pulled her camera out of the backpack and clicked off pictures of the others launching, the Jacksons from Iowa just putting in.

Dorothy and David skimmed up. "See the great egret, Jim?" she asked. *"Casmerodius albus."*

He turned to see a large, white, crane-like bird stalking in the shallows, mottled in tree-filtered sunlight, its curved, slender neck shooting out and its yellow beak snagging a fish.

Jody signaled them as the Smiths from Arkansas launched the last canoe with the Jacksons from Iowa. "Okay, let's head out and give it a steady pull until we reach the turn off into the swamp. We'll be sheltered by trees after that. Let's go."

Jim put his back into the stroke, Dodee too, and the canoe answered, gliding over the water, their flat bottom giving little resistance. They moved up to keep pace with

Jody Sundance. Clyde the Coyote's and Becky the Beaver's canoe hung in there with them, the bantam doctor calling out, "Stroke, stroke," and Jim wondered if he had picked up that little habit during puberty.

They moved out into the open sunshine of the hundred-foot-wide channel, turned left into the wind, and immediately felt the drag as they acted like broadsails on a galleon going the wrong way.

"You okay?" he called to Dodee.

"Yes, but I'm going to shift sides."

"Go ahead. Don't tell me. Just do it and I'll follow."

They kept on, Clyde's "stroke, stroke," falling behind now, only Jody's canoe in front of them.

"Jody," someone called from behind, and she twisted in her seat, then shifted her paddle, effortlessly spinning around. "I have to go back."

"Can we keep going?" Dodee asked. "I don't want to lose ground."

"Go ahead. You'll see a fallen-down tree on the right. Not too far. Wait for us there."

"Okay, Jim," Dodee called back to him, "let's do it."

He dug into the water, feeling good, working, exerting, muscles taking up the slack, and before he got tired, Dodee shifted and he followed, new muscles coming into play. The canoe shot through the water with little whirlpools gurgling down the sides, like it was a low-flying bird, a great blue heron skimming over the surface.

Fifteen minutes went by and their pace had started to wear.

"Is this the fallen-down tree?" Dodee asked.

He looked up to a dead tree, wind-blown at an angle so that it hung up on a neighbor, its sun-bleached branches filled with dead strands of Spanish moss.

"That's a leaning tree, not a fallen one." He scanned up ahead. "I think I see one up there with a channel marker beside it. Not far."

They charged off again, pace definitely slower now, the

wind telling on them, but three hundred feet ahead they came to a massive log, twelve feet long, lying awash in the water with an old Clorox bottle bobbing on a line close by. Jim maneuvered the canoe alongside, slipped his paddle to the other side, and used it to hold fast.

"All right. We made it."

Dodee pulled the water bottles out of the backpack, tossed one to him, and, chest heaving, took a drink. He joined her, the water cool and wet against his dry throat.

"Are all of these cypress trees?" she asked.

He studied the woods lining the channel. "Those ones with the fluted trunks flaring out at the bottom, they're tupelos." He glanced down at the massive log beside the canoe and back up to the moss-laden trees that randomly grew out of the muck to create winding water trails leading deep into a never-never land.

"What's the matter?" Dodee asked.

"Something's wrong. If this big a tree came down, there should be a swath of broken branches and tree trunks. Like a straight path."

"Maybe it floated in."

"And if there's no path here—shit." He jerked around to look back down the channel. "We're in the wrong place."

He saw the red canoes grouped back by the leaning tree, except for one with Jody Sundance heading toward them.

She cupped her hands to her mouth and called out. "We're cutting through the swamp back here, but we're angling your way." She held up her hand to indicate a slanting direction. "You can cut through the swamp and meet us if you want."

"If we don't get lost," Dodee said. "What do you think?"

He held his arm out at a right angle, indicating to Jody they'd cut through, then grinned at Dodee. "We'll be trailblazers. I hate to go back and lose all we worked so hard to gain. And when they come up, puffing and tired, we'll be rested and ready to go.''

''If we don't get lost.''

''Have I ever gotten you into trouble?'' He saw her brows knit. ''Would I lie to you?'' Now she frowned. ''Want some candy, little girl?''

SEVENTEEN

HE TURNED THE CANOE and started through the woods. The sun stabbed through the canopy in light shafts, accenting shadows rippling over black water. He tried to keep it over his right shoulder to maintain direction as they wound around trees, some spots barely wide enough to get the canoe through, pushed aside some low branches, ducked under others, scraped over cypress knees and tupelo roots, the bottom sometimes only inches below the canoe, sometimes less.

"It's spooky in here," Dodee said, peeling Spanish moss from her face. "Promise you won't bring me back here in the middle of the night."

"No chance of that."

They made slow progress with all the twists and turns, but the trees blocked the wind, and the sun warmed the morning, and they paddled in a world of their own. And, spooky or not, a little treasure greeted them at every turn. A bright blue flower bloomed in the crook of a tree. A fresh new sapling had sprouted out of a rotted stump. A mat of water lilies spread like a carpet on the black water surface. The sound of a woodpecker came from overhead, scattered birds flittered through branches—unknown without Jody's or Dorothy's guidance—filling the air with song, and farther off, unseen, but coming closer, the laughter and conversation of the other canoeists.

Jim paddled toward an opening between two cypresses.

"You going through there?" Dodee asked.

"I'm going through there."

"Can we fit? I don't want to get stuck and have to hike out."

"Trust me, little girl."

He gave a couple of power strokes to get some steerage and charged the opening, hearing the roots scrape along the bottom, slowing the canoe, stopping the canoe halfway through.

"Trust you?"

He tried paddling harder, but only succeeded in stirring up the bottom. He tried going backward with the same result. He tried using the paddle as a prop to lift the canoe, but it only sank into the mud. Then he braced the paddle against one of the tree trunks and shoved. Nothing.

"Shit."

"I hate to say I told you so."

"You told me we wouldn't fit. We do fit. You said nothing about getting hung up on roots. Now get out and give us a push." She jerked around to him, mouth gaping, and he laughed. "Boy, are you easy."

"Easy or not, I'm not stepping out in the muck, Jim Dandy."

"Come on back here. That should raise the front end enough for us to scrape back off."

"And tip the canoe?"

"The canoe is not tipping wedged between two trees."

She slowly got to her feet, stepped over the seat, and grabbed onto one of the tree trunks. She stood there, gazing off into the woods.

"What are you doing?"

"I think I see a canoe," she whispered, pointing off to the left.

"Duh. We only have about twenty of them out here."

"No," she whispered again, "this one's yellow."

He blinked at her. "Who's in it?"

"I don't see anyone. I think it's upside down."

"You sure it's a canoe?" She stared off to the left again. He raised his hands. "Well?"

"I think it is."

"Why are you whispering?"

"I don't know. It's creepy."

"Come back here. We'll get un-hung and go take a look."

She crept back to him, squatting down, and he back-stroked, but the canoe went nowhere. He braced the paddle against the tree again and shoved. They inched backward, a little at first, and then slipped free.

"See, nothing to it."

"Yeah, right."

And with her face inches from his, he kissed her. Nice and soft under a warm October sun.

"This is not the place to make out."

"It wasn't a make-out kiss."

"What kind of a kiss was it?"

He shrugged. "Because you're so pretty and your lips were there. It was a kiss of"—he shrugged again—"affection."

This time she kissed him, soft and short. "We better get going, sweetheart."

He braced his paddle across the gunnels while she crawled forward to her seat. He swung the canoe past the twin trees and tried to find a way through to where she had seen the canoe, but saw only an opening dead ahead. He headed for it and popped out into a small channel.

"Hey," Barry Rhodenbarr shouted, pointing a hairy hand, "dig Jim and Dodee."

"Good," Dodee said, waving to the others, "let's get Jody to come find the canoe with us."

"Think the boogeyman is out there?"

The Cinnamons glided up to them. "We thought we lost you two," Phyllis said.

Jim grinned at her. "No such luck."

Clyde the Coyote came up. "You went too far. I knew you would. You got out ahead of everyone."

"We were told to wait by a fallen-down tree. We found a fallen-down tree. A great big log awash in the water with a plastic Clorox bottle float tied next to it. She should have said a leaning tree."

"What kind of a log?" Harold asked.

"One about six feet in diameter."

Clyde nodded. "I knew you'd go too far."

"That's okay," Dodee said, "it was fun exploring by ourselves. Where is Jody?"

"At the head of the column."

"We have to catch up to her." She turned to him. "Jim?"

He fixed a landmark of three large, fluted trunks growing out of a single clump in his mind—oh yeah, like that wasn't a pattern repeated a million times—and dug his paddle into strong power strokes. Dodee joined in, but the front of the column slanted off the small channel and plunged into the trees. Once again they had to squeak through tight places, single-file, zig-zagging around cypress knees and tupelo trees, scraping their bottom on passing roots. Finally they popped out into an open pool where Jody re-formed the troop of Elderhostelers in a small spot of sunshine.

"See you two made it through."

Jim sidled up next to her. "Dodee thinks she saw a canoe in among the trees."

"I think it was a canoe," Dodee said. "A yellow one turned upside down."

Jody's blond eyebrows rose "Where? Can you find it?"

Jim nodded. "I think so."

"You want to come with us?" Dodee asked.

Jody glanced around at the canoes filling up the open pool of black water. "Let's wait 'til we're all here." She back-paddled her canoe up against a tree, grabbed a branch and used it to steady herself, then pointed up into one of the trees where a bird was singing. Everyone fell silent as binoculars sprouted like mushrooms on everyone's tipped-up faces.

"That's a veery," Jody said. "It's a thrush."

"Catharus fuscescens," Dorothy added.

"It's unusual here, probably passing through to South America for the winter."

Jim spotted a warm-brown bird with a tawny chest, singing its heart out as if it were saying its name, "Veery, veery, veer veer veer."

Rebecca, bringing up the rear, followed Topsy and Elaine into the open pool.

"Okay," Jody said, "I think everyone's all here. We're going to head back in a minute. Dodee thinks she saw an overturned canoe, so we'll check it out. But I wanted to point out a few things. Notice the black water here. Ranger Darby mentioned yesterday that it's tannic acid. It comes from the cypress trees, which we should all be able to tell by this time." She patted the tree she held onto. "The trees you see where the trunks spread into a fluted bottom are tupelo gums."

Jim gave Dodee a big phony grin, as if to say "I told you so," and she returned the compliment by reaching down into the bottom of the canoe and giving him a secret hand sign.

"Hank Davis will fill us in more with his lecture this afternoon." Jody raised her arm to take in the tree tops. "If anyone sees any interesting birds, sing out. To use a pun. Okay, Jim, you want to lead the way?"

They retraced the way along single-file, winding through water paths, a torture for someone who had to traverse the swamp, but a fun lark for a group of Elderhostelers. When they came out onto the small channel, the song birds suddenly fell silent as a rust-colored shadow skimmed over the tree tops, about the size of a crow with broad wings and a long tail.

"Wow, did you see that?" Dorothy cried out. "A Cooper's hawk, *Accipiter cooperii*. I haven't seen one in some time.''

Jim found his three-tupelo-tree landmark, then used the sun as a rough guide, keeping it over his left shoulder this time, to lead the way into the woods on the other side; everyone spread out to cover a larger area.

"You know where you're going?" Dodee asked.

"We're moving in the right direction. The thing is, are you sure you saw it?"

"I saw something yellow."

A hundred feet farther on, feeling like a thousand zig-zag miles, they came upon it, dead ahead, as if it had a homing device he had tuned into.

"Over here," Jim called, paddling toward it.

Yellow. A canoe. Upside down. Wedged deep in a tangle of brush and tree branches.

Jody and Becca paddled up in their separate canoes, Harold the Hound with Leo following right behind.

"We ought to preserve this as a crime scene," Harold said.

Jim stared at him. "Who says it's a crime scene?"

"Well, it could be."

Rebecca grabbed the free end of the canoe and tried to yank it out from under the tangle, but only succeeded in pulling herself under.

"I can't get any leverage."

"Get out of the canoe," Leo advised.

"Thank you very much for that suggestion."

"Hold on," Jim said.

He maneuvered his canoe sideways to her, grabbed hold of a branch stub, and reached out to her.

Rebecca took his hand, grabbed the yellow canoe with the other, and yanked on it, taking four tugs to pull it free.

"Yea," Barry said, "ya see, that works too."

Rebecca tried to lift one end of the canoe.

Phyllis screamed. "There's something under there." She clapped her hand to her mouth. "Maybe a big snake."

Jody looked at Rebecca. "Not a snake, but it could be a 'gator."

Jim swung around, backing up on the opposite side of the canoe from Rebecca.

"What are you doing?" Dodee asked, her voice uneven.

He latched on and stared at Rebecca. "You take one side and I'll take the other, and maybe roll it over."

"If we don't tip ourselves over."

"And if there's an alligator underneath?" Dodee asked, voice in the upper registers.

"Then we'll drop the thing and you be ready to paddle us out of here." He looked over to Rebecca. "Ready?"

She shrugged, grabbed one hand on the gunnel and the other on an aluminum ridge that ran down the center of the upturned canoe. "When we get it up, I'll try to twist it to my side, and you lift on yours, and between us maybe we can roll it over."

"And if there's an alligator under there?" Dodee asked again.

He stared into Rebecca's eyes.

She nodded. "Anything moves down there, drop it."

"You don't have to tell me twice."

They heaved the aft end out of the water. And Dodee screamed. Something like a giant turtle swirled out from under.

Except, it wasn't a turtle, not unless turtles wore a green shirt, and green cargo pants with zippers above the knees for turning them into shorts.

"I told you this was a crime scene," Harold the Hound said in a flat voice.

Then Phyllis screamed as the body of the Natural Resources agent rolled on its side.

"Fagedaboudit," Barry muttered. "We ain't gonna get a lecture this afternoon."

Jim stared down at what was left of Hank Davis's bearded face after it had reverted to a lower position on the food chain.

EIGHTEEN

EVERYONE HELPED LOAD the canoes when they got back to the parking lot. The sheriff, alerted by cell phone, had been waiting for them with two Boston Whalers already in the water, and Jody went along to show them the body.

Harold had offered to stay with it and protect the crime scene, but his canoe-mate, Leo the Lion, had ridiculed that.

"Who's going to disturb it out in the middle of the swamp? Can't even see it from anywhere."

Then Harold had offered to go back with the officers in case they needed his expertise, but Sheriff Ward Darby allowed that he might muddle through on his own, especially since they hadn't even determined a crime had been committed.

So Rebecca broke open two coolers of sodas and while they awaited the boats' return everyone milled around Harold the Hound as he told war stories about his days with the FBI.

Jim grabbed a Coke and strolled down to the edge of the boat ramp, gazing out toward the channel. The clouds had rolled in to add to the somber mood.

Leo was right about not seeing the canoe from anywhere. If he and Dodee hadn't paddled so far ahead, or gotten stuck on the tree roots, they never would have found it.

He felt an arm slip under his and turned to Dodee's pale face. "You recovered?"

She gave a little shiver.

Barry waddled his short, rotund frame down beside them.

He stood, hands on hips, and stared out at the water with the same intensity New Yorkers have while gazing down a dark tunnel from a subway platform, willing the next train's arrival. "Why're we waitin' here?" He adjusted the ever-present gold chain around his neck. "It ain't like we can do anything, right? Bernice and I didn't see anything. We were all the way at the back. We ain't involved." He turned to Jim. "Why not take us back, right? We'll probably miss lunch. So, why not take us back?" Jim shrugged. Barry's eyes squinted. "Maybe you should mention it?"

Jim glanced at him, then back out toward the channel.

Barry threw up his hands and walked away.

Leo the Lion strolled down to take Barry's place.

"I had to get out of there." He pushed his straw hat down to his eyebrows. "If I hear one more of Harold's theories on, quote, the crime, unquote," he said, flexing two fingers on each hand, "the sheriff will have a real murder to investigate."

"Maybe he's got something to contribute," Dodee said.

"That would be a shock."

"He was with the FBI."

"Listen to him tell it, he solved all the major crimes of the last century, but he was only in the field one time. Pin him down to it. He spent his thirty-eight years in an administrative job behind a desk in finance." Leo turned to Dodee. "So how great could his expertise be?" He shook his head and pointed out to the channel. "Besides, they're not going to find any crime has been committed. Guy out canoeing alone, way back in the tangles, probably hit his head, or a branch fell on him. He falls over the side with the canoe tipping over on him and that's it. Tragic, yes, but an accident."

Jim took a swig from his Coke.

The problem with Leo's theory was, how did the canoe get wedged under the brush? Hank Davis entangled it before hitting himself on the head?

Yeah, buddy.

But even that didn't work. The canoe had been wedged in upside down.

He turned to Leo. "Don't you have your car here? You could probably leave."

Leo turned down his lips. "Ah, I'll stick around and see what the sheriff has to say."

They heard the sound of a boat engine and a few minutes later a Boston Whaler came around a clump of trees and motored up to the ramp. Everyone came crowding down as Jody Sundance and the short, wiry Sheriff Darby got out, leaving two men in the boat, which spun around and headed back out.

"Very well, folks," the sheriff said, dark sunglasses giving him a raccoon appearance, "give me a few minutes to sort out who I need to talk to and the rest can leave. We don't have any cause to suspect foul play out there"—he jerked his thumb toward the swamp—"Mr. Davis appears to have died of natural causes."

"Didn't look like natural causes to me," Harold the Hound said.

"Harold," Leo said, "stay out of it."

Harold turned on him. "It didn't." He swung back to the sheriff. "My trained eye saw a canoe turned upside down, wedged into the brush, with a body underneath. If he died of natural causes, so did the people in Hiroshima."

Jim bit the inside of his lip. Strip down what Harold said, taking out the bravado, and he had to agree.

The sheriff heaved a big sigh. "I 'preciate your view on this, Mr. Rucker," Ward Darby said, which meant the man remembered Harold's last name, or had found it out. "I said it appeared he died of natural causes, an accident, but we haven't ruled out anything at this stage. Now, if I could see a few people—"

"We don't know anything," Barry said.

"Right," Bernice nodded. "We don't want to get involved."

"Well, that's commendable, but I really want to talk to

the ones who found the canoe, and you too, Rebecca," he said, nodding to Becca the Body, "but I can come by the 4-H Center for that later on."

"I guess you want to talk to me, then," Harold said, "I was there when they found the body."

The sheriff grimaced. "I guess I have to, but who first saw the canoe?"

Jim raised his hand. "Dodee and I. At least Dodee did."

The lean raccoon face nodded. "Very well, I'd 'preciate talking to you for a few minutes. Jody," he turned to the woman at his side, "if you all have two vans, why don't you all start taking these good folks back to the 4-H Center. Can you do that?"

"Okay, we'll load up the van with the trailer. If anyone thinks they have something to contribute to Sheriff Darby, you can stay with me. Otherwise, Rebecca will take you on back."

The sheriff motioned Dodee and Jim to his SUV. He opened the door, pulled a small tape recorder from his pocket, removed the tape and replaced it with a spare from the glove compartment. He announced the time and date of the interview, then asked them to state their names and addresses.

"Very well," he said when that was finished, "this chere is an informal interview. Sometimes we see things we don't even realize and we'd like to capture that. You want to go over how all this came about?"

Dodee told the story, with Jim interrupting to add missing bits, from the time they stopped at the big log with the Clorox bottle until the body drifted out from under the canoe.

"The canoe didn't change position between when you first saw it and the time you actually got to it?"

She shrugged. "I wasn't even sure it was a canoe at first."

"Very well. You saw nothing else unusual?"

Dodee's eyebrows went up. "Unusual? A body came

floating out when they raised the canoe. That's unusual. The whole thing was unusual. I thought it was an animal at first.''

The sheriff nodded. ''Very well.'' He turned to Jim. ''That 'bout everything, Mr. Dandy?''

''If you give me a clue as to what you're seeking I might be able to help you.''

''You saw nothing in the trees or the bushes, say at the scene or when you first approached from the main channel, before you ran aground on the roots.''

Jim shook his head, then, when the sheriff motioned to the tape recorder, said, ''No, I didn't.''

''And you didn't see anybody?''

''No, but now that you mention it, I did notice that Hank Davis was wearing the same clothes he had on Sunday night.''

The sheriff's brow wrinkled. ''How would you know that?''

''Because he came to give us a talk on boating safety and wore cargo pants that zippered off at the knees. I noticed them because I had just bought two pairs''—he raised his leg so the sheriff could see—''for Dodee and me from Cabela's.''

''What do you reckon from that?''

He shrugged. ''I'm just telling you what I saw, sheriff. Isn't it your job to piece it together?''

NINETEEN

As IT TURNED OUT, only four of them had remained behind, Jim, Dodee, Harold and Jody, all the rest had piled into the other van or crowded in with Leo. And when the four got back, everyone had finished lunch and were clearing away.

Jody clapped her hands to get attention. "Okay, everyone. We will not be having our lecture on the Santee-Cooper environment this afternoon, because of the unfortunate accident."

"Not an accident, Jody," Harold said.

"Well"—she held up a hand—"whatever it was, the unfortunate death of Hank Davis, a good friend who will be missed here. I could try to throw something together for you, but I'm afraid it would be just that. So I thought we could just have a free afternoon. It's a couple of hours into Charleston, Georgetown is an hour away—"

"That's where we're heading," Clyde the Coyote said with a nod. "Anyone wants a ride is welcome. Going to see if we can get a look at that treasure they found off the coast."

Jody held out her hand to him. "There you go, that's one invitation. We also have the canoes out in case you didn't get enough muscle aches this morning, and if you've had experience. Also Santee State Park is close by. We'll be picking up our boat ride there tomorrow, but then it will be just in and out. If a number of you want to go, maybe we can get a van together. And, dare I say it, some outlet stores are in the neighborhood."

Topsy the Turtle raised her hand. "Could you tell us tomorrow's schedule?"

"Okay. We load up first thing here for the boat tour of the sunken forest on Lake Marion, then have a picnic lunch before heading back. In the afternoon we'll have a nature talk and walk."

"Then I wouldn't mind going to Santee Park if you're taking a van."

"How many of you would like to go to Santee Park?" Eight hands raised. "Okay, let me grab a sandwich and I'll bring the van down to the Hospitality Room in twenty minutes. For everyone else, I'll see you back here for dinner tonight."

Jim ushered Dodee to the buffet where the cooks had left Saran-wrapped sandwiches for them, along with sodas, juice, tea and coffee.

Harold touched him on the arm. "What about that float you mentioned this morning?"

"What float?"

"The plastic Clorox bottle you found by the fallen tree. What do you think it was there for?"

"Hell, Harold, I don't know. It probably marked the end of a trout line or a fish trap. Or just floated in on the wind and got snagged." He turned to Dodee. "What would you like to do?"

She shrugged.

"I know what I'm doing," Harold the Hound said, picking up three of the Saran-wrapped sandwiches and stuffing them in his backpack. "I'm going out and poke around." He gave his eyebrows a couple of jumps. "Maybe stir up some dust and see where it settles."

Dodee stared up at him. "You know it could have been an accident. This morning."

Harold shook his head. "See, Dodee, sometimes when you get a small-town sheriff, they don't see all the angles." He picked up a fourth sandwich, unwrapped it, and took a bite that left less that half behind. "I don't mean to cast aspersions on his competence. It's just that sometimes a complicated case needs the assistance of a full-time crime lab and the large network of a law enforcement agency.''

"We could go canoeing," Jim said.

"Like the FBI?" she asked.

Harold tapped a finger to his nose and winked. "I haven't figured out all the angles yet, but I'm convinced it has to do with the dam and the hydroelectric plant.''

"We could drive into Georgetown," Jim said.

"If you believe that," she said, "why don't you have agents down here?''

"Because I'm not sure of the connection yet." He chomped down on the other half of sandwich. "Once I have some proof, you betcha I'll get them in. I'll let the sheriff know and call the Bureau.''

"We could go into Charleston if you don't mind a two-hour drive.''

"Have you got any profiles back?''

"No, but I have a couple of suspects," Harold said, closing one eye.

"Or we could go canoeing out on the lake.''

"One of the Elderhostelers?" she asked.

Harold looked around, lowering his voice. "Uh-huh. I'm thinking—''

"Wait a minute." Jim waved a hand between them to cut the conversation. "Why would anybody come on an Elderhostel to blow up…anything? They would just go do it." He saw Harold open his mouth, but Jim held up his hand. "No, I don't want to know." He turned to Dodee. "Do you want to do something or not?''

"You two could come with me," Harold said, eyebrows arching.

Dodee looked at Jim and shrugged.

"No, I don't want to go," he said.

"I'm gonna rent a boat and poke around.''

She held out her hand. "We could just go for the boat ride." She glanced to Harold. "We're just looking, right?''

"Just poking around."

"Or"—she turned back to Jim—"if you don't mind me going, you could take a nap."

Jim stared into her big blues, about to tell her to go the hell ahead, but how competent was Harold out on the water? Probably not very.

"I'll pay for the boat," Harold said, eyebrows arching again.

Jim glanced out to the cloudy afternoon, sighed, and threw up his hands. "Okay, but I'm handling the boat."

"Sure, I don't know much about boats anyway."

"Where are we going?"

"The first murder took place up around Pack's Landing. I thought we'd start there and then come down and check out the scene where we found Davis's body."

"Do you know how to get there?"

"Well, I thought we'd get a map." Harold winked and tapped his fingers against the side of his nose. "I'll talk to Jody and meet you back at the Conference Center."

Jim watched him waddle out the door toward the Administration Building, then loaded up on sandwiches. They made a pit stop back at the room, got a couple maps from Jim's Lincoln, and headed out in Harold's yellow Dodge Neon, Dodee in the back, Jim riding shotgun.

"See if you can find Pack's Landing on the map," Harold said as they drove through the cotton gin/gas station/Bronco-Club metropolis of Davis Station.

Jim took a big bite of ham and cheese sandwich and stuffed it into his cheek. "What did Jody say?"

"She wasn't there."

"And we don't have directions?"

"It's on the map. How difficult could it be?"

Jim glanced over the seat to Dodee, but she steadfastly gazed out the opposite window.

Great, just great. He stuffed his ham and cheese sandwich into his mouth, holding it with his teeth while he slipped on his reading glasses, then took a bite and checked the Santee-Cooper map Hank Davis had passed out on Sunday evening. He found Pack's Landing from the legend, and tried to coordinate it with his AAA state map. Not a lot to coordinate, but if he could get to Route 301 he felt he could wind around and find Rimini, a place that looked to be no bigger than Davis Station.

They stumbled onto 301 and drove through thriving Summerton and bustling Belser Crossroads; then things started to get tricky. They took a road called Lilly Martin toward the lake and turned west onto Old River Road, rolling along in the middle of Nowheresville, USA, until he saw a BOATS FOR RENT sign.

"Turn left here."

Harold slammed on the brakes and screeched into the turn. "Is this Pack's Landing?"

"It's a place where we can rent a boat. We'll find out where Pack's Landing is from there."

They bounced over ruts and around trees until they broke out in a clearing beside a choppy Lake Marion. A small gray house with a rambling porch hung back from the shoreline among some pines. An old Jeep, minus license plates, dozed in its driveway. A line of boats, mostly pontoons, sat on trailers circling the rim of a dirt parking lot, and a weathered cabin squatted at the water's edge serving as an office for a small marina made up of bleached-wood docks and finger-piers; boats tugged at their lines in the slips. A battered Chrysler, vintage mid-eighties, glowered at them like a rhinoceros from a spot next to the office, with a Mercedes SUV, Missouri license plates, parked next to it, an empty trailer hitched to its rear.

Jim opened the door, climbed out into a fresh breeze, and nodded to the tan SUV. "It looks like our fishermen friends from Sunday are here."

"They get around," Dodee said.

A grizzled man in bib overalls and oily baseball cap came out from behind a stripped-down outboard engine, and waddled over to them wiping his hands on a rag.

"You fellers looking for something—oh, sorry, ma'am. Didn't see you there," he said, and touched the tip of his cap.

Harold the Hound put his hands on his hips. "We need to rent a boat for the afternoon. What do you have?"

The man turned to the marina and ran a dirty fingernail over his stubbled cheek. "Well, now, I'm closed for the season. I don't reckon—well, now, I got one boat I ain't pulled out for winter yet. S'posed to do it this afternoon, but I can hold off, I guess." He pointed to a small Seahawk with a forty-horsepower Evinrude engine. "This one right chere."

Harold turned to Jim. "You can run that?" Jim nodded. "Then we'll take it."

The two of them headed for the office.

"Get a chart of the area," Jim called after them, then got Dodee's backpack and the remains of the sandwiches, a small leather bag Harold had brought along, and carried them to the boat.

"I didn't know you knew how to run a boat."

"Lots of great things you don't know about me, sweetie. You don't live on the shores of the Chesapeake without knowing something about boats. My son, Paul, has a Sundance twenty-one-footer and I used to have a small trimaran."

"I'm impressed."

He smiled. "You should be."

The owner came back with two gas cans, hooked one of them up, went over the controls with Jim, then returned to his outboard engine. Harold spread a chart on one of the boat seats and pointed to an X on the chart. "I asked him where they found the body of that boater, and he marked it for me."

Jim cocked his head and stared at the FBI guy.

Harold held out his arms. "What?"

"If, on the off chance he *was* killed, do we want to advertise that we're out snooping around?"

"Yes, maybe we'll smoke the killer out."

"And maybe he'll blow holes in our heads."

"He does and half the Bureau will be down on him."

Jim turned to the engine controls shaking his head. A lot of good that was going to do them.

He started the engine, letting it idle as they untied the lines, and headed out, turning northwest toward Rimini into the dark chop of the cloudy lake.

It didn't take them long to find the spot where the boater had drowned. Hank Davis, the Natural Resources agent, had said it was at Pack's Landing, but they hadn't gotten that far before seeing pieces of yellow police ribbon still hanging in the trees. They circled the area a few times for all the good it did.

"You want me to put you ashore so you can traipse around in the bush?"

"Looks pretty marshy," Dodee said.

Harold shrugged.

Jim shrugged back. "What did you hope to find? Aside from some yellow ribbon, the man could have drowned anywhere and drifted in here."

Harold touched his finger to the side of his nose. "But if the killers see us, they might start to get worried."

Jim studied the tangled-wood shore. Yeah, buddy, lots of eyes looking back at them from in there.

Dodee turned to Harold. "You want to land? If it's not too marshy, we can look around."

Harold shook his head. "I didn't expect to find anything here. I just wanted to get the feel of the place. Let's go down to where we found Davis's body this morning. That's a fresh crime scene. We might find something there."

Jim checked the chart then swung the boat toward deeper water, steering for the channel into the Sparkleberry Swamp.

They sped along the deserted lake and a half mile farther on he spotted *Two For The Road* riding at anchor.

"Looks like our friends," he said, nudging Dodee and

speaking over the roar of the engine. He wondered if they were still fishing for largemouth bass.

"I don't see anyone," Dodee said as they got closer. She turned to him. "You don't suppose something happened to them?"

He throttled back and the boat slowed. Dodee was right. Where the hell were they?

Then a float with a diagonally striped flag came into view and he pointed to it.

"What does that mean?" Harold asked.

"It's a diver's flag. They must be down below."

"Why would they be diving out here?" Dodee asked.

He shrugged and gunned the engine, bouncing along in the chop until they found the entrance into Sparkleberry and swung in under deepening clouds. The temperature had dropped. All they needed now was for it to rain.

They eased along the cut into the swamp until Dodee pointed toward the log where they had hung out that morning. The plastic Clorox bottle still bobbed on the surface nearby. Jim slowed the boat and nuzzled up to the massive log.

"Now that we're here, I don't know what you expect to discover."

Harold reached over the side of the boat and grabbed the Clorox bottle, pulling up the line holding it to the bottom until half a concrete block came awash. He let it go, wiped his hands on his pants, and stuck his fists on his hips. "Can we get in where we found Davis's body?"

"We might be able to get closer, going around to the small channel by the leaning tree, but only a canoe will get us in. In fact, I don't even want to try that other channel. We shear the propeller pin and we're staying out here until someone comes to get us."

Harold rubbed his chin. "Can't see much from out here." He rubbed it some more, then patted the log. "What kind of wood is this?"

Jim shrugged. Who knows? Who cares?

Harold moved to one side of the boat and checked the end of the log. "This has been sawn. Looks like a long time ago."

Dodee turned to Jim. "How do you suppose it got here?"

"Maybe it floated in." He slipped the engine into reverse and eased back toward deeper water. All he needed was to shear the prop pin.

"What's the other end look like?" Harold asked.

"It's probably left over from when they made this channel." He checked the back of the boat, making sure the way was clear. "You finished here?"

Harold rubbed his chin again. "I have the feeling we're missing something."

"Me too," Dodee said. She pointed at Harold. "Like why would they bring Davis all the way out here to kill him?"

"Maybe to draw attention from the dam and the hydroelectric plant."

Jim shook his head. "Oh, yea. That's why they stuck him way back in the middle of the swamp where no one would find him."

Harold swung on him. "You think his death was an accident?"

"I didn't say that. But it's a giant leap to go from Davis's body in the sticks to blowing up the dam and the plant. What reason would they have?"

"Hello." Dodee glared at him. "Terrorism."

Jim shook his head again and glanced up at the sky. "Well, if you two want to see anything else, look fast. The wind is picking up and the clouds are darkening."

Harold shrugged and shook his head.

Jim turned the boat around and shoved the throttle forward, When they shot out of the cut he turned into the wind, screaming down the long axis of the lake. Whitecaps sent water splashing over the boat, soaking them as they plowed ahead.

Great, just great.

He couldn't see the pontoon boat when they got that far; either it had already gone in, or was hidden in the falling visibility.

And then it started to rain.

Great, just absolutely great.

TWENTY

HE EASED OUT OF SLEEP the next morning to see dawn seeping in the window. The afternoon fiasco with Harold, powering the boat back in the cold and rain, shivering and sopping wet by the time he reached the dock, had taken a lot out of him. Now he felt well rested and ready for the new day.

And he thanked God for it.

After all the nights he had sat up with Penny before she passed away, he had come to realize what a great gift sleep was. For the poor it was a relief from oppression, a chance to dream of better things and hope for better tomorrows. For the sick, relief from pain and a time for the body to recover. For the troubled, a time to close one chapter, open another, filled with new possibilities.

The rain had stopped during the night. Once again, God had brought up the sun. Thank you for another day.

Dodee rolled over and peered at him. "Are you awake?" she whispered.

"No, I'm sound asleep with my eyes open."

She snuggled in close and kissed him on the neck.

"What is it you want?"

She raised up on one elbow. "Now is that any way to react when I'm being affectionate?"

"When it happens this early in the morning, it has been my experience you're going to get me involved in something before nightfall that I don't want to step in."

She put her head back down. "Don't worry then."

He closed his eyes and waited her out.

Birds squabbled outside, and someone coughed as they walked by their door, but a pervasive stillness filled the room.

She popped back up on her elbow. "I just woke up thinking of an answer to your question."

He blinked and stared up at the stubbled ceiling. Answer to his question? "What question?"

"Remember yesterday at lunch when we were talking to Harold?"

"The Hound."

"And he talked about someone blowing up the dam and the electric plant?"

"Let's not get into that again."

"All right, sweetheart." She kissed him on the neck again and lay back down. "Sorry."

He stared at the ceiling stubble some more. Was that it? She had given up too easily. And the question, what the hell was his quest— "Okay, okay, what question?"

She giggled. She had won. She knew she would. Just dangling a fishhook out there and he had gobbled it up like a largemouthed idiot.

"Well, dammit, what question?"

"You asked why anyone would want to blow up the dam." She propped herself up on her elbow again. "We're assuming it's some kind of terrorist plot, but suppose it's something completely different."

"Are you building up suspense so I'll blurt out, 'what is it, what is it, tell me quick'?"

She gave him a smile and lay her head back on his chest. He stared back at the ceiling.

"Okay, okay, what is it, what is it, tell me quick."

She popped back up on her elbow. "Have you been listening to Clyde Porter?"

"Clyde the Coyote. You mean when the good Doctor says to his wife, 'I believe I'll have another cup of coffee'? And Becky the Beaver hops to it?"

The Mystery Library Reader Service™ — Here's how it works:

Accepting your 2 free books and gift places you under no obligation to buy anything. You may keep the books and gift and return the shipping statement marked "cancel." If you do not cancel, about a month later we'll send you 3 additional novels and bill you just $4.69 each plus 25¢ shipping & handling per book and applicable sales tax, if any.* You may cancel at any time, but if you choose to continue, every month we'll send you 3 more books, which you may either purchase at our great low price…or return to us and cancel your subscription.

*Terms and prices subject to change without notice. Sales tax applicable in N.Y.

If offer card is missing write to: Mystery Library Reader Service, 3010 Walden Ave., P.O. Box 1867, Buffalo NY 14240-1867

NO POSTAGE
NECESSARY
IF MAILED
IN THE
UNITED STATES

BUSINESS REPLY MAIL
FIRST-CLASS MAIL   PERMIT NO. 717-003   BUFFALO, NY

POSTAGE WILL BE PAID BY ADDRESSEE

MYSTERY LIBRARY READER SERVICE
3010 WALDEN AVE
PO BOX 1867
BUFFALO NY 14240-9952

Play The **Lucky Hearts** Game

and get...
FREE BOOKS & a **FREE** GIFT...
YOURS to KEEP!

yes! I have scratched off the silver card.
Please send me my **2 FREE BOOKS**
and **FREE GIFT**. I understand that I am under
no obligation to purchase any books as
explained on the back of this card.

Scratch Here!
then look below to see
what your cards get you...

DETACH AND MAIL CARD TODAY! (ML-02/02) © 1999 WORLDWIDE LIBRARY

415 WDL DH5S

NAME (PLEASE PRINT CLEARLY)

ADDRESS

APT.# CITY

STATE ZIP

Twenty-one gets you
2 FREE BOOKS and
a **FREE GIFT!**

Twenty gets you
2 FREE BOOKS!

Nineteen gets you
1 FREE BOOK!

TRY AGAIN!

Offer limited to one per household and not valid to current
Mystery Library™ subscribers. All orders subject to approval.

"I mean the treasure they found on that old Spanish galleon off the coast." He brought his hand up to play with her breast. She rolled her eyes. "I'm trying to have a serious conversation."

"It's too early in the morning."

"They're storing the treasure in a bank in Georgetown."

"I haven't had any coffee."

"Worth two or three hundred million dollars."

"And there's a connection here somewhere?"

"What better way to rob that bank? You blow up the hydroelectric plant, which cuts off the electricity to its alarm system and causes complete chaos."

"You're buying into Harold's theories, aren't you? Lock, stock—"

"No, I'm just saying—"

"And you think one of the group's involved? As I said before, if someone wanted to blow up the dam, why would they come on an Elderhostel to do it?"

"I'm just saying, isn't it a possibility?"

"Anything is possible, Dodee." He pulled her head down and kissed her. "Just do me a favor. Don't get caught up in Harold's suspicions. They feed on themselves until you end up suspecting everyone." He kissed her again. "Now, if you'll excuse me I have a little bladder problem I have to attend to."

He went to the bathroom and washed and shaved, splashing aftershave on his face, and stared into the mirror as he combed his hair.

There were better ways to rob a bank in Georgetown than blowing up the electric plant. Like just take out a substation. A lot less dynamite and a lot less trouble.

Of course, if it really were a terrorist group, what better way to collect two or three hundred million buck-ohs and make a big splash with one stone?

He dressed in jeans, chino shirt, and trail shoes; came around the corner of the closet, and stared down at Dodee, covers up to her neck, big eyes studying him.

"I'm going to get coffee." He turned toward the door, then turned back. "If you're going to rob a bank, why kill Hank Davis?"

A big grin spread across her face.

"No, forget it." He turned toward the door. "I don't want to know." He got to the door and turned around again. "Okay, I want to know."

She shrugged. "He's the Natural Resources agent. Maybe he came across something and they had to waste him."

"Waste him?" He shook his head. "You sound like a moll in a cheap detective story. I'll bring you coffee."

He hurried down the walkway in the morning air, sunny but cold, making a mental note they'd need jackets if they were going on the sunken forest boat ride. He turned into the Hospitality Room and smelled the rich aroma of coffee.

Simon Cinnamon, sitting with the Smiths from Arkansas, waved to him. "Morning, Jim," came his deep bass voice.

Jim waved back and continued into the kitchen, poured himself a cup of coffee, and came back to sip it in the doorway. Clyde Coyote and Becky Beaver quick-walked up from the shore, pumping arms bent at the elbow, heads erect, bodies stiff, the sun highlighting their clouds of expelled air. They slowed as they circled the window walls, puffed around the parking lot, cooling down, then came on in.

"Morning Clyde, Becky," Jim said. "How did you make out on your trip into Georgetown yesterday?"

"Very nice little town." His eyes squinted. "Only it was a two-hour drive, not one as Jody Sundance said. I have to report that to her."

"Coffee, Clyde?" Becky asked.

"Yes, I believe I will, dear."

"Did you get a chance to see that treasure from the galleon?"

"No, I didn't." He shook his head twice. "That was a

mild disappointment. The place was locked up with as many guards as the White House.''

"We went to the Rice Museum," Becky said, coming back with Clyde's coffee.

"Poo. Don't even bother, is my advice. Seven or eight display cases with little placards beside them. Three dollars. Not worth half that for my money.''

"The historic part of the town was pretty."

"Yes, very quaint. A long boardwalk running along the river with boats moored to the docks. The salvage boat was there, the one that brought the treasure in. It was docked next to a Chinese junk called—what was that called, dear?''

"The *Mandarin*.''

"Yes, had the history there. Made in Singapore and somehow it was stored in Wisconsin for fifty years. You could charter it for a dinner cruise.''

Jim nodded. "Were there guards around the salvage boat?''

"It wasn't really a salvage boat. More like a shuttle to run the treasure in, from what I could find out. Looked like a small Coast Guard cutter. No guards about. Deserted. I believe they already removed the day's treasure.''

Jim glanced over Clyde's shoulder to see Harold the Hound sitting in an easy chair, popping bite-sized Heath bars into his mouth, pretending indifference, but no doubt listening intently to everything they had to say.

One more thing to factor into his conspiracy theory? And if the FBI guy didn't make the connection himself, Jim bet all the sweet parts of his body that Dodee would make it for him. Which brought her back to mind.

He refilled his mug, a second one for Dodee, and took them back to the room, kicking the door with his foot.

Dodee opened it, fully dressed in a white blouse, a light flax jacket with slacks to match, and tan slip-ons. "I thought you were bringing me coffee.''

"Here it is," he said, handing it to her.

"No, I meant right away. Where were you?''

"I got to talking with—one of the group." He watched her eyebrows rise. Shit, she'd find out anyway. "Clyde the Coyote."

She sipped the coffee and gazed at him over the steaming mug.

"Go ahead, ask me." He held out his free hand. "Yes, we talked about the treasure stored in a bank with more guards than the White House. Is that it?"

"I haven't said a thing, sweetheart."

"And if you add this to Harold's suspicions, I'll punch you right in the nose."

She smiled and batted her eyelashes.

TWENTY-ONE

BUTTERED FRENCH TOAST smothered in syrup, sausage, and coffee. He set them down next to Phyllis, grateful that no spaces remained at Harold's table to entice Dodee. Maybe the two would conspire on the boat trip, but for now he would have some peace.

Topsy smiled at him, green eyes peering through her small oval glasses. "Where did you go yesterday afternoon, Jim? We didn't see you at dinner."

"Harold wanted to rent a boat and so we tagged along. Big mistake. We got caught in the wind and the rain and had a time getting back to the marina. We picked up some fast food on the way back."

"We ate at a restaurant in Georgetown," Simon said, buttering a sweet roll as Phyllis stared at him and shook her honey-blond head.

Dodee brought two glasses of juice back from the drinks table. "I believe you said you believed you'd have a glass of juice this morning."

He frowned and glanced over to the next table where Clyde and Becky were engrossed in something Farouk was telling Harold.

Dodee bent over and whispered in his ear, "I'm going to the ladies' room. Be right back."

He watched her go, took a bite of French toast and turned to Simon. "Did you ride into Georgetown with Clyde?"

"No, we went in by ourselves," Phyllis said. She pushed her plate back and sipped from her coffee cup. "Jody said it was only an hour so we took off, but we wouldn't have gone had we known it was two hours.''

"Clyde said the same thing.''

Simon took a bite of buttered sweet roll. "Phyllis wanted to do some shopping and sight-seeing and I knew Clyde was into that treasure thing.''

A chair suddenly clattered to the concrete floor as Harold jumped to his feet at the next table. "I got it!'' he said in a voice that carried throughout the room. Then he bent down, said something to those at his table, and rushed over to Jim, taking Dodee's empty seat. "Where's Dodee?''

"She went to the ladies' room.''

He nodded, and kept nodding as he glanced in that direction, turned back and nodded some more. "I figured it out.'' Nod, nod. "I knew I would. You were a help.'' He glared intently across the room, like by so doing he could will Dodee to appear, but when she didn't, he turned back. "I have to go,'' he whispered. "Tell Dodee I solved it. I just have to find out a couple of things and then I'm going to the sheriff. Without you, Jim, I wouldn't have found the key.'' He hopped to his feet. "Tell Dodee I'll piece it all together for her at dinner. You're gonna be surprised.'' Then he headed for the door.

Simon's brow wrinkled. "What was that all about?''

Jim grimaced and shrugged. "He's full of conspiracy theories.''

"Like blowing up the dam.''

"Who's blowing up the dam?'' Topsy asked.

Jim shook his head. "No one. It's all in Harold's imagination.''

And he didn't tell Dodee about it when she returned.

Jody called for attention at the end of breakfast, clapping her hands. "Okay, everyone, we're heading out for our boat trip this morning. Vans will pick you up in a half hour, same drill as the last two days. There are restrooms at the park, just in case. It's chilly this morning and we'll be out on the water so you'll want to bring heavier jackets, if you have them. We'll have a picnic lunch there and tonight we're having a special dinner, a local dish called Frogmore Stew, so you want to be sure to be here for that. Any questions?'' She glanced around the room. ''Okay, I'll see you in half an hour.''

When they got back to the room, Jim told her about Harold.

''What did he say?'' she asked.

''I just told you. He jumped up from his table, knocked over his chair, and said to tell you he had solved it. He just had to find out one or two things and he was going to the sheriff.''

''What one or two things?'' Jim shrugged. ''That's all he said?''

''He said we were going to be surprised.''

''Like how?'' She took her jacket from the closet. ''You didn't ask?''

He took the jacket and helped her into it. ''He said he'd tell you all about it at dinner, and you can bet he will if there's something to it.'' He held the door for her. ''And if there's not, well, he'll tell us anyway.''

She shook her head. ''Sometimes, Jim Dandy, you have a decided lack of imagination.''

''No, I have a decided desire to mind my own business.''

He ushered her into the first of two vans in the parking lot and sat next to her in the middle seat.

Jody turned around from the driver's seat and stared in the direction of the Conference Center rooms. ''We're missing one. Anybody see Harold?''

''He's not coming,'' Jim said.

She turned to him, eyebrows raised. ''He told you that?''

He nodded. ''Said he'd see us at dinner.''

Clyde bent forward in the back seat. ''I believe he drives a yellow Dodge Neon.''

''Yes, he does,'' Becky said. ''I saw him leave earlier.''

''And I don't see Leo's car,'' Clyde said.

Farouk jumped out of the other van and rushed over to his white Toyota Sienna with the roof rack.

"Leo's not coming, either," Jody said. "He has some business he couldn't get to yesterday."

Farouk took out a jacket, shut the door, and ran back to the other van.

Jody put the van in gear. "Okay, then, we're all here." She started out and waved for Becca the Body in the second van to follow. They rode through Davis Station, back along Rev. J.W. Carter Road to Route 95, and headed south. "Because of all the lakes and all the rivers and swamps," Jody said, "we can't go anywhere direct. We always have to go around and take the interstate."

Dodee turned to Clyde the Coyote. "You had breakfast with Harold this morning?"

"He sat at our table."

"Until he jumped up and knocked over his chair," Becky said, shaking her head, her gray hair tied in a tight bun.

"What caused him to do that?" she asked.

Clyde shook his head. "I declare, I don't know. He just, whoosh, jumped up and shouted something like 'I got it,' excused himself, and rushed out the door."

Jim turned to him. "Remember what the conversation was about when it happened?"

"Yes. I vividly recollect because I was doing the talking. I was telling everyone of our trip to Georgetown. If you want specifics, I had just told them of the heavily guarded bank where they kept the treasure from the Spanish galleon, and how they wouldn't let us in to see it."

TWENTY-TWO

THEY EXITED THE INTERSTATE three stops south and passed a blue Taurus coming the other way.

"That looked like Leo's car," Becky said.

They followed the blacktop as it curved through Santee State Park down to a parking lot across the street from Fisheagle Wildlife Tours, two long pontoon boats tied to the dock with a sign inviting them to explore the sunken forests of Lake Marion. They piled out of the vans and Rebecca turned the second van around and headed out.

"Hey," Barry said, his red baseball cap turned backward atop his head, "where is she goin'?"

Jody pulled on her jacket. "She has things to do back at the 4-H Center. I'll call her when we get in and she'll come pick us up." She clapped for everyone's attention. "We're going to be out on the water for a few hours. We do have a Porta-Potty head on board, but if anyone wants to use a real restroom, now is the time to do it. Otherwise, let's load up."

A breeze blew across the lake, waves flashing in the sunshine, and brought with it a taste of winter.

Jim waited for Dodee to bundle up and take his arm and they started for the boat, holding up at the pavement as a tan SUV passed by, pulling *Two For The Road.*

"There's our two fishermen again," he said.

"Uh-huh. They get around."

They crossed the street to the Fisheagle pier. A flat plywood roof covered the pontoon boat; a metal boarding plank connected it to the dock. A short, wiry man stood by in a green jacket, plaid shirt, and khaki pants. His tanned face had white spots around the eyes, about the size of dark sunglasses.

"Good morning, folks," the wiry man said, "welcome to Fisheagle Tours. My name is Ray Darby and I'll be your captain for the trip. We'll be flying at an altitude of two feet this morning, but I hope we won't hit any turbulence."

Laughter rippled through the group.

"Are you any relation to Sheriff Darby?" Simon Cinnamon asked.

"Ward's my cousin. How did you meet him?"

Jody waved a hand. "That event over at Sparkleberry? We were there when they found the body."

"Really. That was tragic. Hank Davis was well liked around here, yes ma'am. A good man."

Jim turned to see Dodee had disappeared, then saw her back up on the road, taking pictures of the boat and the area. How many of those would turn into paintings when she returned to her studio? She hurried and caught up with him and they followed the Cinnamons onboard, six-foot-two Simon with yellow porkpie hat covering his curly hair, and five-foot-one Phyllis in a purple scarf. Upright plastic lawn chairs had been set up in pairs along the sides with an aisle down the middle. Jim motioned Dodee into the seats behind the Cinnamons and she placed her backpack under the seat, leaving the camera strapped around her neck. Everyone else followed onboard except for Farouk, who was sauntering down from the restrooms. Oxra called to him, waving her hand for him to hurry up, but the tall, lean man walked with the unhurried grace of a Bedouin chieftain coming in from the desert.

"I know it's a bit chilly," Captain Ray Darby said, "and if it gets too bad we can pull down clear plastic curtains, but once we get across to the other side, the trees should give us a wind break and I think, I hope, you'll find it a pleasant trip."

He gave them all a quick rundown on where the life preservers were, in the unlikely event they would need one, plopped himself into the captain's chair, started the engine, and pulled out into the river.

"Good morning again," Ray Darby's voice came over a loudspeaker as he pulled down a mike from the overhang. "As I say, we're heading across to those trees you see, but we can't just strike off for them because we'll hit snags and run aground. There's a channel out chere, part of the waterway through the lakes and canals and locks all the way to Charleston. But a funny thing happened when they flooded this lake, yes ma'am."

When they reached the middle of the lake, they turned west, zig-zagging along, following day markers indicating the channel.

"A funny thing happened when they flooded this chere lake. It was in the depths of the depression when the project began, and by the time the dam had been completed things in Europe were starting to heat up. They had started out cutting down trees the lake would cover, and then, fighting economics and rising water and men called up for World War Two, they decided just to leave the trees where they were. They would rot out over a couple of years anyway and no one would have to worry about them."

He turned half around to face the boat, pulling the mike on a flexible rig around with him.

"Well, guess what, folks?" He steered, one eye on them, the other on the channel. "The trees didn't rot. Sunk as they are in fresh water, without the air to get to them, and maybe helped by the tannic acid runoff from the cypress swamps, they are as solid as the day the water rose. They cut the first-growth trees, big old trees that God planted before the white man came, cut them off at the waterline when the lake drained low in the winter, but they're still down there, ready and waiting to snag an unwary boater not paying attention to the channel. And they have. Caught me unawares many a time. The good thing about it is, this sunken forest provides safe habitats for young fish fry to grow into big fish to provide *my* fish fry. Oh, yes, ma'am.''

Jim shook his head at the corny joke, but he watched as smiles and laughter broke out among the group.

That was one of the great things about being on an Elderhostel. Everyone had witnessed enough dings and scars in life to want to grab some giggles when the occasion presented itself. You only had to be mildly funny, for they were ready to laugh. Which made for good company.

Except, of course, for the occasional Harold the Hound, and even he was harmless.

''So, allow me to be your guide this morning, pointing out some of the flora and fauna, as we wend our way through some stubby dead bushes that are in reality the tops of trees, and glide over, hopefully, some others cut just under the surface, that had maybe been a hundred feet tall and hundreds of years old. Kings of the forest trapped in time.''

Captain Darby swung the pontoon boat around a day marker and, as far as Jim could tell, seeing something only in his mind, headed off toward the trees. And as they approached, a cloud of birds, black above and white below, broke into the air, swirling overhead like a tornado.

''Swallows,'' Dorothy the Dove called out. ''Tree swallows, *Tachycineta bicolor.*''

Jim shook his head. Where did she get all this knowledge? He checked her earrings to see they were tigers today.

When they reached the brush, true to Captain Darby's word, the wind abated. They wove in and around the dead treetops; hard to believe they were rooted sixteen or twenty feet down. They came upon living bushes and trees growing on top of the dead ones, upon carpets of water lilies and swamp flowers, with someone or another pointing out birds as they went along, like the small red-eyed vireo. A smaller black-throated blue warbler, a rare sighting in that area, had everyone peering through binocs, and became

Barry Rhodenbarr's favorite because it called out "beer, beer, beer, beer."

They moved out into a channel, creeping along, and back into the bush again, slipped by a dense thicket laced with Spanish moss. Suddenly the air exploded with the beat of wings as two bald eagles, great brown and white birds, swooped down from a high branch, seized the wind, and grabbed for the sky.

"Fagedaboudit," Barry cried out in glee and awe. Jim noted that his favorite saying seemed to cover all situations.

"Bald eagles," Dorothy said, as if there could be any doubt.

Jim smiled as they gathered the wind beneath their wings, and he remembered the song about heroes. Penny had been the wind beneath his wings. And now that she was gone? Well, God, always there, always love, always strength. And the kids and grandkids, of course.

He turned and studied Dodee's profile, the short, loose curls the color of ripened wheat, a smooth face with hairline wrinkles around cornflower eyes that seemed to take everything in. She had a smallish nose, and soft lips that, as she turned to him as if she felt his eyes upon her, spread in a shy smile.

"What?"

"Just thinking how really pretty you are."

She gave his thigh a squeeze, and he leaned over and kissed her.

"Hey," came Barry the Bear's voice from the seat behind, "none a that. Fagedaboudit."

"Shut up, Barry," Bernice said. "You love birds go right ahead."

Dodee broke off the kiss and Jim could see a slight blush on her cheeks.

He pressed his lips together and nodded. Dodee. She was now the wind beneath his wings. The one who gave joy to life, the veneer to cover up the everyday grunge, a salve to the dings and scars of the world.

He hoped he was for her as well.

The engine roared as it churned in reverse, pulling the boat back from a tangle of woods, then eased off to an idle, and Captain Darby swung around to face them, yanking his mike around with him.

"Now if you don't want to hear a gory story, ladies, plug up your ears. Back in the twenties and thirties liquid lightning was the mainstay of economics around these chere parts, yes ma'am, and kept right on going, despite all the revenuers could do. A course, these good old boys would get into a territorial dispute from time to time, and since these were the days before industrial arbitration, don't you know, occasionally their mediation would be of the violent persuasion. Well, the woman of the man who ran this chere still we're talking about, had a reputation for this sort of mediation, prematurely sending both revenuers and corn mashers to that great still in the sky. One day someone or something found the woman at an inauspicious moment and decapitated her. And her body was found right chere." He waved his arm to indicate the water around the boat, then turned to them with wide eyes. "But, yes ma'am, they never…never…found…her head."

"Now there's a woman who knows how to give head," Barry Rhodenbarr muttered in the seat behind, then grunted, as if something sharp had suddenly jabbed him in the ribs, like Bernice's elbow.

Captain Darby swung back around in his seat. "I told you it was a gruesome story," he said into the loudspeaker. He backed the boat up and started off in a new direction. "Let's see if we can find something more pleasant to talk about."

Jim stood up and stretched his legs, glancing back at their wake, and then to Topsy Horwitz sitting alone in the back seat by the rail. Her lips were drawn and a sadness he hadn't seen in the last few days had returned to the green eyes half hidden behind her glasses. He ambled back and dropped into the seat beside her.

She looked up and gave him a sad smile. "Hi, Jim. I guess I'm taking a sorry break from the vacation break I was taking from sorriness."

He grinned and it echoed in a real smile from her. "I've been keeping an eye on you and you've looked like you were having a good time."

"Oh, I am. The vacation thing helped a lot. It's just that sometimes I miss him, like now as I'm thinking this trip would be so nice to share. Tell me it does get easier."

He shrugged, then nodded. "One of the things that makes it so rough, I think, is that we spend so much time taking care of them at the end, and then, boom, they've gone on. Suddenly all the care-giving is over and we have nothing to do. We're left alone, not only by ourselves, but with an emotional desert to walk through."

"And maybe feeling a little guilty?" Her questioning eyes stole a look into his from behind her small oval glasses.

"Uh-huh. Sometimes I'd ask Penny if she wanted me to bring her anything and she would say no, only to have her call out for something before I got down the hall." He shook his head. "I couldn't figure out why she didn't tell me while I was in the bedroom, until I realized what she really wanted was company."

Topsy took a deep breath and let it out in a sigh. "And toward the end I just wanted to get it over with, because I knew that's what he wanted, and then I'd feel guilty about it because it meant he would be dead, and I didn't want him to go."

He chewed on the inside of his lip. "Guilt hangs around like a dull toothache. I think we have to try to logically reason it out. Even if we might have wished, from time to time, it was over, we did nothing to bring it about. Even your husband, as you say, wished it was over. I've sometimes thought since that Penny was ready to go, but it was her body that was hanging on, as if it knew that once she left, it was an empty shell with nothing to sustain it. I comfort myself in knowing that no matter how happy she had been, and happiness is only in moments anyway, we could never touch the happiness she is experiencing now."

She nodded silently a few times. "But how can we be sure?"

He shrugged, then turned in his seat to her. "Let me tell you about a priest friend of mine. A holy man. He was telling me once about how the saints really looked forward to heaven. Hungered for it, he said. And then he mentioned that if he died and found it was all untrue, he was really going to feel cheated." He smiled at her. "That told me it's okay to have doubts. The big thing is to keep on trucking, as my kids say. And strange as it may seem, rather than weakening my belief, he strengthened it."

She cocked her head and let out another sigh.

Something flashed out on the water and he nodded toward it. "Look at that, a white heron."

"It's a snowy egret." She put her hand to her mouth, eyes lighting up. "Oh, I shouldn't have so brutally contradicted you."

"Looks like you're back on vacation."

TWENTY-THREE

DODEE SNUGGLED CLOSE to him on the leeward side as they ate. The picnic consisted of bag lunches, two sandwiches, four cookies, and a small can of fruit cocktail, with sodas and juices from a cooler. They ate at bench-tables beside the parking lot. The sun had not warmed the day, and back on their side of the lake they caught the full strength of the wind again, making for a chilly meal.

Across the table, the tall, lean-faced Farouk, his jacket engulfing a shivering Oxra, ate contentedly in a rough wool shirt as if it were a spring day on the Steppes, while the older Smiths from Arkansas and the Jacksons from Iowa huddled together at the next table. But Barry the Bear sat content in a short-sleeved shirt with his red baseball cap sitting backwards on his head, shoveling food into his mouth.

Jim took a sip of Coke, only adding to the day's chill, and looked across to Jody. "How many more of these canoe trips do you have planned?"

"We have the river trip tomorrow." Jody's brow wrinkled. "Oh, you mean Elderhostels? This is the last canoeing Elderhostel for the year."

"I was going to say, it's getting damn chilly."

"We'll head back"—she stood and raised her voice—"We'll head back as soon as Rebecca gets here with the other van. I called her and she's on her way. It's supposed to warm up tomorrow for our trip down the river. I hope."

"Tell me," Simon the Seal said, yellow porkpie hat

cocked on his curly head, "what's this special dish we're having for dinner tonight?"

"See," Phyllis held out a hand, "here he is on his second sandwich, with one of mine snatched away for a third, and already he's inquiring about supper."

"What they don't know, my dear, is that I am a general in the Army."

She stared at him. "And your point is?"

"All the world knows the Army travels on its stomach."

"Oh, gimme a break," Barry said with a groan.

Jody swallowed a bite of sandwich. "Frogmore Stew is our dish tonight. Everyone likes it."

"Can we get the recipe?" Jim asked.

"Uh-huh. It's pretty simple. Bring a big kettle to boil and for each person, add a quarter of a pound of sausage, cut into three-inch chunks, boil fifteen minutes, add two to three new potatoes, again per person, continue boiling another fifteen minutes, add two small ears of corn, like in the frozen food section and boil for fifteen minutes. Well, if the ears were frozen, bring the water back to a boil for another fifteen minutes. Finally, add half a pound of shrimp with the shells on, again for each person, and cook for only three to five minutes, otherwise the shrimp gets tough. Drain off all the water and serve with cole slaw, rolls, and lots and lots of napkins. You eat it with your fingers."

Barry turned his rotund body to Jim. "Why ya want the recipe? Ya gonna cook it?"

"Jim's a good cook," Dodee said.

"You ate his cooking?" Simon asked. "And you're still alive."

"Well, that's kind of tricky. The only time I ate his cooking was on our last Elderhostel. We went to a cooking school in Baltimore and cooked our own dinner every day."

"That sounds like something I'd like," Topsy said. "How was the food?"

"For us it was great, but we had a couple of chefs die while we were there."

"Fagedaboudit," Barry said. "From eatin'?"

Jim held up his hand to her. "Don't go into it. We went there, we had a great time, we did a lot of cooking and learned lots of stuff, and that's it."

"And you bought me a Henckels chef's knife, remember. I love it, and I think of you every time I use it."

"Yeah, but what about the chefs dyin'?"

"Don't go there, Dodee."

She ran two fingers across her lips.

"Is that where you met?" Phyllis asked.

"We met in New Jersey on another Elderhostel," he said.

Phyllis looked at them. "So, how did it happen? You just walked up and said, 'Hi, my name is Jim'?"

Dodee glanced at him and then smiled. "We were studying bonsai, miniature Japanese trees. He volunteered to come help me dig up a tree—"

"Not volunteered. Coerced."

"—on the side of the road."

"Big mistake."

"And the police came along and arrested us. We were in jail for a couple of hours together."

Phyllis's mouth hung open. "And you're still together?"

Dodee reached out and took his hand. "Um."

"Not me," Barry said. "I'da split."

"That's 'cause ya got a split personality," Bernice said.

Elaine, Topsy's roommate, turned to Jody. "What's on for this afternoon?"

Jody raised her voice again. "When we get back, we have a nature talk in the Walter Cox Building. Then for those who have thawed out, we'll go for a walk." She turned at the sound of a van rumbling down the road. "Hey, here's Rebecca. Everyone ready to load up?"

They gathered up the remains of their lunches and scrambled aboard the vans, Jim and Dodee in Jody's.

"Brrr," Elaine said from the back. "Crank up that heater."

"Ya cold?" Barry asked, throwing out bare, hairy arms. "It ain't cold. Come to Brooklyn sometime and I'll show ya cold."

Jim put his arm around Dodee, who bundled in close. She gazed up at him. "Armstrong heater?"

"Use that expression, lady, and you're telling your age."

The van headed out and by the time they reached the interstate the heater was putting out big time, but Oxra, sitting in the second seat where she got its full force, and with Farouk's jacket and arm around her small body, still shivered.

Jim leaned forward. "You okay, Oxra?"

"I think I am catching something. A cold or something."

"I have some ibuprofen in my room," Dodee said. "I'll give you some right off and maybe you can kick it."

"Thank you, I think I need something."

When they got back to their room, Jim stretched out on the bed. "I could take a nap right now. Turn off the world and burrow down deep."

Dodee dug into her suitcase and came up with the pills. "You're not going to the nature talk?"

He stared up at the ceiling for a moment. "Well, I guess I am."

"No, sleep if you want. I'll take these to Oxra and head on over." She bent and kissed him.

"You could always stay and nap with me." He watched her eyebrows rise. "I meant a real nap."

She kissed him again. "I think I'll take in the nature talk. Besides, I want to see what story Harold's come up with now."

He listened to the door click shut and continued to stare at the ceiling. Screw Harold. He'd come back with some more wild theories. And Dodee would soak it up like a clue sponge. Always piecing puzzles together. Worse yet, succeeding.

But someone definitely screwed with Davis's body. The canoe didn't tangle itself up in the swamp. And maybe the sheriff did have a dynamite box. But to make a leap between that and the hydro-plant? Unless Harold really had come up with something.

Without you, Jim, he'd said, *I wouldn't have found the key.* What key?

Ah, shit. He got up, grabbed his jacket, and headed for the Walter Cox Building.

When he came in, Jody was introducing J. Douglas Cracken, a member of an old South Carolina family from the eighteen hundreds. She mentioned J. Douglas had a degree in something he didn't hear—probably bugology from all the dead beetle and butterfly creatures he had in flat cases—and was a professor at Clemson University.

Jim sat down next to Dodee as the bugologist started talking, and looked around for the FBI guy. "Where's Harold?"

"He's not back," she whispered.

Sonofabitch. He should have taken the nap.

Meanwhile good old J. Douglas talked about the environmental protection that takes place on Santee-Cooper lakes, and about stamping out yellow fever and malaria, both once prevalent in the area, with malaria still a threat to return. Two million people a year die of it in Africa.

Jim looked over to see the Cinnamons come in with Farouk, but not his wife. "Did you give Oxra the ibuprofen?" he asked Dodee.

"Made her take it while I was there and left some pills for later."

J. Douglas brought out his tray-boxes, full with local beetles, with the comment that there were some 350,000 different kinds of beetles in the world. Then he smiled and showed them one that looked like a beetle, walked like a beetle, and talked like a beetle, therefore it was a spider.

"Arachnids include the spiders, daddy-longlegs, scorpions, and ticks."

"Wait a minute." Jim raised his hand. "A tick is a spider, an arachnid?"

"Yes," J. Douglas said, "they're arachnids. Ticks are the most misunderstood of all the arachnids. Spiders have eight legs as you know. The thing about ticks is that when they're first born they have six legs, so you'd think they were an insect, but after the first molt they get another set of legs to make it eight."

J. Douglas moved from the beetles to flies and dragonflies and walkingsticks.

"What are those ugly things in that tray," Phyllis called out. "Are they what I think they are?"

"Oh," J. Douglas said with a smile, pointing to creatures four inches long, "those are roaches."

"Yech. And you have them around here?"

"Yes, these are all local—"

"That's enough for me." She turned to Simon. "We are never, understand me, never moving to South Carolina."

Which brought a bit of laughter.

"That's why we don't call it a roach," J. Douglas said. "We call it a palmetto bug so you tourists keep coming."

Which brought more laughter.

They moved on to butterflies and moths, which brought a lot of oohs and aahs from the women.

"Pretty aren't they?" Dodee asked, turning to Jim.

"Not even Solomon in all his glory."

J. Douglas tapped the tray with his finger. "All butterflies have pigmentation scales on their wings, so that if you rub them off, if they're yellow, they will rub off yellow, except these two." He pointed to two in the case. "They are of the Morpho family, meaning change. If you rub the scales off them they're clear like a refracting prism, so their color depends upon the angle the light hits them."

When J. Douglas finished with the trays, they went outside. The afternoon had warmed up and the wind had died, making it a shade on the chilly side of pleasant. He led them around the Walter Cox Building and stopped them at the interface where field merged into woods, motioning with the palms of his hands facing down, signaling for quiet.

"Hear that warbling?" he whispered. "I think that's a painted bunting. People come from all over to see it." He stole forward, everyone following with binocs ready, then stopped and turned to them. "It's probably the most gaudily dressed song bird in North America. If we can get to see it, the male has a royal blue head, a red eye ring, a chartreuse cape on its back, red underparts, black on the wings."

"A painted bunting?" Topsy asked.

Dorothy nodded. *"Passerina ciris."*

J. Douglas glanced at her, lips turned down as he nodded. "It's one of the southeast's most endangered birds, declining seventy percent over the past thirty years." He waved for them to follow. They stole forward until he held up his hand for them to stop.

And suddenly there it was, a small bird, about the size of a sparrow, then two more showed. Jim heard cameras click all around him before the birds flew off.

J. Douglas led them through the woods along the water's edge, and gave them a new theory about cypress trees. "We now believe they act like buttresses to stiffen the spreading roots, much as buttresses stiffened medieval church walls. This gives them the ability to withstand the high winds of hurricanes." And finally, he pointed out a pitcher plant, which grew in poor soil, but modified itself to catch insects to increase its nitrogen supply. "Flies are drawn by the odor, enter the throat of the pitcher, slide down the slick sides and sink into the enzyme soup, bingo, swallowed up alive."

Jim shook his head. He felt just like the flies. If Dodee kept getting sucked into Harold's theories, they could both end up in the soup.

TWENTY-FOUR

"I WANT TO GET SOME ICE," Simon Cinnamon said as the nature walk came to an end, pointing to a fork in the trail that led back to the dining hall.

"Get some sodas, too," Phyllis said, then turned to face what remained of the group. "Would all of you like to stop by for a drink? Simon packed enough bottles to open a bar."

Dodee shrugged and looked at Jim. He nodded. "Yeah, we'll come."

That got the Rhodenbarrs onboard.

Then Farouk turned down his lips and shrugged. "Of course."

"I have some snacks," Topsy said. "I'll bring them."

"Oh, we have some too," Dorothy Gramm added.

"Great, we can have a party."

Jim motioned toward the dining hall. "I'll go with Simon and pick up the sodas."

"Yeah, me too," Barry said.

So they ended up splitting along sexist lines, the women heading back with Phyllis.

The men broke out of the woods by the 4-H Center's challenge course, two wooden platforms, one twenty feet high, the second thirty, held up by a triangle of telephone poles ten feet on a side. On one corner two lines stretched to another pole fifty feet away, designed for walking on the bottom rope while holding onto the top, but a slip brought a twenty-foot drop into a sand pit. On the second corner a series of rope swings reached across to yet another pole, this one designed to hand-walk across and back. A wooden wall made up one side of the triangle with knobs and blocks attached to the outside to simulate cliff climbing. And the back side, which faced the dining room, contained ten vertical ropes tied to thirty horizontal ropes to form a rope lattice for climbing, fives kids at a time, to the wooden platform thirty feet up.

"Looka that," Barry said, pointing to the challenge course as they started by. "Ya wouldn't get me on that swing thing. Fagedaboudit."

"We had those for training in the Army," Simon said, shifting to his deep general's voice, "only higher and longer. Yes, sir, I slogged through them many a time, but I wouldn't want to do it now." Then he pointed to the rope lattice leading up to the top platform. "That's more my speed now."

"I could do that," Barry said.

Jim rolled his eyes. "Yeah, right."

"Yeah, I could." Barry stuck his hands on his hips. "Climb it like a money, up one side, down the other."

"I believe you."

"I could," he said, jutting out his jaw.

"I could still do the rope lattice," Simon said, leading the way over to the obstacle and looking up.

"Tell me about it." Barry glanced up and then turned to Jim. "Ya think I can't? I challenge yez. The last one up buys the sodas."

Farouk's lips turned down as he gazed up at the top, then grabbed onto the lattice and started climbing.

Jim shook his head. "What are you doing?"

"All right, go for broke," Simon said, pulling down his yellow hat and grabbing on. "The last one to the top."

Jim threw out his arms in a big shrug. "This is crazy. What are you trying to prove?"

"Yeah, well I'm goin'." Barry took off his gold chain

and stuffed it in his pocket. "Look down at ya from the top, chicken."

"I'm telling you, somebody's going to get hurt."

But they continued on, Farouk already up seven rungs while Simon was working on the third, and the short, stubby Barry on the second.

Jim shook his head. Talk about doing something stupid. He took a deep breath, let it out, shook his head again, and grabbed on. Really stupid.

He climbed up three rungs, feeling it jerk back and forth, unstable under his feet.

"Used to do this all the time," Simon said to someone, maybe himself, "no, sir, no problem."

Jim climbed another couple of rungs and looked up to see Farouk halfway there.

Really, really stupid.

He grit his teeth and kept climbing, not looking down, moving an arm up at the same time as the opposite foot, one after another. The cool afternoon had suddenly warmed up. He should have taken off his jacket. Then at the halfway mark, he moved out of the tree-line's wind shadow and caught the breeze full in the face, like a hurricane trying to blow him off the rope lattice.

Really, really, really stupid.

He looked up to see Farouk standing on the platform, a crazed look in his eyes, arms thrown in the air, like a desert warrior signaling his troops to attack. "I am a hero, yes."

Jim shook his head, grabbed the next rope rung and hauled himself up, puffing and panting, fighting the cold wind, sweating at the same time.

Keep going. Don't look down. He looked down.

Simon climbed six rungs below and a little ways to the right of him; Barry was stuck on the fourth from the bottom, staring up and to the left at him.

Jim grabbed the next rung and moved up, and again, and again, fighting the wind. Keep going. Too late to turn back now. Come down on the other side with the wind at his back.

He reached the bottom of the platform and the rope pressed flat against the wood, making it hard to grab and pinching his fingers when he did.

One more step. And now he had the platform edge in his hand. Sonofabitch, he was going to make it. Another rung.

And there was nothing on the platform to grab.

He bent over the top, snagging fingernails in a crack between boards, hanging half on, half over the side. Sonofabitch, what was he doing here?

Farouk sat staring at him with his wild eyes, big smile on his face. Oh, yeah, smile. He's about to fall to his death and the cocksucker's smiling.

He looked up to see Farouk standing on the platform, crazed look in his eyes, arms thrown in the air, like a desert warrior signaling his troops to attack. "I am a hero. Yes!"

Farouk reached out his hand and Jim grabbed it, held on, and scrambled over the side, rolling over onto his back, staring up at the blue sky, heart pounding, lungs pumping like a jackhammer.

Sonofabitch. What was he doing here?

He rolled over and sat up, looking over the lake spread out before him like silver carpet, the trees and forest on the other side reaching to eternity.

He sat on top of the world. Sonofabitch.

He climbed to his feet and threw up his fists. "Yes!"

He bent at the waist and looked down. "Barry." The stocky New Yorker still clung to the fourth rung. "Barry, get up here, you dumb shit."

Then he saw Simon at the halfway point, hung up in one of the loops by his right arm, his dangling feet scrambling to find purchase, a grimace of pain on his face that looked up to him as the yellow porkpie hat floated to the ground.

"Farouk, quick, Simon's in trouble."

He spread-eagled on the platform, swung his legs over

the side, clutching a crack between the boards. He reached for Farouk's hand, but the man was already over the side.

Sonofabitch, what was he doing here?

He stepped down to the next rope rung, holding onto board-cracks, then grabbed the top rung on the lattice, breathed a sigh of relief, and moved off the platform, climbing down, hurrying now, and pulled up next to Simon, Farouk on the General's other side.

"You okay?"

"I think I dislocated my shoulder." Simon held his right arm next to his chest. "The wind caught me and I slipped off."

There was a good deal of stress in Simon's eyes, and a gray cast to his milk-chocolate face.

Oh, God, was he having a heart attack?

"I can't figure out how to get down."

"We'll get you down," Jim said. "Barry." The man still clung to the fourth rung. "Barry, run and tell Phyllis to bring the car."

"I can't move," Barry shouted. "I'm gonna fall."

"Jump, you're only four feet off the ground."

"No, I'm eight feet—"

"Get down, you shit. Simon's in trouble. Get down or I'll come down there and throw you off."

"Jeez, okay, okay. Gimme a break."

"I don't want to alarm Phyllis," Simon said.

"We need the car," he said, staring at Simon's pallor. Shock or heart attack? Or maybe just stress? "In case something's broken," he added.

Simon took a breath and then nodded.

"Here's what I'm going to do. I'll straddle you, arms on each side, then you can lean against me and we'll walk down the rope."

Farouk threw an arm around Simon's shoulder before Jim could move. "I will do it." He straddled the General and smiled into Jim's face, the same crazy grin he had at the top. "Longer arms."

"Hey, I did it," Barry said from down on the ground, holding out his hairy arms and grinning like he had climbed Mount Everest. "I'm down."

"Go get the damn car."

"Okay, okay, jeez, gimme a chance to catch my breath."

"Okay, Simon, let's do it."

Step by step, Simon leaning back against Farouk for support, they walked down the rope, at last stepping off onto hard ground.

Simon's breath came more easily now, and the stress eased in his dark eyes, but he still had a way to go. "Don't tell Phyllis about this," he said. Jim nodded.

Yeah, right, like Barry would keep it a secret?

Simon nodded to Farouk. "Thanks for getting me down."

Farouk smiled his crazy grin and shrugged.

Jim picked up the yellow porkpie and handed it to Simon.

Simon grimaced in pain as he put it on left-handed. "If I ever try something like that again, Jim, shoot me."

"Count on it."

TWENTY-FIVE

A BURGUNDY MERCEDES sedan came charging around the lines of trees and bounced over ruts in the road, kicking up a cloud of dust.

"Oh, shit," Simon said, "here's Phyllis."

It bounded onto the field and barreled up to them before slamming on the brakes.

The driver's door flew open hardly before it had stopped, and Phyllis jumped out of the car, racing up and standing on tiptoe to throw her arms around Simon's neck. "Are you okay, honey? Tell me you'll be okay."

"Ow, ow, be careful of my shoulder."

"What should we do? Did you call an ambulance?" She turned to Jim. "Should we call an ambulance?"

Two more cars came tearing up before he could answer, his own blue Lincoln from the same direction with Dodee at the wheel, and coming from the camp entrance in the opposite direction, a blue Taurus driven by Leo the Lion.

Dodee hopped out and came running up, trailed by Barry and Topsy. "Do you need an ambulance?" she asked, cell phone in her hand.

"I'm okay," Simon said. "It's just my shoulder."

Phyllis held him at arms' length. "You're all right? It's just your shoulder?"

"Yes, it's no big deal. I'm all right."

Phyllis turned on Barry. "I thought you said he was having a heart attack."

"Who's having a heart attack?" Leo asked, his furrowed face intense.

"Hey," Barry held out his hands, "gimme a break."

Phyllis put one hand to her own chest and turned back to Simon. "Tell me, you're not having a heart attack?"

"I'm not having a heart attack."

"Jeez, he looked like he was havin' a heart attack, the way he wuz hangin' there."

Dodee put her arms around one of Jim's. "He's okay?"

He nodded.

"What's going on?" Leo asked, his dark eyes shaded under his straw hat.

"Hanging where?" Phyllis asked.

"Up there." Barry pointed up the rope lattice.

Simon glanced heavenward and muttered, "Oh, shit."

Now Phyllis turned on him. "What were you doing up there?"

"We weren't doing anything."

Barry held out his hands. "The last one up wuz supposed to buy the sodas."

Jim let out a long breath that sounded in the ensuing silence like it could be heard in Munich.

"You were climbing up there?" Phyllis said, breaking the silence in a shriek that could no doubt be heard in Munich. "For sodas?" Munich and maybe points east. "What are you, crazy?"

"Hold on," Simon said, raising up to his six-foot-two height and putting on his Commanding General's voice, "now everyone relax—"

"Relax, bullshit," answered the five-foot-one Commander-in-Chief. "What did you think you were doing? You think you're a kid?"

Dodee whirled on Jim. "Were you climbing, too?" Her cornflower blues scorched him.

"Now," he said, and hesitated, realizing he was about to say "relax."

Farouk patted Jim on the back and then himself on the

chest. "The Jackrabbit and the Falcon. All the way. To the top." He threw his fists in the air. "Yes!"

Dodee glared at Jim again. "Have your lost *your* mind? I expected more sense from you."

"It wasn't my idea. Barry suggested it."

"Oh, yeah, sure, blame it all on me. Fagedaboudit. I didn't go climbing way up there. I stayed down low."

"Because you froze after four rungs, you shit. Do you need to change your pants?"

Simon cleared his majestic throat, "Now everyone—"

"If you say 'relax'"—Phyllis swung her little body around, her hands on her hips, and glared up at her husband—"I'll punch your lights out. God, you're worse than the kids. I think you've been jumping into foxholes without a helmet too long."

"Hey, I'm hurt here," he said, deep voice changing to a whine. "Isn't anybody going to help me?"

"Right," Jim said, stepping forward, grateful to change the subject. "Let me take a look."

"You a doctor?" Barry asked.

"I'm a physical therapist."

"We should get Clyde the Coyote," Phyllis said.

Simon shook his head. "Let Jim do it."

He took Simon's arm, holding one hand on his back, and worked it around, bringing a grimace of pain to the man's face. "Oh, that hurts. Can we get back to the room? I need a drink."

Phyllis stared at Simon for another minute, then her face softened and she turned to Jim. "Is he all right?"

"I think it's just a sprain. Take him back to the room and I'll get some ice. You can check with Clyde if you like." He turned to Dodee. "Come on, let's get some ice."

Dodee walked silently beside him to the Lincoln, Barry tagging along, but it spilled over when they got in the car. "Damn it, Jim Dandy, you should have known better than to climb up there."

"It was no big deal."

"You could have fallen and broken your neck. What was the sense to it?"

He grinned at her. "You sound like Phyllis."

"Phyllis is right. You all acted like school kids."

He pressed his lips together and drove on. But Phyllis had spoken out of concern, love rather than anger. Was Dodee telling him something in a roundabout way? While he was trying to figure out how he felt about her, was she doing the same about him?

He stopped at the dining hall and hurried up to the ice machine on the porch, Barry tagging at his heels.

"Get the sodas," he said as he filled a plastic bag with ice.

"Me?" The eyebrows rose on Barry's stubbly face. "Why me? The last one to the top wuz supposed to buy. Simon never got—"

"Get the fucking sodas."

"Okay, jeez, I'll get 'em. I was only sayin—"

Jim turned on him.

"I'm gettin' 'em, I'm gettin' 'em." Barry held up his hands. "Simon's hurt. I should do it, 'cause I'm a nice guy. I wuz gonna do it. Gimme a break. Fagedaboudit," he declared, ending with his all-purpose expression.

Jim left the ice on the porch and crossed the dining hall to the kitchen. He found a freezer and rummaged around in it, coming up with a large bag of peas and diced carrots. Then he went back to the car, picking up the ice along the way, and drove back to the Conference Center.

"What are you doing with the peas and carrots?" Dodee asked.

"You'll see."

They knocked at Simon's door and entered to see him propped up on the bed, a glass of caramel-colored liquid in his hand.

"How's our patient?" Jim asked. "Get Clyde to look at him?"

"I couldn't find Clyde," Phyllis said.

While Dorothy and Topsy passed out snacks—crackers and cheese, petit fours, chips and dip—everyone joked and laughed, now that the danger was over, about climbing to the top so they didn't have to pay for sodas, and about Barry frozen on the fourth rung.

"Hey," Barry said, transferring his gold chain from his pocket to loop around his neck, "I stayed down low in case youse guys needed me to run for help. Later I wuz gonna climb right to the top. Besides, it was the fifth rung. An' I paid for the sodas. Ya know, bein' managimous."

"Oh, yeah," Bernice said, glancing to the ceiling, "you're managimous all right."

"What I'm sayin'. If I ain't managimous, I ain't nothin'."

Jim got a hand towel from the bathroom, wrapped it around the frozen peas and carrots, and slung it over Simon's shoulder so it rested on the clavicle and the scapula.

"Still hurt?"

"It's eased off some. This is the first time I've been iced down with peas and carrots."

"Old therapist trick. Makes a good ice-pack. Keep it on for half an hour." He turned to Dodee. "You said you have ibuprofen?"

"I have ibuprofen," Phyllis said, handing him a glass of orange soda with vodka.

"Give him four. It will cut the pain and inflammation."

She pointed to his drink. "I could put milk of magnesia in there."

"Very funny." He sat down on the floor next to the dresser. Dodee dropped down and sat cross-legged with her back to him, leaning against his chest. He kissed her on the neck.

Simon turned to Phyllis as she gave him the pills. "I guess I was a damn fool."

She smiled. "Everybody hear that? The General admits to being a damn fool."

"It has to do with being a man," Topsy said, eyes smiling behind the oval glasses. "Always have to prove something."

"I don't have that problem," Bernice said, holding out her hand to Barry, bracelets shifting on her wrist. "He's never proved anything."

"And also to do with age," Phyllis said. "Not only proving we can do it, but we can *still* do it. Growing older gracefully." She patted Simon on the cheek. "Never mind, you're still *my* General."

"Yes, I am, ma'am." He turned and gave a left-handed salute to Farouk. "But if it hadn't been for you, I'd still be up on the ropes."

Farouk stopped stuffing chips and dip into his mouth long enough to grin.

Topsy took a bite out of a petit four. "I read a quote about age. From Jack Falkson; I think it was Falkson. At twenty, we worry about what others think of us. At forty, we don't care what they think about us. And at sixty"—she held out a hand—"we find they haven't been thinking about us at all."

"Ain't that the truth," Bernice said.

Dodee turned to Jim. "Want some snacks?"

"Never turn 'em down."

She retrieved a tray of cheese crackers and offered them to him. "Anybody seen Harold?" She passed the tray to others.

"That guy," Leo said and grimaced. "If I hear about someone might be bombing somebody one more time, I'm kicking him out of the room."

"We missed you today, Leo," Dorothy said.

He stood up next to Farouk, both the same height, tall and lean. "I had some business I had to take care of. I'll be along tomorrow for the big trip down the river."

Topsy squatted in front of Jim and held out a tray of petit fours. "Have some before I eat them all."

He took a couple. "You seem to be enjoying yourself."

Topsy smiled and nodded, then looked into his eyes. ''You never answered my question the other night,'' she said in a private voice.

''What question is that?''

She glanced across the room to Dodee, then back. ''So, you fell in love again?''

''I guess I didn't, did I?''

''You are evading the answer.''

''I guess I am, aren't I?''

She glanced at Dodee again. ''She's a beautiful person, looks and style. You gave me some good advice. Let me give you some. Life is short and none of us is promised tomorrow. Decide and tell her.''

TWENTY-SIX

THEY HAD ONE MORE round of drinks and then started out for the dining hall, well lubricated, boisterous, and somewhat erratic. The General, arm in a sling Jim had made for him, yellow porkpie cocked at a jaunty angle, led the way. Farouk and Leo trod right behind him, and Jim was surprised to see they were all the same height, about six foot two. Leo and Farouk, both thin and gangly, had appeared to be taller.

The wind had died, leaving a pleasant evening; a couple of the brighter stars popped out as the sun set behind them.

Dodee came up and put her arm under his. "Harold's not back." She glanced up at him. "Think we should call the sheriff?"

"No I don't. He could be out having a steak dinner somewhere."

She shrugged. "Or lying in a pool of blood." He broke stride and stared at her. "Well, he could."

"Talk about melodramatic."

"He said he was going to check on something and would be back for dinner. Maybe—"

"Maybe he's still checking on it."

"So what do we do? Just ignore it?"

He took a deep breath and let it out. "If he doesn't show up by bedtime, we'll call. How's that?"

She shrugged, but made no response.

The General led the way through the buffet line when they got to the hall. "This can't be Frogmore Stew," he said, deep voice putting out the decibels, like he was feeling no pain. "There's no frogs in here. They should call it Frogless Stew."

Which got laughs from Dorothy and Topsy, who looked like they were feeling little pain themselves.

Jim loaded his plate and carried it to the table. Serve it with plenty of napkins, Jody had said. She wasn't kidding about that. If his pile of un-peeled shrimp, along with cocktail sauce, wasn't enough to stack up dirty napkins, he had four short ears of buttered corn, to say nothing of the three-inch chunks of juicy sausage and four buttered potatoes, everything mouth-watering and delicious and all eaten with his fingers.

When he finished, Dodee added six more shrimp and an ear of corn to his plate.

He smiled at her. "Are you trying to fatten me up for something?"

"I can't eat them and you look like you're really enjoying it."

He shook his head and pushed the plate back. "I can't eat another thing."

She leaned over to him. "Harold's not here. You said to wait and see if he showed up by dinner."

"I said by bedtime." He searched the room. No Harold. And no Oxra either. He saw Farouk putting napkins over a plate of food. The way Oxra had been feeling, Jim didn't think she would be enthralled with sausage and un-peeled shrimp. "Maybe Harold's back at his room."

"What would he be doing there?"

He peeled one of the shrimp she had given him. "He could be suffering from the same flu bug as Oxra."

"And if he's not?"

He ate the shrimp and peeled another. "We'll tell Jody." He popped the second in his mouth and started on the third.

She stood up. "Like me to bring you a piece of apple pie?"

He finished off the shrimp and glanced around before

spotting Clyde the Coyote two tables over. "I believe I will have a piece of pie. And I believe I'll have some ice cream on it. And I believe I'll have some sprinkles on the ice cream."

She leaned over and whispered in his ear.

He smiled up at her. "These shrimp would have to be oysters for me to take care of the horse as well."

He ate the corn she had given him, and the pie, and the ice cream with the sprinkles, becoming a charter member of the clean-plate club. They strolled back hand in hand to the Conference Center, but when they reached it and Harold's yellow Neon was still missing, he realized his options were running low, the most unsavory of which included spending the night alone in his Lincoln.

"Are you going to call the sheriff?" she asked, pointing at him.

He stared over her shoulder. Darkness had settled in and a big, nearly-full moon rose over the lake.

"I said, are you going—"

"I'm thinking. If we call the sheriff, he's not going to do anything tonight. Harold could be in Charleston living it up for all we know."

She folded her arms. "Then let's us go look for him ourselves."

He blinked at her. "And where would you suggest—"

"The hydroelectric plant."

"What are we supposed to do? Go rummaging around—"

"Check the parking lot for his yellow Neon."

He sucked in his breath and let it out. "Check the parking lot and that's it?" She nodded. He shrugged and waved her toward the Lincoln. "You owe me for this."

It took them an hour and a half to find the plant, driving along deserted back roads with only an odd light in a house here, a shuttered store there, a parked lumber truck next to a closed gas station, no signs pointing anywhere, and even the rapidly filling moon being swallowed by the dark of the woods around.

Lots of wrong turns. Each a frustration. Little conversation. Afraid of the cutting remarks that would spill out if he opened his mouth. And maybe she afraid of provoking them.

They finally pulled up to the well-lit plant, an island in a black sea, and eased into the parking lot beside what looked like the administration building. Deserted but for a handful of cars. None of them a yellow Neon.

"Satisfied?" he asked, managing to keep the venom out of his voice.

"What about over there?" she asked, pointing to the generating plant buttressed to the dam.

"Do you see any cars over there?"

"Maybe if we drove over—"

"There's no cars there, Dodee. He's not here." He hung his hands on the steering wheel. "You know, while we've been out goose-chasing, he could have come back to the Conference Center. Could be snug in his bed."

She reached out and put her hand on his arm. "Okay, at least we gave it a shot."

But when they got back, there was no yellow Neon.

"Now will you call the sheriff?"

"And what will I say? Hello, Sheriff, one of our Elderhostelers is missing."

She reached into his glove compartment, pulled out his cell phone, and held it out to him.

"This is stupid. There's not going to be anyone there at this time of night."

"There always has to be someone there."

"We don't really know he's missing."

"You can tell him that." She jiggled the phone. "Make the call, Jim Dandy."

He sucked in a breath and let it out. "You owe me for this." He punched in Information, got the number of Sheriff Darby's office, then punched that in. "Owe me big time."

"Sheriff's Department," came a woman's voice, sounding sweet and young.

"Hi, this is James P. Dandy. I don't suppose I could talk to Sheriff Darby?"

"The sheriff's gone for the day. Can you tell me what this is about?"

Jim told her about talking to the sheriff earlier and about one of their Elderhostelers being missing.

"You're out at the Cooper 4-H Leadership Center? Do you have a number there where he can reach you?" Jim gave his cell phone number. "Well, thank you Mr. Dandy. I'll let the sheriff know. He'll be in touch if he needs more information."

He closed the phone.

"What did he say?"

"She." He slipped the cell phone in his pocket and climbed out of the car. "She said he'll be in touch."

She climbed out her side and looked at him over the Lincoln's roof. "That's it?"

"That's it." He locked the door and came around the car.

"Harold might be dead by then." He shrugged. "You should have told her about the dynamite. That Harold knew something about it. Call her back."

"What?"

She held out her hands. "Call her back and tell her about Harold and the dynamite."

He sucked in his breath and let it out. "You're gonna owe me, really big time." He punched REDIAL.

"Sheriff's Department."

"Hi, this is Jim Dandy again, I just talked to you. I hate to bother you, but"—he gave Dodee a phony grin—"my girlfriend insists I tell you that this might be somehow connected to the dynamite the sheriff asked us about."

The line went dead for a few seconds, and when she

came back on it sounded like the tail end of a giggle. "Yes, sir. I'll be sure to pass that information along."

He slapped the phone shut. "There. That's it. No more."

"What did she say?"

He closed and locked her door. "She said she'd pass that along."

"She won't."

He put his arm around her and steered her toward their room. "You're probably right."

"Not after you told her that your girlfriend made you do it."

But halfway across the parking lot, his cell phone rang. He turned and held it out to her.

"Don't give it to me."

"You were the one who wanted to talk to the sheriff."

It rang again.

"Maybe it's not even him. It might be one of your children."

It rang again.

He shook his head. "Big time." He slapped open the phone and answered, "James Dandy."

"This is Sheriff Darby."

"Yes, Sheriff"—he grimaced at her—"I hate to bother you, but I'm out here at the 4-H Center, and one of our Elderhostelers is missing."

"I was told this has something to do with the dynamite?"

"Well, it might. Harold—you met him the other day—he said he had one more thing to check out and then he was going to call you. Has he called?"

"Who is this?"

"James P. Dandy. One of the Elderhostelers out here at the 4-H camp."

"And who was supposed to call?"

"Harold the Houn—ah," he turned to Dodee.

"Rucker."

"Harold Rucker. You met him. He's retired FBI."

"Oh. Him." He sounded like he had just looked into a commode someone hadn't flushed. "What has this to do with the dynamite?"

"Harold was convinced it had something to do with the dam." He shook his head. He sounded stupid. He didn't believe it. Why would the sheriff? "Look, I don't know if this has any validity, but that's what he was saying, and now he's been gone all day and his car isn't here. I just thought you should know in case there's a connection."

"What kind of car?"

"A yellow Dodge Neon."

"Okay, Mr. Dandy, I appreciate your concern."

Jim slapped the phone shut.

"What did he say?"

"He said he appreciated our concern."

"Is he going to do anything?"

"Oh, yeah. He's issuing an all-state bulletin even as we speak."

For which he received a poke in the ribs. Sonofabitch. He had to stop making smart remarks.

But she paid him back for the phone calls by the end of the night. In bed. Snuggled under the warmth of the blankets. They went on a ride to the bottom of the sea again, slower this time, less frenzied than on opening night, but with the same primordial call of grunts and groans and sighs at the end.

"How much do I still owe you?" she whispered, her still-heavy breath warm against his ear.

"Owe me? Oh. Paid in full."

She curled up against his chest, as if trying to contrive a way to maintain as much skin contact as possible, and tucked her head under his chin.

"I hope you're comfortable," he said.

"Um, I think so. You have a comfortable body."

He ran his hand over her back, feeling the smoothness of her skin, and allowed himself to dip into the sea of sleep, slowly settling—

"Maybe we're missing something."

That popped his eyes open. Missing something?

"I said, maybe—"

"I heard. What do you mean?"

"What did Harold say this morning before he left?"

He shook his head. "Dodee, darling, I love"—oh, God, what did he love?—"sleeping with you, but why do you pull these wild questions out of your, your whatever just as I'm about to fall asleep?"

She patted a smooth hand on his tummy. "I'm sorry. Go to sleep, sweetheart."

He closed his eyes. The L word. He'd almost said—what? That he loved her? Maybe that wouldn't have been such a bad thing. As Topsy said, no one is promised tomorrow. Except if it was a lie. Then he'd be no better than Harold, spouting off wild accusations.

Where *was* Harold? Clyde had been talking about the treasure from the Spanish galleon when Harold had run out. Which only added to the reasons for blowing up the damn dam.

Unless Dodee was right about missing something. Like what?

"I don't know," he said.

But the only answer he got was her slow-paced breathing.

Sonofabitch, she had done it to him again. Got him wide awake, wrapped up in a bunch of questions, then slipped silently off. He smiled and kissed the top of her head. Screw it. Tomorrow was another chapter.

TWENTY-SEVEN

THEY DROVE TO A REFUSE site beside the Edisto River where construction was going on and scarred trees hung tenaciously to life. A big sun hung in the clear sky, but the night chill still clung to the air.

Jim wore a windbreaker, red chamois shirt and his two-in-one cargo pants. Only his feet in sandals, were exposed. Dodee also wore her cargo pants, a red two-layer shirt, light jacket, with her feet in white socks and sneaks. Chances were they would doff the windbreakers when the morning warmed and their paddling exerted some internal heat, but to get started on their big canoe hike down river, he was glad of the extra protection.

On the other hand, the two bruisers brought along to help manhandle the canoes, as well as Jody and Becca the Body, wore short-sleeved shirts and shorts, bare skin heated by young blood so they weren't even goose-bumped.

He hated them.

Barry Rhodenbarr had his thick hairy arms exposed, but a sweater flopped over his back with the sleeves looped in a loose knot around his thick neck.

As insurance on the long trip, Jody had insisted everyone carry a change of clothes wrapped in a plastic bag.

Jim had stuffed his in Dodee's backpack.

Even so, he couldn't see any of the Elderhostelers doffing their duds behind a tree. Still, if it was a matter of being warm in dry clothes or freezing in wet ones, he'd make the change if he had to do a jig in the buff.

He and Dave Gramm and the Jacksons from Iowa helped the bruisers slide the red canoes down a two-foot red-clay bank onto the narrow sand strip at the water's edge. He picked out a canoe and dumped in Dodee's backpack—the dry clothes, water bottles, and two bag lunches—along with a paddle that reached to his nose

"Everybody," Jody clapped her hands. "Okay, everybody, listen up. Boy, for a small group, you surely are rowdy this morning." She motioned to the two bruisers. "John and Rico are going to take the vans to meet us downriver at a state park so everyone give them a hand of thanks."

Jim glanced around as they clapped, checking the smaller-than-normal group for the missing. Oxra still wasn't feeling good and Farouk had elected to stay with her. Simon's shoulder felt too tender to attempt the trip, but Phyllis teamed up in a canoe with Topsy when her friend, Elaine, had decided to go into Charleston. Dorothy Gramm wasn't there either, but David had teamed up with Leo the Lion.

Harold the Hound remained among the missing.

"The bottom falls away quickly from the shore so be careful launching," Jody said. "Remember to brace the canoe while your partner gets in. On a river, like here on the Edisto, the water is generally flowing faster and deeper in the center than along the shallow banks, which slow it down. But when we come to a bend, the outside curve will flow faster and deeper, while the inside curve will be slower and, because it's dropping sediment, maybe get very shallow. They had something about this on television recently, about how the bends in a river will slowly eat away the banks in the outside curves until sometimes it will break through between two wide curves, leaving an oxbow lake behind. If Farouk were here he could tell us all about it. He's restoring some of them on the Missouri river as wildlife refuges."

Jim put on his PFD and helped Dodee into hers, zipping it up the front and patting it on her chest.

"Are we having fun?" she asked.

"Okay, everyone," Jody called, "I'll lead the way and Rebecca will bring up the rear. Call out if you get into any trouble. After you launch, stay in this area until we're all ready to go. We'll stop halfway down for our bag lunch, but there's no potty pauses until we pull out at the state park." She made a circular motion like a western trail driver and pointed toward the center of the river. "Okay, let's do it."

Jim heard a scream and whirled around to see Clyde and Becky floundering in the water, their upside-down canoe pushing them along with the current into an overhanging tree branch. Yet, even as he noticed, one of the big bruisers zipped by him and plunged into the water, manhandling the canoe and helping them to shore.

Clyde the Coyote looked down at his wet clothes and turned to his wife. "I believe you did not brace the canoe for my entrance."

Becky the Beaver jerked her head up. "I believe I did."

"I believe you did not."

"I believe I did and you did not stay low in the canoe as I believe you were told."

"Okay," Jody clapped her hands, "everybody's all right. Good thing the vans are still here. You can change into your spare set of dry clothes and we have a few dry PFDs. Nothing's harmed."

Clyde nodded and shook water off his hands. "I believe I'll have my spare set of clothes."

Becky raised her chin. "I believe you can get them yourself."

Jim glanced around to see a lot of faces trying to hide smiles as Becky took out her dry clothes and tossed the plastic bag to Clyde, and they both stomped off to separate vans.

Jody gave a spread-armed shrug, but a smile lit up her

freckled face. "Okay, let's be careful launching. We want to have a calm, dry trip."

Jim braced the end of the canoe between his legs and turned to Dodee. "I believe I'm ready for you to crawl down to your seat."

"I believe I'll give it a try."

After she was seated with her paddle braced across the gunnels, he pushed off and climbed in, slipping into the seat and giving a couple of quick strokes to get away from the bank.

They rendezvoused in the middle of the river with Phyllis and Topsy as the Rhodenbarrs came barreling past.

"Jeez, Bernice, gimme a break. Stay on one side or the other."

Jim watched them go and turned to Phyllis and Topsy. "How are you two doing?"

"We're doing fine," Phyllis said, up front. "Topsy's handling the steering, aren't you girl?"

"I got a lot of practice when we did the swamp."

"I'm surprised you came without Simon."

"I'm not helpless, Jim."

"No, I just thought you'd stay to keep him company."

"If he's going to pull some fool stunt and hurt himself, he gets no sympathy from me. Besides, I've been looking forward to this part of the trip and he told me to go."

When all the canoes were launched, Clyde and Becky in dry clothes and a dry canoe, they started down river. Jim kept in the middle on the straightaways and swung to the outside bends to pick up added push from the current, overhanging tree branches and snags in shallows sliding by, scaring up a blue heron and great egret along the way, and an osprey that called out as it flew off. Somewhere at the back of the line someone started singing "Cruising Down the River on a Sunday Afternoon," no one complaining that it was actually on a Thursday morning. They passed an occasional river cabin, nestled in the woods, with small rickety docks. At one point a handsome woman in her early thirties stood on the bank dressed to the nines, as if she were heading for an elegant luncheon, or had just returned from a church breakfast, or was plying her trade to a paddling clientele.

Oh yeah.

They came upon a flock of swallows, that filled the air with a trilled chatter and the beat of their wings as they lifted in a swirling cloud, on their way to winter grounds in South America. A red-shouldered hawk studied them from high in a tree set back from the bank. And, giving contrast to drab trees in dormant dress, colorful butterflies danced on their dainty way.

When he finally followed Jody the Jaguar onto a sandy bank at an inside bend in the Edisto, the sun and the exertion had done its job. Jim pulled off his jacket and unzipped the lower part of his two-in-one pants legs, making them into shorts. He helped Dodee out of her jacket, stuffed it all into the backpack, and followed her up onto the sandy bank. He curled one arm behind his head and pulled down on the elbow with the other hand, putting a seventeen-second stretch-stress on his back muscles, then repeated it on the opposite side, and glanced around.

Two cabins, deserted this midweek morning of October, gave each other a cold shoulder as one faced up river at the bend, the other down; tall grass and two oaks occupied a no-man's triangle in between.

"How far do we have to go?" Dodee asked.

"We're about halfway," Jody answered as she rewrapped the band around her blond ponytail. "Figure what we've done, and that's what we have left."

"Before we can go to the toilet?" Barry asked, pronouncing it "terlet," as he climbed out of his canoe and trudged up the bank.

"Have to hang in there."

"Maybe I gotta go walk in the woods."

Topsy and Phyllis edged their canoe up on the sandy bank. "This our lunch stop?" Phyllis asked.

"Welcome to chez sandbank."

They ate sitting in the canoes pulled up dry on the bank like a bunch of Indians before the white man came, a bunch of well-ripened Indians.

Jim took a bite of ham and cheese sandwich and turned to Jody. "Are we still going to the power plant this afternoon?"

"Uh-huh. It won't be so bad." Jody looked at her watch. "It's eleven now. By the time we're finished paddling and touring the plant, we'll get you home good and hungry for dinner."

"We having Frogmore Stew again?" Jim asked.

Jody laughed. "No, that's a one time per trip entry. Did you like it?"

"Messy, but I liked it."

"Yeah, ya liked it," Barry said. "See the pile a shrimp and sausage he put away?"

Topsy peered at him from behind her oval glasses. "How *do* you keep so slim?" She turned to Dodee. "Does he eat like this at home?"

A small flush came into Dodee's face and she shrugged. "I don't know. I live in Kansas and Jim in Maryland."

"No, I don't," he said, trying to bail her out. "When I come on a trip like this, for a week, when I don't have to do my own cooking, I go a little wild. At home I watch what I eat and I exercise an hour or more a day. That's the key to staying in shape. Dodee"—he nodded to her— "leads a senior citizen aerobics group."

"It's called a chronologically challenged group and I only assist."

"And I see Clyde and Becky walking every morning." He turned to the bantam man. "What do you think, Doctor?"

Clyde swallowed a bite of lunch. "Exercise is essential in maintaining an optimum body weight. However, the benefits far exceed that. It strengthens the heart, helps keep the vascular system flowing, eases arthritis, relieves stress, builds bone, and provides good muscle tone for continuing an active lifestyle.''

Jim held out his hands in affirmation.

Leo the Lion tipped his hat down over his eyes and grunted. ''Whenever I get the urge to do anything, I lay flat on my back until it passes.''

''I also use weights and stress machines,'' Jim said. ''It's important to keep up your body strength. We've shown that you can take people in their late eighties and nineties, those barely getting around with a walker, put them through a mild series of muscle-building exercises, and they end up walking by themselves again. But it's better to maintain muscle than try to regain it.'' He glanced over at Clyde. ''I'm talking from a physical therapist standpoint.''

''You have no argument from me.''

''Three things you can do to take control of improving your health. Quit smoking, if you smoke. Eat a sensible diet with plenty of fiber. And exercise. The only caveat is to start out slow and easy and with guidance.''

Phyllis smiled at him. ''Does that include climbing rope ladders for sodas?''

Dodee shook her head. ''That's not exercise, Phyllis. That's stupidity.''

Jim held out his hands. ''It was not my idea.''

''Jeez, go ahead,'' Barry said. ''Blame it on me. What am I, a punching bag?''

TWENTY-EIGHT

HE PADDLED LAZILY as Dodee took pictures of an old
house, seeing something in it he didn't. The exuberance of
the morning had given way to a lassitude of early afternoon,
their chez sandbank long gone upriver. Up ahead and on
the other side of the river, Jody led the parade, followed
by the Smiths from Arkansas, everyone else strung out behind. He watched her swing her canoe into shore, and from
out of the shelter of the ten foot high river bank stepped
the two bruisers who had dropped them off.

"You have to go to the bathroom?"

"Don't remind me," Dodee said.

"Looks like relief is just a hundred yards away."

She put down her camera and picked up her paddle, dipping it into the water with renewed vigor. "Now is not the
time to tarry."

He guided them across the river and as they closed in he
saw a concrete ramp cut into the bank. The two bruisers
carried two canoes between them, one on either side, up to
the parking lot, where a brown SUV waited, a star on its
rear door. The khaki-uniformed Sheriff Ward Darby leaned
on it with one hand, the other on his hip, ankles crossed,
the dark raccoon-liked sunglasses turned to Jim and Dodee
as they touched shore.

"Oh, shit."

Dodee half turned. "What's the matter?" He nodded toward the sheriff. "Oh," she said. "I wonder if he's heard
anything about Harold."

"I don't know, but he's staring at us, like he's waiting to ask questions."

"Well, he'll have to wait 'til after I come out of the restroom. Can you bring the backpack, sweetheart?"

"Go. I'll bring everything."

She did, without further encouragement. He helped one of the bruisers carry the canoe up the hill, only fifty feet, but he was huffing and puffing like the big bad wolf by the time he dropped the thing on the ground. He continued on to the sheriff, who disengaged himself from the brown SUV.

"You called me last night?" the sheriff asked.

"Dodee and I, yes. She's in the bathroom."

"That would be the girlfriend who made you do it?" Jim shrugged and nodded. "Understand." He motioned to the canoes. "You all were out on the river all morning?"

"Uh-huh. We left after breakfast and had lunch halfway down." He worked his shoulders in a circular motion. "Thought I'd be more tired than I am, but we were with the current and taking our time."

"Nobody turned back?"

He glanced at the canoes being pulled up from the river. "We all made it. There was no place to turn back even if we wanted."

The sheriff gave a quick nod.

Jim realized he hadn't been making idle chatter. "Did you hear from Harold? Harold Rucker?"

"That was my next question," Ward Darby said, turning to Jim so he could see his own reflection in the sunglasses. "Obviously you didn't?"

"If he came back last night, no one saw him. And I didn't see his car this morning."

"A yellow Dodge Neon? What year?"

"I don't know."

The sheriff rubbed his hand across his jaw. "Tell me again what you told me last night."

He gazed at Dodee, out of the restroom and heading his

way. "Well, all this is Harold's theory. He might be retired from the FBI, but his ideas were way out."

"He was with the FBI, but never a field agent."

"He thought the purpose of the dynamite was to blow up the dam." He glanced at Dodee as she wrapped both her arms around one of his, and back to the sheriff. "First he thought it might be a terrorist attack, then an environmental extremist. Also that it had something to do with the bodies you found in the lake."

The sheriff nodded to Dodee. "How'd do, ma'am. I don't suppose you would have anything to add to Harold's speculations?"

Jim rolled his eyes, wondering what was coming next.

But Dodee only repeated what he had said. "All we know is he left yesterday morning saying he solved the case and needed to get one bit of evidence before calling you."

Darby nodded. "And you have no idea what that could be?"

Dodee glanced up at Jim. He sighed and held out a hand. "Okay, this is wild, but when Harold jumped up from the table, one of the men had been talking about the treasure from the sunken ship being stored in a bank in Georgetown. Like someone was going to blow up the dam to cut off the electricity so they could rob the bank." He shrugged. "I told you it was wild."

"Last night I would've agreed." Sheriff Darby folded his arms and stared down the ramp where the bruisers were pulling canoes out of the water. "This morning we found his yellow Dodge Neon in the parking lot of the hydroelectric plant."

Dodee opened her mouth to say something, but Jim squeezed her hand, cutting her off. All he needed was for her to blurt out it hadn't been there the night before, and then try to explain how they knew.

"Maybe he met someone and drove off with them."

The dark sunglasses turned to him. "That's probable. If it is, I'd like to get my hands around his neck. What bothers me more is that he might be a nut case, trying to blow the place up himself. At this point I don't even know if the man you met is really Harold Rucker. I'm waiting for confirmation from the FBI on that.''

"We're visiting the electric plant this afternoon," Dodee said. "Want us to keep an eye out for Harold—"

"Thank you, ma'am, I do not. If Mr. Rucker shows up, please call me right away. Otherwise, I want no more calls in the middle of the night. I don't want any more wild theories. I have enough for a million years. I'd 'preciate you keeping out of police business." He turned to Jim. "You too."

"Yes, sir."

With that the Sheriff strolled down to where Jody and Becca the Body were helping to load the canoes.

Dodee held onto his arm and glanced up at him. "Why did you squeeze my hand?"

"I didn't want to have to explain what we were doing at the plant last night. We're already too deep into this as it is."

"But someone drove Harold's car into the parking lot this morning. If he's not there, what does that tell you?"

"It tells me we are staying the hell out of police business."

She turned and nodded to where the sheriff and Jody were talking. "I guess that means we probably won't be visiting the plant."

"You don't know that. They could just be passing pleasantries."

The sheriff left as they finished loading the canoes and tying them down.

"Everyone out of the bathroom?" Jody asked, and made a head count with her finger. "We're heading back to the 4-H Center." Dodee gave Jim an I-told-you-so glance as Jody went on. "We'll have about fifteen minutes there if you want to change. But make it quick. The vans have to go on other business so we'll be picking up our bus, and maybe some of those who couldn't make the canoe trip. Then we'll head out for a tour of the Jefferies Power Plant.'' Jim gave her back a no-you-don't smile. ''Okay, let's load up.''

He picked up the backpack and followed Dodee on board. She took the window seat behind the driver, Rebecca. He sat beside her, putting an arm over her shoulder.

She rested her hand on his leg. ''Tired?''

''From the paddling?'' He shook his head. ''You?''

''I think I'll be okay if someone gives me a massage this evening.''

He shook his head. ''I have to do everything.''

He stared at her as the van charged down the highway, dark profile against the sunny window. Was there something going on in that head? The sheriff had been emphatic. Stay the hell out of police business. But if the sheriff was right about Harold trying to blow up the plant himself, you could bet your sweet ass James P. Dandy wasn't getting in the way. Except he couldn't see lumpy Harold skulking around planting dynamite.

Trouble was, the Dodge Neon hadn't been there last night. How did it get there this morning? Unless Harold *had* parked it there and gone off with someone. Except who? And where had he spent the night? And was Harold the Hound really Harold the FBI guy? If not, had the sheriff checked the Neon for dynamite?

Or had someone planted it there?

He closed his eyes and tried to picture the Conference Center's parking lot that morning when he went for coffee. Except for the Neon, all the cars had been there, wet with dew. And everyone, except Harold, had been at breakfast. If someone in the group had planted the car, it would have had to have been done after they started down river.

So who was missing?

Oxra was sick. And Farouk, who stayed behind to take care of her. Dorothy Gramm. Where was she? Right there were the two highest suspects on Harold's list. And Simon with his hurt shoulder. Elaine, Topsy's roommate, had gone into Charleston. Or so she said.

And Leo?

He glanced around, not seeing him, but he could be in the other van.

He bent over and whispered in Dodee's ear, "Was Leo with us on the river?"

She turned her face to him, brow wrinkled, eyes wide, nose raised.

He put a hand on her chin, turned her head, and whispered directly into her ear again. "Was Leo with us on the river? I'm trying to figure out who could have planted the car."

She looked at him again, then she reached up and turned his head, whispering right up into his ear. "We are staying the hell out of police business."

TWENTY-NINE

HE SMILED AS HE TURNED toward the front of the van, buffeted by the passage of two big lumber trucks coming the other way.

She had nailed him with the staying-the-hell-out-of-police-business comment. He had left himself wide open and she had driven an eighteen-wheeler right into his solar plexus.

Sonofabitch.

But she would crumble in the end.

It was one of the things he'd learned about her. Along with how she could change a blank piece of paper into an image with a few bold strokes of a pencil, some whimsy that reflected her laughter, or her tenderness, or anger, emotions visible in the drawing if only the observer engaged his imagination.

But with it went her obsession to assemble pieces of a puzzle. He had planted the possibility that one of their number had moved Harold's car. Now it fermented like rising yeast inside her head. She would no more be able to contain that speculation than you could cork an erupting volcano.

In the end, she would crumble.

And when she did?

Zingo.

Yet, when they arrived back at the Center, she still hadn't erupted.

Sonofabitch.

He changed out of his cargo pants and sandals into jeans

and trail shoes. He left her mutating from canoe-paddling to walking clothes and strolled down to the Hospitality Room.

Oxra sat there next to Farouk, small enough to be his child rather than his wife, except for the gray streaks in her long black hair, piled this afternoon on top of her head. She had a sweater draped across her arm. "How was the canoe ride, Jim?"

"It was fun," he said, picking up a handful of miniature Heath bars. "It was long." He made two circular motions with his elbows. "I'm surprised I'm not sore. How are you feeling?"

"I'm much better, thank you. At least I think I'm going to live now."

"She is much better, yes," Farouk said, giving him a firm nod.

An anemic horn tooted and they turned to see a yellow bus arriving.

Oxra stood up, Farouk towering over her. "Dodee going?"

Jim nodded. "She should be along."

Dorothy Gramm came in carrying an empty coffee cup, wearing painted speckled-trout earrings. She set the cup on the kitchen pass-through and turned to them. "We all going?"

"We are going, yes," Farouk answered.

"I'm waiting for Dodee," Jim said, and watched the three of them leave and, through the windows, join Dave Gramm on the way to the bus.

There they were. The major suspects of Harold the Hound. If the object was to blow up the dam, all the players were in place. He'd be an eyewitness—

He blinked. What the hell was he saying? Did he want to be there when the thing blew?

Phyllis and Simon walked by, heading for the bus.

Dodee came by and he knocked on the window for her to wait, grabbed another handful of miniature Heath bars—

if he was going to be scattered all over the landscape, he might as well be scattered full of candy bars—and hurried to catch up.

"Sure you want to go?" he asked and watched her nod as he followed along. "Because we could take a nap or go for a walk."

"No, I want to go. Don't you?"

He shrugged and nodded and followed her onboard the bus of doom. If something was going to actually happen, he wanted to be there to protect her.

Was that love?

"We been waitin' for yez," Barry said, as Jim came down the aisle. "Thought ya wuz grabbin' a nooner— ugh." He grunted in pain and turned to his wife. "Jeez, Bernice," he said, rubbing his side.

Jim flopped into a seat next to Dodee near the back, behind Topsy and across from Phyllis and Simon.

The bus lurched, circled out of the parking area, and rolled down the road.

On their way to doom?

Topsy, alone in her seat, swung her legs up on it, leaned against the window, and gazed over the seat back. "What kind of things do you carry in your gallery, Dodee?"

"Paintings," Jim said, giving her a smile.

"That's the way I started out, sweetheart," she said, putting a hand on his leg. "We've added other things as we've gone along, especially since my daughter, Alison, has taken over managing the place."

"That must be nice for you," Phyllis said, talking across Simon.

Dodee nodded. "It allows me more time to concentrate on my own work, and"—she glanced at him—"to take trips with a strange man."

"What things do you carry now?"

"We have a lot of sculpture, pieces in stone and metal, and some in wood. We have some experimental things, combinations of paint and sculpture, a small section of one-off designer outfits, jackets and skirts mostly, some textile hangings, and a few pieces of exquisite furniture, individual pieces, wooden chairs, an inlaid table. Some of the wood they are using is coming from old barns and old houses being torn down for new roads and highways. Even so, it's very expensive.''

"Oh, we know that.'' Phyllis motioned to Simon. "We're renovating an historical home—well, not we, but we're on a committee, a big old mansion in the heart of downtown. It will eventually be a museum, and to get the wood to make things like stair banisters and paneling in the library, we've been buying it from Mountain Lumber Company. They extract old stumps and logs buried in rivers like the Mississippi, and from old barns and houses, and turn it into lumber. The stuff is beautiful, but through the roof. We're competing with people who are doing the same thing all over the country, personal homes as well as community projects like ours.''

"Old wood is bringing top dollar now,'' Simon said in his basement voice.

"Give us one of your cards, Dodee. Maybe we can use a sculpture or painting in the house. Is your daughter married?''

"Allison? No, she was going out with someone, but it turned into friendship. But my daughter Wendy is married to a pediatrician—''

"My son-in-law, the doctor,'' Jim said.

Dodee gave him a smirk and went on, "And I have one grandson, whose picture I just happen to have with me.'' She pulled out her wallet. "His name is Corbett Jr., but we call him Corby to differentiate from his father.''

"Oh, I'd like to see,'' Topsy said. "And I just happen to have some pictures of my grandchildren.''

Dodee handed her picture to Topsy. "We were calling him Two, but we quit that because we thought it might stick. Imagine going through life being called Two.''

"Oh, he's beautiful,'' Topsy said, holding the picture.

Jim stared at her.

Of course, what else was she going to say? You gotta really ugly grandkid, I mean ug-ly? Yeah, buddy, that works.

"While this conversation has been scintillating, ladies," he said, moving to the empty seat behind Dodee, "talking about babies and all, I think I'll tear myself away and study the insides of my eyelids."

"Good idea," Simon said, following. "I think I'll join you."

Jim spread out on the seat and rested his head on the back.

"What do you think happened to Harold?" Simon asked. "I heard you were talking to the sheriff."

"They found Harold's car, but the man is still missing."

"Found it at the power plant I heard?" Jim nodded. "What does the sheriff think?"

"He thinks Harold met someone and they went off together. Maybe we'll see him when we get there. I can't see anyone taking his wild theories seriously."

"Unless there's a connection to the other bodies on the lake." Simon shifted in his seat and leaned across the aisle. "I served on a courts-martial once. A corporal was accused of blowing a sergeant away, and then going on to kill four others to cover it up. Before it was over, against the advice of counsel, he broke down and confessed. He and the sergeant were having an argument in the field, and when it got heated, the sergeant pulled out his gun, and the corporal pulled out his and it went off. So he said. When asked why he killed the others, the corporal said because they were witnesses. After you killed the first, might as well do the others if that will get you off. They can only hang you once."

"What happened?"

"They gave him corporal punishment."

THIRTY

HE STARED OUT THE WINDOW of the bus of doom as they passed the Jefferies Power Plant administration building, searching the parking lot for a yellow car, and breathing easier when he saw none. Someone must have moved it away, so, obviously, it probably hadn't been full of explosives.

They pulled up to the building that housed the generating equipment for the dam and parked in its lot. They were met by Daniel Marsh, mid-thirties, shock of wild brown hair and eyes to match, dressed in a blue uniform with an identification badge over his left breast and four pens stuck in a plastic pocket-holder.

"Good afternoon, everyone, and welcome to the Jefferies Hydroelectric Power Plant. I'll be your guide today, and if you have any questions, please just sing out." He motioned to the grassy slope beside him. "This is part of the dam that holds back the water of the Santee-Cooper, and as you probably know, water will seek its natural level. If there is a weak spot, the water will find it and break through. We had one such spot right here, some flaw in the concrete mixture or an air hole in the way it was poured, and we had to lower the level of the lake to fix it. Fortunately it was fairly high up. One of the things we don't want to do is lower the level of the water. There are one hundred and seventy-one thousand acres of water in the Santee-Cooper Lakes and each surface inch is worth a million dollars in electricity. So you can imagine what happens if we have to drop it three or four feet, to say nothing of the time it takes to do that."

"Has there been consideration given to tearing down the dam?" Dorothy Gramm asked. "It's been shown that dam construction upsets the ecology. It destroys water-edge forests and wildlife habitats." Her husband, quiet but intent, stood beside her. The thing was, Daniel Marsh looked nonplussed, nodding as she carried on. "For instance, sturgeon, once one of the most important commercial game fishes, was almost wiped out. Now that some dams have been destroyed, the fish are starting to reproduce in the lower Missouri."

Daniel Marsh held up both hands, palms facing her, as if she had a gun on him. "I don't believe we ever had sturgeon in these waters, ma'am. But you're right about the Missouri and the Mississippi; sturgeon were plentiful throughout that area, and in tributaries in Arkansas, Iowa, Illinois, Kansas, Kentucky, Louisiana, and even up north in Montana and the Dakotas."

Dorothy's mouth dropped open, obviously surprised the young man knew so much about fish. "So you see the need—"

"But those were channel dams, ma'am. Made for barge traffic. From what I've read, a lot of that traffic was only marginally economical at best. In fact, the Corps of Engineers was just recently in the middle of a brouhaha for trying to build more locks and dams in spite of one of their reports saying it wasn't needed."

Jim cast a look to Farouk, but the engineer for the Corps stood silently by with his arms folded.

"Now I agree that if a project is not economically viable," Daniel Marsh said, "or even marginally viable, ecology ought to take precedence. After all, we have to get involved to protect the environment for our children. And I guess you all have to protect it for your grandchildren. What kind of world do we want to leave them?"

Marsh turned and held out his hand to the power plant.

"But this is not a marginal facility. We produce one-third of all South Carolina's electricity, without using up fossil fuels and throwing contaminants into the air. The Jefferies Power Plant, because of our low electricity rates, supports industries and makes jobs available in what was a depressed area when it was built. It has also brought better health to the area. We eradicated malaria. At one time sixty percent of our children suffered from it. Finally, we do have a good record of taking care of Santee-Cooper's environment. We refrain from doing lots of things, like spraying for mosquitoes, because of the ecology. Does that make sense?"

Jim turned to Dorothy. The guy had completely floored her. Did Daniel Marsh have that depth of knowledge, or had someone primed him for Dorothy Gramm? But that made sense only if someone suspected she might be involved in blowing up the dam.

He glanced around. Which might explain why the parking lot was empty except for their bus.

"So," Marsh said, "we all have to be involved in protecting the environment, especially people like you who are—" he suddenly stopped, as if searching for the words.

"If you say 'old,'" Phyllis said, "you're dead meat."

Daniel Marsh grinned. "People who are advanced in wisdom."

"Marvelous," Barry called out. "Talk about gildin' the lily."

"Why don't we go inside and I'll show you how it all works."

Jim held up his hand. "I notice there aren't any cars here in the lot."

"Good point. The plant is automatic, everything is run electronically from the administration building. If something goes kerplunk in the middle of the night, then we have to rush over and manually pull levers and turn wheels and generally make a mess of everything. Otherwise, it's computerized."

Daniel Marsh led them inside and they were immediately engulfed in the roar of the plant. Five turbine housings rose up from a wide expanse of concrete floor, and one more, the nearer, looked like it had been laid out in a large circle on the floor but had never been built. Commercial windows interspersed with concrete columns walled the building on the down side, to the left, and on the right, a high concrete wall, part of the dam, which displayed dials and registers and an open staircase leading to rooms sixteen feet up.

Jim saw two men handling brooms and four others looking at dials and copying something onto pads.

"The plant is named after Senator Jefferies," Marsh said, raising his voice above the roar of the turbines, "who first presented the idea to the U.S. Senate. Later he became governor of the state."

Jim looked back to the men with the brooms. If everything was automatic, why were they here?

"The construction of the plant began in nineteen thirty-nine and took three hundred million yards of concrete to complete."

Or were they plants by Sheriff Darby in case someone whipped out a bomb?

"Supposedly two men are buried about here." Marsh stamped his feet a couple of times. "They got buried in concrete as it was being poured and couldn't stop."

You can't trust Elderhostelers.

"It cost thirty-one million dollars to build and power came online in February of 'forty-two, in time to supply energy to Charleston's defense industries engaged in World War Two."

They might decide to attack with canes.

"Today we not only supply power to South Carolina, but through a network of links, to Texas, Florida, Canada, all over."

Except, if Harold was right, maybe one of them had something more lethal in their pockets. He smiled. What would Dodee be able to make out of that?

"We are eighty-five feet under the lake level here and water flows down tubes through the concrete wall"—he pointed to the lake side of the building—"shoots under our feet, and spins the blades of the turbines, generating electricity. It's not how much water is in the Santee-Cooper Lakes, but the eighty-five-foot height, or wall of water, that supplies the pressure on the turbine blades."

Farouk raised his hand. "It is the water-head pressure, not flow?"

"That's right, the more head the more power we can put out."

"Reminds me of a woman I knew," Barry muttered.

"They are constant speed?" Farouk asked.

"One hundred and twenty RPMs."

"Not variable?" Farouk flopped one hand back and forth. "Either on or off?"

Marsh nodded. "On or off."

"Of course."

Clyde got Marsh's attention. "Is it cheaper to generate electricity with hydropower?"

"Hydropower, oh yes."

"Then why not put out maximum power all the time?"

Marsh nodded. "Good question. The answer is the Corps of Engineers." He turned to Dorothy. "Those same Corps of Engineers we were talking about earlier. About fifteen or seventeen years ago, they made us cut back because the flow was silting up Charleston Harbor. The interesting thing is, the Corps is paying us for the difference between what we can generate and what they're regulating."

"When the lake rose," Dorothy asked, "what got flooded out?"

"In some cases it swallowed whole towns, yes, and family farms two hundred years old. But for most, it was a windfall. This was in the middle of the depression, farm prices were depressed and jobs were scarce. Most folks ended up with more land than they started with."

Simon raised his hand, showing the light palm of his

milk-chocolate skin. "And what about the black sharecropper? What did he end up with?"

Daniel Marsh raised his hands and shoulders in a massive shrug, and for the first time looked less assured. "I don't know. I wish I could tell you they fared as well as everyone else, but knowing the times, and the way it was here in the south?" He gave another massive shrug. "I can only say Santee-Cooper provided a lot of jobs in its buildings and in the industries it spawned." He looked around. "Why don't I take you up on top and we'll show you how the Pinopolis Lock works; it takes boats from Lake Moultrie down to the Tail Race Canal, which links us through the Cooper River to Charleston Harbor. There's an elevator we use for freight for those who can't climb the stairs."

"That's me," Barry said, "I ain't walkin'."

Elaine called after him, "A freight elevator is just right for you, Barry."

Dodee turned to Jim and raised her eyebrows.

He raised his eyebrows back. "I can take the stairs."

He took her hand and they started up. He glanced over the railing to see the cleaning men and the dial-readers shifting position to follow, except for one who trailed Barry and Bernice to the elevator.

Maybe it was crazy to think of an Elderhosteler blowing up the dam, but someone was taking it seriously.

By the time he exited onto the power plant's concrete roof, taking the stairs had lost its appeal. The wind whipped up whitecaps on the sunny lake and he zipped up his jacket. Dodee shifted around to his lee, cuddling into his side.

"At least I'm good for breaking wind."

"Especially after eating Frogmore Stew."

"What? Oh. Not funny, sweetie."

Marsh pointed to a narrow pier running one hundred feet straight out into the lake with a white metal box sticking up at the end. "There's a phone out there for boaters to call when they want to use the lock. It's a demand system. We get a call and come up and lock them through. If you'll step over to the lock itself, I'll show you how we connect boaters to the Tail Race below."

Jim followed the others, down a small staircase alongside the lock, just enough to get out of the wind.

"That feels a lot better."

"What are those black things for?" Dodee asked, pointing to three-foot-wide floats seventy-five feet down in the empty lock.

"Boats tie up to them when they come in the lock, and they ride up and down with the water level."

He turned back to the main part of the roof where two men were sweeping and four others were checking out doors and testing the railings.

"What are you looking at?" Dodee asked.

He motioned toward them. "If this building is so automatic, why have those guys been busy ever since we got here?"

The wheaten eyebrows arched over her cornflower blues. "They're watching us?"

He nodded. "Makes me think we'll get out alive."

"Is that why you didn't want to come?"

Suddenly, water started roiling from the bottom of the lock and Daniel Marsh came to the top of the stairs.

"I've opened the gates, which allows water to flow into the lock. Once it reaches lake level, the top gate opens, a boat enters, we close the gates, drain the water, and open the bottom. The boater's on his way. The lock is seventy feet wide and we can take a boat up to one hundred and fifty feet in length, or a number of lesser boats together. At the time the lock was built it was the largest single-lift lock in the world."

Oxra came up next to Jim and stared over the rail.

"How are you feeling?" he asked.

She flopped a hand back and forth. "Better, but not really good. I told Farouk he should go this morning, but he would not without me. If I had stayed back this afternoon, he would have stayed also, even though he's been looking forward to seeing this plant.''

''What did he do all morning?''

''He has a woodworking magazine he brought along. *Fine Woodworking*. He was happy, but he should have gone.''

Jim turned and stared across to the administration building.

Someone had moved Harold's Neon into the parking lot that morning. If not Harold, who? Someone who had to know his car.

And if they wanted the police to think it had something to do with blowing up the dam, that someone had to know Harold was spreading those rumors.

He turned back to stare down into the lock, roiling water climbing up the sides.

Harold had said they planted the bodies in the swamp to draw attention away from the dam.

The rising water marched up the far wall, overtaking a recessed ladder, rung by rung.

But what if they planted the car here?

To draw attention from…where?

THIRTY-ONE

A BROWN SUV WITH A BIG star waited for them in the Conference Center parking lot as they pulled in. The short, wiry figure of Sheriff Ward Darby stood beside it with feet planted wide and arms folded. When their yellow bus pulled to a stop and the doors opened, he climbed aboard.

"Evenin' folks," he said in his southern drawl. "I'd 'preciate it if you all could gather in the Hospitality Room. I promise not to keep you long. Thank you."

He stepped off the bus and everyone followed. The afternoon had chilled into evening. The October days might contain a vestige of summer, but the nights bore a foretaste of winter, and Jim welcomed the warmth of the big glassed-in room.

Jim sat in a corner easy chair with Dodee sitting between his spread legs, leaning against him, his arms around her waist. Some of the group had run off to the bathroom, but eventually everyone crowded in. The Smiths from Arkansas sat right at the door, like they were ready to bolt for dinner, while the Jacksons from Iowa sat directly across from them by the kitchen, bookmarks for everyone else spread around the room. The wiry sheriff rested his backside against the pass-through while his deputy, a young man with a serious face and shifting eyes, stood beside him, the man's hand resting on his sidearm.

"We're all here," Jody said.

The sheriff unfolded his arms and stood as tall as his short stature allowed. "I'm sorry to be a bother, but we've

a bit of a problem you all might be able to help us with."
He looked over to where Jody was standing. "Am I disturbing your supper?"

She shook her head. "We can delay it if we need to."

He nodded and for the first time took off the dark glasses that gave him his raccoon look, although the impression remained in that the circles were now white from where they had been shaded from the sun.

"Harold Rucker is missing. I think you know that. This morning we found his car in the parking lot of the Jefferies Power Plant, placed there sometime last night or this morning."

"Harold said someone would bomb the plant," Leo the Lion said. "Maybe he was there checking it out. Did you search for him?"

"He's not there."

Barry jumped up from his seat and held out his hands. "Hey, we don't know nothin'. We had nothin' to do with it. We don't wanna get involved. Can we go?"

The sheriff stared at him for a long minute and Barry sat back down.

Simon raised his hand. "Could someone have met him and driven off?"

Sheriff Darby pressed his lips together. "We found traces of blood and skin in the car."

"Have you run DNA on it?" Simon asked.

"No." Clyde shook his head. "That would take weeks. But what about blood type? You could give that a quick check."

"And you are, sir?"

"Doctor Clyde Porter. I guess I was jumping ahead of you there, Sheriff. Sorry."

"We have checked the blood type against his records in Washington and it's the same as Mr. Rucker's—"

Topsy gasped. "Are you saying he's dead?"

Sheriff Darby heaved a big sigh. "No, I'm not. I'm just giving you some of the facts as we've found them, ma'am.

Maybe he cut his finger at one time or got in an accident. What I am saying is that we don't know where Mr. Rucker is, and seeing that we have his car, we have to investigate this as a missing persons. And, please, everyone, if Mr. Rucker does show up, call me immediately. But evidence at this time points to foul play. That's why I'm here. I'd just like to ask you all some questions, one at a time, to piece this thing together. I won't keep you long. I know you're anxious for your supper. I assure you I am too." He pointed to Jim and Dodee. "We already talked earlier. Have you anything to add?"

He shook his head, but Dodee leaned forward.

"Does this mean you're sure Harold is really Harold Rucker?"

"Fairly sure, ma'am. They faxed us a picture. It's either him or someone with a near likeness. Okay, I'll ask you all not to talk about this until I have all your statements. That will give me your individual impression without clouding it by what someone else might have to say. Who would like to go first?"

Barry jumped up. "We don't know nothing. We had nothin' to do with it. We don't want to get involved."

"Okay, sir, I'll take you first. The rest of you give your names to George here"—he motioned to the deputy—"and we'll go in order."

Jim followed Dodee to their room. He went into the bathroom and when he came out she was standing at the window, staring at the sun setting behind the trees and across the lake. He went up and put his arms around her.

"You're not saying very much."

She turned her head, smiled up at him, then turned back to the sunset. "I'm staying the hell out of police business."

He shook his head. Damned if she wasn't. Still, she had to crumble in the end.

"I hope nothing has happened to Harold," she said. "He might have been a busybody, but he was harmless."

He said nothing, only continued holding her, feeling the

warmth of her back against him, drinking in her closeness
and the smell of her perfume.

"Maybe we're looking at this all wrong."

He smiled at the cracking of her resolve.

"Maybe it's not Harold's blood and stuff. Maybe Harold's the perpetrator—"

"Oh, yeah, the perp."

She swung around in his arms. "Are you making fun of
me? Yes you are." She gave him a poke in the side.

"Ouch. You have this violent streak in you I haven't
seen before. Maybe I better get another room."

She raised her nose, lowered her eyelids, and slipped her
arms around his neck. "You're sure you want to do that?"

"Do what? I've just had a short-term memory loss. Sure
I want to do what?"

He kissed her, holding her close. It felt like she belonged
there. They had grown together over the past few months—
past year—and whatever he felt was more than casual
friendship. Something much deeper resided inside. He just
wasn't sure—

"Maybe," she said, breaking the kiss, "Harold is not as
innocent as he seemed. You listening, Jim Dandy?"

"I'm all ears."

"Is that what I'm feeling?"

"Don't be crass." He patted her on the butt for empha-
sis. Or the fun of it. "Okay, Harold is not as innocent as
he appears. He's a serial killer, destroying life. And Total
and Rice Krispies and Corn Flakes and—ouch. You're doing it again. I'm gonna report you to the sheriff."

"Do you want to listen to this or not?"

He stared at her until her eyebrows arched. "I guess I
do."

"Suppose Harold was using everyone, babbling about
the dam and conspiracies and playing the fool to cover up
something?"

"Like what?"

"That's it. I don't know."

"You didn't see Harold when he ran out the other morning. Whatever it was he thought he had discovered, he was on fire with it. Said I helped him find the key. Said we would be surprised. He might have been acting, but we're talking Academy Award performance if it was. I don't think he would have been able to do that if he had been"—he let it hang a moment—"the perp."

She sighed and shook her head. "Then, to quote you, what could it be?"

"And to quote you, I don't know." He patted her on the rear end again. "C'mon, let's get some dinner. We'll think clearer on a full stomach."

As they left their room, they heard the bus drive off and when they got down to the dining hall, Barry and Bernice were still at the buffet table, but, surprisingly, everyone else was already seated.

"How did you get here so fast?"

"Jody held the bus for us until we were all finished talking to the sheriff," Bernice said. "We came down in that."

"I'm gonna have some Herby's potatoes and peas," Barry said, spooning them on his plate.

"That's herb potatoes."

"Herb, Herby's, that's what I'm havin'."

Jim loaded up with two pork chops, applesauce, the Herby's potatoes and peas, and a salad with blue cheese dressing.

"Take two chops," he said to Dodee.

She shook her head. "I can only eat one."

"Take two. You might find a friend who's hungry."

"Find a friend?" she asked, but took two.

They sat down opposite Leo the Lion. Topsy sat next to him and Elaine sat next to her.

"What do you think of the sheriff, Jim?" Leo asked. He laid his hand palm-up on the table. "It looks like Harold knew what he was talking about all along. About the dam and the plant, I mean."

"That's a change in your thinking." He scanned the table. "Anyone learn anything when the sheriff questioned you?"

Topsy leaned forward, eyes peering through oval glasses, and spoke in a low voice. "All he told me was to make sure I called him if Harold showed up. But where is he? That's what I'm wondering."

"Who knows?" Leo shrugged. "Maybe someone threw him down an elevator shaft or something."

Jim took a forkful of herb potatoes and peas. "Were you sitting at the breakfast table before he left on Wednesday? What were you talking about?"

"Nothing memorable." Leo held out his hands, fork in one, knife in the other. "In fact, Harold wasn't saying anything for a change. Clyde was talking about that treasure from an old Spanish ship. Suddenly Harold jumped up like he was having a heart attack and ran out of the place."

"That was it? Anything before that, maybe?"

Leo's lips turned down. "The weather. Politics. General conversation."

"You talked to the sheriff first," Topsy said, glancing from Jim to Dodee. "What do you think happened?"

Dodee put down her fork. "We don't know anything either." She wiped her mouth with her napkin. "Jim called the sheriff Wednesday night because Harold said he would see us at dinner, but he never showed up."

Leo picked up his empty coffee cup. "What's crazy is, Harold had a million theories. He was an innocent, like a Sherlock Holmes looking for a crime to solve. Maybe because he was retired from the FBI and had nothing to do. Or because he was writing his book." He pushed back his chair and stood, tall and lanky, taking in the whole table. "It would be a damn shame if he stumbled onto more than he could chew and it got him killed."

THIRTY-TWO

JIM AND DODEE WERE strolling toward the Walter Cox Building with the Gramms when Dorothy stopped them halfway. "Hear that?" They listened to the call of a night bird. "That's a chuck-will's-widow, *Caprimulgus carolinensis.*" They heard it again: *chuck-will-wid-ow.* "They get their name from their call," she said.

They entered the auditorium to see the seats arranged in a semicircle like on the first night. Jody stood up front chatting with those already there. Others followed them in until just about everyone had showed up.

"Tomorrow night we're going to be making T-shirts," Jody said, "for those who want to give it a try. We do this with the children who come here in the summer, so we thought we ought to do that with all who are children at heart."

"What a nice way to put it," Topsy said.

Barry nodded. "Gimme a break. Yez just sayin' that 'cause ya don't wanna say we're old."

Phyllis threw up a hand for attention. "I prefer to say, those who are mellowing into fine wine."

Dodee smiled and glanced at Jim. "Except some have over-ripened into vinegar."

"Or some," Dorothy said, also looking in Jim's direction, "those who haven't taken a shower yet, have ripened into Limburger."

Jim held out his hands. "What is this? Beat up on Jim night?"

"Oh, I didn't mean you. But you have to admit, you do make a Jim Dandy target."

He held up his hands in surrender. "All right, all right, get it out of your system."

"As I was saying," Jody called, then raised her voice another notch, "as I was saying... Boy, I think you all are as bad as the kids. Give you one thing and you're off and running. But as I was saying," she added quickly, as if to forestall them from starting in again, "tomorrow we're going off to the Bidler Forest. We'll need to have our walking shoes on, it's a three-mile hike, all on a raised-wood walkway. I think you'll enjoy it, adding to our bird-watching collection, I hope. And then tomorrow night, our last, we'll be making T-shirts for those who want to. Normally, that's what we do tonight, but someone has borrowed the equipment, so we'll do our Elderhostel Swap tonight."

"What are we swapping?" asked the female half of the Smiths from Arkansas.

Bernice raised her hand and her bracelets slid down her arm. "If we're swapping husbands, I got one I'll give away."

Barry snapped up in his seat. "Fagedaboudit."

"After the rope-climbing trick," Phyllis said, "I might have one myself." She jerked around to the Rhodenbarrs. "Except, not for Barry."

"Jeez."

Topsy grinned, running her hand through her poodle-cut hair. "I'm open for giveaways, but not for Barry."

"Oh yeah, jeez. Like Jim sez, this is beat up on Barry night? Okay, I can take it. We got broad shoulders, huh, Jim? We can take it, huh, Jim?"

He smiled. "Barry, if you think I'm swapping Dodee for you, fagedaboudit."

"As I was saying," Jody called out again, "you all are not as bad as the kids, you all are worse. What we're swapping is information about other Elderhostels we've been on, those we like, those that were only so-so. I know, I just know, you all want to rave about the time you spent here at Santee-Cooper. Right? No, don't get started again. But if we have attended one that isn't so good, we should inform Elderhostel, because they want to know and will pull out their support if things aren't run right.''

Jim raised his hand. ''There's also an Elderhostel Notebook on the Internet, where you can report on one you've attended and ask about one you're planning. A lot give advice on the coordinator, which can make or break a program. Like Jody has made this a great program for us.''

That brought a round of applause.

Jody gave a slight curtsy. ''Thank you all. Okay, anyone have an Elderhostel they'd like to share?''

Dodee raised her hand. ''We went on a cooking one in Baltimore. And we had great fun.''

Jim nodded. Oh yeah, just great.

''We stayed at a hotel right downtown,'' Dodee continued, ''and we learned a lot about cooking.''

And how to hide dead bodies.

''And some tricks of the trade.''

And how to poison someone without using poison.

''We used the college's teaching kitchen for hands-on cooking, making our own dinner every night, and we're still here to talk about it.''

Just barely.

''The chefs recommended All-Clad pots and I bought some when I got home and love them, and they also recommended Henckels knives and a friend of mine''—she turned and patted Jim on the knee—''bought me one as a present.''

''I think I would have preferred roses,'' Phyllis said.

''Okay,'' Jody called out, ''cooking in Baltimore. Anyone else?''

Becky the Beaver leaned over to Clyde. ''Want to tell them about Sarasota's Asolo Theater?''

And Clyde stood up. ''We attended an Elderhostel at the Day Spring Episcopal Center in Florida. Good accommodations and food, and a great program run by Laura Smith, who is both an actress and a director. We attended three or four plays, met with the cast and talked to them, saw how the plays were staged and we discussed them both before and after we went. We met a lot of couples who had come back to this Elderhostel a second time. It was a great week.''

"Okay, very good. Theater in Sarasota, Florida. Anyone else?"

Elaine told about going to Grants, New Mexico, where they studied the Cities of Cibola, about the Pueblo people in the area, and visited Chaco Canyon and had super meals. One of the Smiths told the group about visiting St. Vincent and the Grenadines and sailing on a seventy-eight-foot catamaran.

Dorothy stood up, fluffing her hands through her Hamill-haircut. "We've been on sixteen Elderhostels—''

"Jeez, sixteen? That's a lot.''

Phyllis shook her head. "I met a couple who had been on sixty-four.''

Jim leaned forward. "I heard of a man who had attended over two hundred and twenty and was signed up for eight more.''

"Jeez, what does he do, live on 'em?''

"Wait a minute,'' Dorothy said, "you want to hear my story or not?''

"Yes, we do,'' Jody said. "Everyone listen.''

So everyone shut up while Dorothy told them about her Elderhostel to study Maori history in New Zealand, and the visit to the Great Barrier Reef and Ayers Rock in Australia. "Oh yes,'' she said, finishing up, "g'day, mate.''

Topsy glanced around. "I've only been on one other Elderhostel. That was with my husband before he died. The trip was thirteen days and we went to Antarctica. I want to tell you I never saw so much ice in my life. It was put on by Marine Expeditions of Toronto in conjunction with Elderhostel, and they did everything well. We got to see a bit of Buenos Aires, eating at various restaurants, and then Ushuaia, the southernmost town in Argentina. Then it was onboard ship, where we had good food, good lectures, and small, but clean, cabins. As for Antarctica, our trips ashore were wet rides in Zodiac boats.''

"Jeez, the Antarctic. So what d'ya think?''

Topsy smiled. "A great place to visit, but I wouldn't want to live there.''

When the meeting was over, Jim and Dodee strolled back with Topsy. Jim pointed to the Hospitality Room. "Think I'll go in and see if I can find a newspaper.''

Dodee turned to Topsy. "He's going to snarf some miniature Heath bars.''

"No, I'm not.'' He took another step. "At least I wasn't.'' Another step. "But it's not a bad idea.''

"I'm going on to the room, sweetheart. If you brought me a Heath Bar, I wouldn't say no.''

"Aha, see. You make fun of the snarfer, but you want to be a snarfee.''

He held the door for Topsy and followed her in.

"This week is flying by,'' Topsy said. "Tomorrow and then the trip back.''

"Have you enjoyed it?''

The door opened behind them and Clyde the Coyote came marching in. "Is the paper here? I missed it this morning.''

"Jim was going to look at it,'' Topsy said, then smiled. "Or was Dodee right and it was only an excuse?''

Jim turned to Clyde. "You can have it.''

"I just want to see if there's anything new about that old galleon off the coast. It must be fun, recovering treasure from underwater.''

Jim reached down in the bowl of miniature Heath bars— only six left—and scooped up five, tossing one to Topsy.

"I shouldn't be eating this.'' Then her eyes brightened behind her oval glasses and she peeled off the wrapper. "But I am on vacation.''

"The question is, are you enjoying it?"

"I am. I was even all right talking about Antarctica. In fact"—she opened her mouth and popped the Heath bar in—"I'm enjoying it so much, I might even stay on vacation for another week after I get home."

"As the guys in AA put it, one day at a time."

The door opened and Elaine's plump frame came through. "Any of those little Heath bars left?"

Topsy turned to Jim and pressed her finger to her lips.

He smiled. "I think there's one left."

"Only one? Oh well, sorry about taking it."

Clyde turned from the newspaper. "You can have them all, as far as I'm concerned."

"I think I'll head out and give Dodee her share of the booty. See you in the morning."

THIRTY-THREE

THEY STARTED OUT an hour late. Becca the Body's van had broken down, but they got it going. So they arrived at the Bidler Forest parking lot an hour late. Everyone piled out of the vans and Jim and Dodee walked with the Cinnamons toward the Visitor's Center.

"How's the shoulder?" he asked.

Phyllis opened her mouth to say something, but Simon held up a finger to her and she closed it, raising her nose in the air and looking away.

"My dear wife was probably going to mention something about my brain, but my shoulder's fine." He went to move it in a circular motion and gave a small wince. "Mostly fine. A couple of days in my hot tub and it will be good as new."

Phyllis turned to Jim. "Are you leaving this afternoon?"

"We're staying until tomorrow."

Dodee took Jim's hand. "Who's leaving?"

"Leo mentioned it at breakfast," Simon said.

Phyllis nodded. "And I think Clyde and Becky. I don't know about Oxra and Farouk. We didn't want to be here alone if everyone was bailing out."

Jim smiled. "'Fraid of the boogeyman?"

"With God knows what happened to Harold and those other two bodies in the swamp, I like the idea of safety in numbers."

He couldn't argue with Phyllis on that.

The sheriff thought the first death was accidental, and

maybe so. He also said the same thing about the Natural Resources agent, but on that Jim had to agree with Harold.

Thing was, Harold's theories had only gained validity when he ended up missing. Like he knew too much and someone took him out.

Took him out, ha. That sounded as bad as Dodee's "waste him."

But if someone planted the yellow Neon, wasn't it logical to assume they did it to draw attention away from the real...caper?

Oh yeah. Take him out, waste him, caper.

Yet for that to work, someone would have had to have known Harold was blabbering on about bombing the dam. Only the Elderhostelers knew that. Besides Jody and Rebecca.

If it was one of the group, who? And if it wasn't the plant, what?

They entered the Visitor's Center. A small lecture area to the right, items for sale to the left, windows around that faced onto the woods.

"I'm going to hit the head," he whispered to Dodee. "It's supposed to be a three-mile walk so you might want to go yourself."

"Thank you, daddy."

"Screw you."

"Promises?"

He ran into Leo in the restroom. "I hear you're leaving this afternoon?"

Leo nodded. "Got to get back to business."

"Hope you have a safe trip back. You were here in the spring. How was it then?"

"It was warmer, had a few more bugs, but aside from the people, it's about the same."

When he emerged he saw Dodee coming out of the ladies' room. "Aha, see. You listened."

"I always listen to you, sweetheart. I just don't always pay attention."

They had a short lecture by a chunky female ranger on the Bidler family, who came down from the north and bought big land holdings after the Civil War and went into the lumbering business. The land for the Sparkleberry Swamp had been purchased by the state from them. The ranger also pointed out some of the birds they would see, and the different kinds of trees they would encounter, some of which went back fifteen hundred years.

"There might even be one that goes back to the time of Christ," she said, pale blue eyes sweeping the group, "somewhere in the deep forest. We say that because we haven't completely surveyed the whole area, but probably not."

Jim turned to see Farouk standing beside him. "How about old wood like that? That would be worth something."

Farouk's lips turned down. "A lot of wood, yes, not old wood."

"Fifteen hundred years—"

"Cut the tree, the wood is green."

"Okay," Jody called out, "I apologize again for our late start. We now have a choice of a really, really early picnic lunch, or going through the forest and having lunch when we finish."

"Later," Simon said.

"Let's walk first," Dorothy said.

Only Barry opted to eat then, and when he was outvoted, bought himself four candy bars.

Jim followed Dodee out and they started along the five-foot-wide boardwalk built up two feet above the forest floor and swampy bottom. It was chilly, but the trees blocked the wind and the sunshine made it seem warmer than it was. The ranger pointed out trees—swamp cottonwood, red bay, water locust—and birds—thrushes and warblers—as they went along, but Jim felt natured-out and just strolled along enjoying the walk until the ranger turned to them at one point and indicated what was left of a rough-hewn wooden slab sticking into swamp muck.

"During the depression, and even after, moonshiners would set up stills out here where the revenuers couldn't smell the corn cooking. We believe this is one such still."

"When we were in Woods Bay," Simon said, adjusting his yellow porkpie, "the ranger pointed one out, and the same when we took a boat ride to the sunken forest."

"No doubt," she said, "they were all over the place."

Dodee swung to Jim, blinked, and swung back to the ranger. "How about in the Santee-Cooper Lakes before they were flooded?"

"No doubt. After they finished the dam, the rising water swallowed whole villages and forests. It's probably more a question of where they weren't than where they were."

The ranger started off again and Jim took Dodee's hand. "What are you thinking?"

"I'm thinking I should stay the hell out of police business."

He nodded and walked along beside her. Sonofabitch, she zinged him again. But if she had an idea, how long could she contain it?

Twenty feet farther she looked up at him. "Unless you really want me to tell you?"

He shrugged and kept walking. Now he had her. All he had to do was wait—

"Okay, I'll tell you."

He gave her a big grin.

"Well, if you don't want to know…" She turned, but he caught her hands and pulled her over to the side railing. She pointed at him. "You heard what the ranger said? It got me thinking about the old Spanish galleon and finding treasure underwater. That's what Clyde was talking about when Harold ran out of the breakfast hall."

He waited for her to go on, but she had fallen silent. "And your point is?"

"Suppose finding a treasure under the water triggered

Harold's thinking. Suppose it wasn't the galleon, but a cache of whiskey left over from the corn cooking days. Did you ever read *The Moonshine War* by Elmore Leonard?''

"I've read a lot books by—"

"A man hid a bunch of barrels of moonshine to use for his retirement."

He stared down into her eyes. "You're saying that maybe someone hid a cache of moonshine, and then the rising lake water covered it?"

"Why not? Everything fits. And why whoever killed Harold—"

"Now he's killed?"

"It explains why they planted his car at the power plant. To keep everyone away from the lake where they are probably pulling up barrels right now."

They were falling behind and he took her arm, leading her along the boardwalk. "That's really a stretch. Think about it. Clyde's going on about treasure from under the ocean, and right away Harold jumps up and says to himself, 'Eureka—'"

"Eureka?"

"'Eureka, there are tons of moonshine at the bottom of the lake and that's why people are getting dynamited.' That's one hell of a big jump in logic."

"But isn't it possible? Don't you think we should at least call the sheriff and tell him about it?"

"Oh, yeah. Remember how happy he was the last time we called? I'm sure he'll be ecstatic about this."

They caught up with the others before she turned to him again. "Whatever it is, I don't think it had to do with the power plant."

He nodded. "I think you're right."

"And that leaves something in the lake."

"Or in the swamp."

Her eyebrows raised. "Moonshine in the swamp?"

He shrugged. "It would have to be a hell of a lot of moonshine to be worth killing someone over."

"Then what?"

He shrugged again.

The group had stopped, gathered on the boardwalk around an immense tree; Simon stood on the ground, helping Phyllis down.

"What's going on?" Jim asked Farouk.

"Going inside the tree. Hollow inside."

He stepped back and stared up to the top. "How did it get hollow? Lightning?"

"Maybe Indians make a house."

He looked up it again, the width maybe six or eight feet in diameter. "If it was solid, that would be a lot of old wood."

"Green wood," Farouk said and stepped off after Phyllis climbed back on the boardwalk.

"Yucky down there," she said. "Big inside, but yucky."

He turned to Dodee when their turn came. "You want to see?"

"Sure," she said, and climbed down.

They had to bend down, on hands and knees to crawl in, but they both fit in the dimness inside, light coming from a hole somewhere high up. All that kept the tree upright was six inches of solid wood around the rim, the roundness adding to the strength like a monocoque structure.

He chucked her under the chin. "Want to set up house?"

"I want to get out before I have an attack of claustrophobia."

They crawled out and onto the walk and the ranger took up the point again.

By the time they finished the three-mile hike, everyone was ready for lunch. Jim helped Farouk, Becca the Body, and Jody line up three picnic tables and they all sat down in the bright sunshine, but a cold breeze kept them huddled together.

Jim opened his bag lunch of ham and cheese sandwiches. It could have been horseshit as hungry as he was.

"Are these good," Phyllis said, sitting across the table, next to Farouk, "or am I just starving?"

"They're good," Dodee answered, working ham and cheese and bread around in her mouth.

Jim stared at Farouk. "You keep talking about old wood, yet whenever I point out one of these old trees you say it's not old wood."

"Old trees, green wood."

Jim hung his head and shook it. "Of course. What am I thinking? Wood doesn't start aging until it's cut."

"Cut down and dried many years. It is cut for its richness. Big demand. Old houses restored, or fine one-design pieces of furniture."

"Expensive?"

"Big bucks." He pointed with his index finger and cocked his thumb to simulate a gun. "Like robbery. People buy houses and barns to get wood."

Phyllis nodded. "Tell me about it. I'm head of that committee I told you about, restoring an old house and it's costing us a fortune. These new dot-com billionaires are buying it all up for their mansions. We need solid wood for paneling and banisters, and that's not including shaping it. We really need American Chestnut, but, ha ha, try to get that."

Farouk nodded. "Sometimes I get an old stump or log, in my work, old wood, very good."

Jim stared at him. "Chestnut?"

"Sometimes."

"In your work? Opening up side channels along the Missouri River?"

"Yes."

Jim continued to stare at him, but Farouk had finished. "What, you just find the logs out in the field? Wouldn't they rot?"

"When we dynamite the dams, we pull up old logs, old stumps, preserved under the water and mud."

"Under the water." He blinked at Farouk. "Like under

the lake. Like the sunken forest on the boat ride the other day?''

"Of course."

Jim swung around to Dodee to see her cornflower eyes staring back into his.

THIRTY-FOUR

JIM TURNED AS THE VANS circled the parking lot and headed for the administration building. He glanced into the Hospitality Room, then down to the water's edge where Dodee stood, arms hugged around herself. A cold wind whipped up whitecaps that flashed on the sunlit lake. He strode down and wrapped his arms over hers, pulling her back against him.

"Just checked with Jody. The lake is eighteen to twenty-two feet deep, on average. Something else, remember the pontoon boat we took through the sunken forest? The captain said they left the trees to rot, and when they didn't they came back and cut off old-growth trees below the water line. If odd stumps and snags found in the Missouri are worth big bucks, as Farouk says, how about a whole sunken forest?"

She slipped around in his arms to face him. "I've been thinking a horrible thought. Suppose Harold isn't dead?"

He turned her and himself so he had his back into the wind, putting her in the lee of his body. "What's so horrible about that?"

"Maybe he's hurt. Maybe they shot him, but he got away and he's wounded out there."

"Out where?"

"Wherever he was going to find his clue," she said and buried her face in his chest.

He glanced up to the Hospitality Room.

Where would Harold go to find out if someone was stealing trees from the bottom of the lake? Which, on the face of it, didn't make a lot of sense.

"You're not talking," came her muffled voice from down in his chest.

"I'm thinking. We're still missing something. How would anyone hope to load up lumber trailers and haul them out without getting noticed?"

She pulled back and stared up at him. "Maybe they did notice. Maybe Hank Davis found out and that's why he was killed. And his friend, who the sheriff said accidentally drowned, maybe he was killed for the same reason."

He glanced back up to the Hospitality Room where Farouk, Leo, and the Cinnamons were looking in their direction.

The scary thing about Dodee's reasoning was that it was all starting to make sense.

The Natural Resources agent had been investigating a fish kill. If someone was dynamiting trees from the bottom, the concussion would send a lot of finny friends to that big bass pond in the sky. And if Hank Davis came upon them in the middle of it? As the Mafia would say, he sleeps wit' da fishes.

"Except"—he gazed down at her—"they still had to cart the logs out of here. It's a state resource. Even with all the other lumber trucks on the highway, someone had to notice them loading up at the lake. Don't you think someone would call the sheriff?"

Her lips turned down at that, and then her eyebrows arched. "Maybe they did."

"Sonofabitch, Dodee, you're saying the sheriff is in on it? Then why ask us about the dynamite box in the first place?"

"Maybe because it fell off a truck and they were desperate to get it back before someone else started asking questions. Think about it. He ridiculed Harold from the beginning."

"Maybe because he was ridiculous."

"And when you reported Harold missing, did he care? Only when you mentioned the dynamite. And when he met with all of us last night, why did he ask us to let him know the moment Harold showed up?"

"If he showed up."

"Because maybe Harold got away and he's afraid he'll call his friends at the FBI."

He peered into her big blues. If her reasoning was scary before, now it was petrifying. And if she was right, they could be high on the sheriff's shutting-up list.

She nodded. "I think they only wounded Harold and he may be still alive out there."

"Where?"

She wrinkled her brow, turned down her lips, and raised her shoulders. "I don't know."

He chewed on the inside of his lip, and thought back to the last time he had talked to Harold. If he eliminated everything that had to do with the dam and the plant, the galleon off the coast and the treasure in the Georgetown bank, what was left?

"Harold said he'd figured it out. That he knew he would. I thought, yeah, right, but now?" He shrugged. "He also said he had just a couple of things to find out and then he was calling the sheriff."

"See? What if he did call and the sheriff's in on it?"

He chewed on his lip some more. "Harold also said that without me he wouldn't have found the key."

"What key?"

He shrugged again. "The only thing I helped him find was the big log in Sparkleberry Swamp. Maybe, and we're loading up a lot of maybe's here, but maybe the Clorox bottle—"

"You said it drifted in."

"Not dragging half a concrete block it didn't. Someone deliberately put it there. But to mark the log? Harold said we'd be surprised. I'd be surprised at anything we found out there."

She pressed her lips together. "We never checked the other end of the log. One end was sawn, but if the other had been dynamited from the bottom, would there be evidence of it?"

"I don't know."

"But what else do we have to go on?" She stood back from him. "You know what this means? We have to go out there. No"—she held up a hand to stop him from speaking—"think about it. We can't call the sheriff. We don't know if he's in on it or not, but if he is, we could be signing our own death warrant."

He heard the sound of a car and turned to see Clyde and Becky wave as they drove away. People were starting to clear out. A few today, everyone tomorrow.

He drew in a deep breath and let it out.

"We could call the FBI."

"And by the time they got here?"

"But we don't even know—sonofabitch. Why didn't the sonofabitch mind his own damn business?"

He turned toward the dining hall where the vans and canoe trailers were parked.

Great. Just absolutely great.

"Okay, we need a canoe and a way to get it to Sparkleberry Swamp. I'll go check on it. You put some warmer jackets in the backpack, and water, and grab a few handfuls of Heath bars for energy." He looked up at the sun, rolling on its downward journey. "And grab a flashlight just in case."

He hustled along the shoreline, past the fishing pier and toward the swimming pool, wind whistling in his ear, whitecaps beating against the beach, and saw the red canoes stacked on the trailer outside Rast Hall. He found paddles leaning beside the storeroom door, ready to be stashed, and five PFDs slung across the trailer tongue. The thing was, rather than the six canoes on a trailer, he needed just one, but how to get even that to the swamp?

He strode around Rast Hall, past the dining room, to the

administration building and tried the doors. Locked. One lone van sat in the parking lot and he hurried to it. With no one around to give or deny him permission, he could take it and apologize afterward. Dodee's motto. Only the last time they had tried they almost ended up in jail.

The van's locked doors mooted the question. Sonofabitch. When one thing goes south, why did everything else have to go with it?

He strode back to the canoes. If he had some line maybe he could tie one onto the roof of his Lincoln.

The blast of a horn spun him around in time to see Leo the Lion wave. Another one heading out. He wished he was with him. Then Leo braked the car, backed up, and drove across the field to him, rolling down his window.

"Didn't know that was you standing there, Jim." He stuck out his hand. "I'm heading out."

He shook the man's hand. "Good to meet you, Leo."

"What are you doing with the canoes?"

"Ah, Dodee's got it in her mind to take one out." He heard the toot of another horn and looked up to see a white Toyota minivan with a roof rack, Farouk behind the wheel, Dodee in the passenger seat. "Here she is now."

"Well, I better get on the road. Maybe we'll meet on another Elderhostel someday."

"Never can tell."

Leo drove off as the minivan pulled across the grass to him and Dodee hopped out.

"I told Farouk about Harold and the logs and he's agreed to help us."

"Of course," Farouk said, coming around the car.

Jim nodded. "No one's around. I couldn't get permission to take one of these"—he slapped a canoe—"but we can always apologize when we get back."

Dodee smiled. "That sounds familiar."

A chain tied the canoes to the trailer with a lock, but it was unlatched and they pulled one free, manhandling it onto the roof rack. Farouk produced a line and padding from the back, tied the canoe to both bumpers and to either side of the attached roof rack.

"You look like you know what you're doing," Jim said.

"Oxra and I take canoe many times back home in Missouri."

Dodee gathered three red PFDs and they hopped in, Jim in front with Farouk, Dodee between them in the seat behind, and they sped out of the 4-H Center.

She showed him the backpack. "Got everything you wanted. I also threw in your cell phone in case we have to call for an ambulance."

"I have," Farouk said, opening a compartment on the console between the seats and holding it up. "We can take this."

"Jim's is already in the backpack," Dodee said.

"Okay," he said, replacing the cell phone and slapping the compartment shut.

They zoomed into the outback town of Davis Station with no one knowing how to get to Sparkleberry Swamp. Jim ran into the Bronco Club, a small drinkery, got directions and they zoomed off again, speeding along Rev. J.W. Carter Road, trying to beat the late afternoon sun.

THIRTY-FIVE

THE AFTERNOON WANED as they turned onto the Sparkle-berry Road, bounced over its rises and dips, humps and bumps, and into the deserted parking lot nested in a circle of trees. The top branches swayed in the wind, but down on the ground, when they pulled to a stop next to the concrete boat ramp, a cloud of dust overtook them and lingered in the air, settling in an eerie stillness. They untied the canoe, Jim in the back, Farouk in the front, and carried it to the water's edge.

Jim glanced at the sinking sun.

He sure in the hell wished he had Harold's rented power boat. It'd make for a faster trip out and back, and faster getaway if they ran into trouble.

Farouk set the front end in the water and Jim eased it in until just the aft end rested on the concrete pad. Dodee came down carrying the red PFDs.

Farouk held up a hand. "Wait." He grabbed one of the PFDs and turned back to his minivan. "I call Oxra."

Jim rested a foot in the canoe to hold it in place and faced Dodee. "Maybe you ought to wait with the car."

"Bullshit. You're not leaving me here alone, Jim Dandy."

"Farouk can leave you the keys. If anything hap—"

"I'm not staying, Jim."

He glanced up at Farouk talking on his cell phone and shook his head. "I should have thought about it back at the camp. I just want to keep you safe."

"I'm not staying, James P. Dandy. That's it."

He took a deep breath and let it out. "Okay. Get the backpack."

He slipped into his PFD as he waited, listening to birds squabbling in the trees for the choice spots to bed down.

Farouk came back down the ramp zipping up his own yellow PFD. "Ready?"

Jim nodded to Dodee as she slammed the side door of the minivan.

"You want to lock this?" she called.

Farouk spread his arms in an exaggerated shrug.

She hurried down with the backpack. Jim helped her into a PFD and turned to Farouk, who motioned for him to climb into the canoe.

He crawled forward, keeping low. It had been a long time since he took the front seat, but from what he had seen, Farouk knew his way around a paddle. Besides, he wasn't ready to argue with the wild look that always flirted around Farouk's eyes. He sat down and braced the canoe until Dodee climbed in the middle, dropped the backpack, and sat on it, hands on the gunnels. Then Farouk shoved off with one foot and slid into the back seat. A couple of power strokes and they were off, gliding through the still water provided by the tall cypresses and tupelos that sheltered the boat ramp and the parking lot.

That all changed as soon as they reached the channel.

The wind that had been playing with the treetops now hit them with full force, not enough to knock them down, but higher than on Tuesday, and feeling even stronger as they headed directly into it, chasing the setting sun.

He put his back into it, power strokes until his muscles tired, then shifting sides, Farouk matching him all the way, but with the increase of wind, and Dodee's weight in the middle, they earned each inch of progress. He was glad to have Farouk along. He and Dodee would have never made it.

He searched the brush line on either side of the channel,

tall trees sending long shadows, looking for other Clorox bottles marking other logs. The only place he could see where anyone could haul away the log was at the boat ramp, where fishermen came and went all the time.

"How can anyone hope to drag logs out of here and not get noticed?" he asked Dodee.

But it was Farouk who answered. "No need for secret. Need for permit."

Jim gave a couple more strokes, then switched sides. "What do you mean? You don't think they're loading up logs?"

"No."

He gave two more strokes, waiting for Farouk's explanation. None was forthcoming.

"Why blow up trees if they're not going to take them out?"

"To make study. Tree here, tree there. Enough money, get permit. Keep secret no one else get permit."

He stopped paddling and looked around to Farouk. "You can do that? Get a permit?"

"Of course."

"Why not just get the permit and forget about a study?"

"Too much money, too much time. Many agency approvals. Need lawyers, need environmental studies, need big bucks."

"And if there aren't that many trees, it's not worth it?"

Farouk gave a quick nod. "Of course."

Jim nodded. Of course.

"We're losing ground," Dodee said.

He swung around and dug his paddle in again. They passed the small side channel everyone else had taken on Tuesday, marked by the leaning cypress trunk Jody had called a fallen tree. He switched sides and Farouk followed.

"You know, this is all suddenly making sense. No one's pulling out truckloads of lumber, so no one notices, so no one calls the sheriff. That means the sheriff is probably not in on it. We could call him now and get the hell out of here."

"I have the cell phone in the backpack," Dodee said.

"No," Farouk's voice came from father back. "We wait and see what we find."

Jim pointed ahead. "Might as well, there's the Clorox bottle marker."

He added more power to his strokes, the goal in sight renewing his vigor.

Only one hangnail of logic nagged at him. If the sheriff had nothing to do with their scam, then all the original reasoning came back into play.

Someone had moved Harold's car to the power plant to draw the police away from here. But for that to work, someone had to know the sheriff would take it seriously. Which they knew he would because of Harold's ranting about blowing the place up. Which meant they had to know of Harold's ranting. Which meant they had to be part of the Elderhostel group. Which meant someone who had not been along on the Edisto River trip. Which meant two people, one to drop off the car and one to pick up the drop-offer.

Which meant—sonofabitch—Oxra and Farouk? Farouk who knew about dynamite. Farouk who knew about wood and getting permits. Farouk who had called someone from his cell phone back at the parking lot.

Jim glanced around, searching for a way out if he and Dodee had to abandon ship.

Not a lot of fun places around.

The swamp provided the only shelter, and that's where Hank Davis had ended up. Maybe Harold as well.

He turned to the sun, flirting with the horizon, and fixed the direction in his mind. If he had to make his way back in the dark, he'd be going in the opposite direction.

They turned in toward the plastic bottle and the massive log, awash but clearly visible now. Farouk steered them

alongside and Jim hooked it. He turned to see Farouk studying the log.

Dodee got to her knees. "Any sign of Harold?"

Farouk straightened up, wild eyes ablaze in the horizontal rays of the setting sun, and patted the log. "American
Chestnut."

Dodee turned to him. "How much do you think it's
worth?"

Farouk's brow darkened as he studied the length and
diameter of the trunk, some calculator going off behind the
wild eyes. "Maybe two hundred and fifty cubic feet, twelve
board feet per cubic foot." He blinked. "Three thousand
board feet of American Chestnut." He blinked again.
"Twenty thousand dollars."

"What? And how many trees are buried in the lake?"

"Hundreds," Jim said.

"Which is worth?"

"Millions."

Dodee gasped. "Millions? No wonder someone is trying
to get this wood out of here, even if it means killing someone to do it." She glanced at Farouk and back to Jim.
"Right?"

He stared at her without answering, concentrating on a
sound playing in the background, that of an outboard engine.

"What's the matter?" she asked.

"Someone's coming."

They all turned, gazing back in the direction of the parking lot. Long shadows reached across the water. Then a
pontoon boat cleared from behind a cypress, coming full-
on up the middle of the channel, *Two For The Road* em-
blazoned in red across its side.

Farouk swung to him. "They take us back."

"No," he shouted. "Let them go."

But Farouk jumped to his feet. "Here," he called, waving his arms, "over here."

Great, just great.

The bows of the pontoon boat turned and angled toward them.

Just absolutely great.

He turned back to the log as the canoe started drifting away and latched onto it with his paddle, the aft end swinging out toward the channel.

"Dodee, we gotta get out."

"Over here," Farouk called, "over here."

The roar of the engine flew across the water.

"What do you mean?" she asked.

"Over here."

"Those are the guys who killed Harold."

The boat was almost on them.

"They killed Harold?"

Farouk jerked around to him. "Who killed Harold?"

Jim glanced out to the channel. One man in the boat. With a rifle. "Sonofabitch."

He dove for Dodee as a crack rang out.

He hit her in the back, driving her over the side, the canoe tipping with them, turning over, another crack from the rifle as the water rushed up to meet him, and smashed him full in the face, and closed over him, a polar chill sucking out all noise and thought, until the sound of bubbles slipped past his ear.

THIRTY-SIX

HE REACHED FOR HER in the twilight water, touched her hair as she headed for the surface and grabbed on, pulling her back down, fighting both the buoyancy of their PFDs, and her hands trying to yank free. The dark shape of the log loomed out of the murk in front of him. He dragged her around the end, moving behind it before breaking the surface.

But the tree trunk, barely awash, provided little cover.

She came up bubbling and coughing and spitting. "What are you doing?" she yelled.

Another shot rang out and a slug slammed into the log to give her an answer.

He yanked her under again, turning from the log and heading for the swamp. He felt his feet touch bottom and drove them along, bumping into root tangles and smashing his knees.

Great, just absofuckinglutely great.

He popped out of water too shallow to stay under, snatched hold of her PFD and lugged her behind a big cypress, clamping a hand over her mouth. She wrenched it away, trying to gulp in air.

"We've got to get out of here," he whispered in her ear.

"What about Farouk?"

"He's in with them. We've got to get out of here. Now."

He grabbed her hand and hauled her along, shallow water now, but the bottom mucky and sucking at his shoes every step.

Another shot slapped into wood five feet to his left and high.

A lousy shot?

Or the boat rocking?

He plunged on, crawling over roots, zig-zagging from tree to tree, tugging Dodee after him, trying to build up a sight barrier between them and the boat.

Another shot, ten feet to the right. It wasn't the boat rocking. The guy had cut the engine and was shooting at sound. Which meant they were out of his line of fire.

So far so good.

Oh, yeah.

Feet sinking into the ooze. Tripping and scrambling over hidden roots and cypress knees like they were charging through an obstacle course wearing lead boots. Spiderwebs and Spanish moss slapping him in the face. Maximum energy for minimal distance.

Oh yeah, just fucking wonderful.

And on top of it all, he felt the adrenaline seeping out of his body, leaving his muscles bone weary.

"Jim," Dodee called between gasps, "I need to rest."

He ignored her. Can't rest. Any minute now and Farouk would come paddling in after them.

In fact, why hadn't he? Canoe was full of holes? Had to chance it.

He splashed behind a tree, found some exposed roots, and dropped into the mud, dragging Dodee down beside him. Blood pounded in his head, heart thumping, air charging in and out his lungs like a two-way vacuum cleaner.

Sonofabitch, he wasn't eighteen anymore.

Sonofabitch, he wasn't fifty anymore.

He turned to her, gasping, trying to get words out. "You...you...okay?"

She held a hand over her heart, chest heaving, sucking oxygen, and nodded for an answer.

He glanced up at the treetops and then to the woods around, twilight, with nightfall coming on fast, but fast enough to hide them from the boat? And even if it was, how the hell would they get out in the dark?

He gazed back toward the channel, shifting back and forth to get a view of the open water and the boat. Nothing. Not even the sound of an idling engine. Only the silence of the swamp. Which he'd take right now. Better than feet sloshing through the water after him. Or slugs smashing into his body.

She tugged at his belt and he faced her. "You okay?"

She nodded. "But…but what do…we do now?"

He scanned the nearby trees, trying to fix them in his mind while he could still see. His clothes clung cold and clammy to his skin, heat starting to seep from his body.

"We wait for darkness."

"What about Farouk?"

"Fuck Farouk. He has to be in on it."

"Why?"

"He could have taken Harold's car to the parking lot and left it there. Oxra picked him up. And it all makes sense. He knows how much the trees are worth, how to use dynamite, how to survey underwater areas, and about getting permits. And that phone call before we shoved off? How do you think that pontoon boat got out here so fast?"

The fading light deepened her big blues into dark gray. Her lips quivered, signaling a creeping cold invading her body as well. "I screwed up asking Farouk to come, didn't I?"

He shrugged. "No more than me, sweetie. I should have made you stay back at the 4-H camp."

Stars started popping out, the North Star already visible as the sky deepened into velvet, and the shapes around them turned into grotesque figures, witches' hands reaching for them from a haunted hollow.

The outboard engine started up, idling, telling him they hadn't given up.

Big surprise.

A shaft of light shot across the darkness. Narrow beam,

maybe a three-cell flashlight, limited, but could fix on him if he got in the way. It swung left and right, sending long fingered shadows scurrying before it, searching, probing.

The outboard engine kicked up a notch, changing the angle of the beam. Then the light snapped off. Replaced by oblivion.

Millimeter by millimeter shapes took form as his night vision seeped, thick as syrup, back into his eyes.

The outboard kicked up a few more notches, held for a few minutes, then roared to full lift and headed out.

"They gave up," she said.

He stood, helping her up and wrapping his arms around her. "You okay?"

"Okay? I'm freezing my rear off, my clothes are sopping wet, it's pitch black all around, someone's shooting at us, and you ask if I'm okay? I'm having a Jim Dandy time."

"Don't start."

"Damn, didn't I tell you not to bring me into this swamp in the middle of the night?"

"We have each other."

"True." Her hand brushed his cheek. "And if I have to be in this situation, I'd rather it be with you than anyone else."

"Me too. If you have to be out here in these conditions, I'd rather you be here with anyone else but me." He grunted as he got a small poke in the ribs. "Come on. We got to go."

"Go? Look around, sweetheart, we can't see shit."

"You can bet those guys haven't given up. Probably heading back for bigger lights and reinforcements. I don't want to be here when they return. We'll move up this side of the channel and when we reach the leaning tree, we'll try to make it back across to the road."

"It's pitch black."

"It's all I have to offer right now. The darkness will make it rough going, but it will hide us if they come back. I'll take whatever ally I can get."

"And if we make it across the channel?"

"*When* we make it across the channel, we'll either hike out to the highway, or try to get Farouk's cell phone from the minivan." He turned to her. "You wouldn't happen to have my cell phone in your pocket?"

"Wish I did, I'd call a taxi. It's in the backpack somewhere under the canoe."

"You are death on my cell phones, Dodee. The last one smashed in Baltimore; this one is lost at sea in South Carolina. Probably wouldn't have worked soaking wet anyway."

He took her by the hand, checked for Polaris, using the North Star as a guide, and started out.

But his prediction of rough going was an understatement. The boggy bottom sucked against every step. Bushes loomed out of the blackness to slap him in the face. Lurking roots either tripped him up or he stepped on one and slipped on its slick surface, sometimes dumping him into the water, sometimes taking Dodee with him. He rested only when he stopped to listen.

Silent night. Except for the cry of an occasional night bird. If frogs and toads and turtles were about, they were buried deep in the mud to get away from the cold. He just hoped the snakes and alligators were down there keeping them company.

A scream pierced the air and sent Dodee climbing his body. "What's that?"

"A screech owl."

"How do you know?"

"I know screech owls. We have them at home. Too bad Dorothy isn't here to give us the Latin name."

"You're not just saying that to calm—"

He put his hand on her lips.

It floated across the water, faint at first, but rapidly growing louder, the outboard engine returning.

Sonofabitch.

He searched the woods for a recognizable feature. Nothing. Much less Jody's leaning tree. If he had to guess, he'd give their progress as two hundred feet.

A long stream of bright light shot out, big broad beam now, a billion candle power, directed not at them, but sweeping straight down the channel, like where he and Dodee might be had they headed straight across the water for civilization.

A second light snapped on, sending out another broad beam, this time sweeping the woods. Two people onboard now.

Fucking Farouk.

Of course.

The second beam swept along with the boat, poking holes through the woods as it came.

He dropped to his knees behind a tree and pulled Dodee down beside him, hugging her close, and peeked around the trunk.

A blast of light smashed him in the eyes, then moved on, leaving him blinking in the dark.

Suddenly the outboard engine raced, as if thrown out of gear, and the first beam of light swung off the channel to join the second on a spot fifty feet back the way he and Dodee had come. Both beams transfixed a figure, half hung up on a low tree branch, half in the water. A man. The light-beams held there for a moment, then swung away, leaving behind a negative burned onto Jim's retinas, which slowly developed in his mind.

They had just found Harold the Hound.

THIRTY-SEVEN

DODEE LET OUT A LITTLE CRY and he put a hand to her lips. "It's okay," he whispered to her. "Okay."

"It was Harold," she said in a whimper.

"I know. Nothing we can do for him now."

She started sobbing and he hugged her, smoothing down her hair, encrusted with dirt and twigs and Spanish moss, just as he used to do to his daughter, Cee Cee, when some childhood heartbreak overwhelmed her. And in the darkness, in the cold, in wet and clammy clothes, a ton of mud caking his feet, with only the stars and God as witness, he admitted to himself the depth of his feelings for the bundle he held and soothed. He said a silent prayer, asking God to help him get her to safety.

He opened his eyes and saw a shadow on the pool of water where they crouched, and swung around to see, climbing above the horizon, filtering through the trees, the moon, a big, yellow, helium-filled balloon, slowly exerting its majesty over the night sky.

He raised her head and kissed her softly on the lips.

"I'm sorry for getting you into this," she said.

"You always say that, sweetheart, when we get into one of these things, and I always tell you it's as much my fault as yours."

"But this time—are we going to get of this?"

"We'll get out of this. I'll get us out of it."

He kissed her again.

Brave words. Long odds.

But he'd get her out of it, or die trying.

"And when I do, sweetie, you are really, really going to owe me big time." He helped her to her feet. "C'mon. We got to keep moving."

"Ah," she gave a little scream and jerked away, swiping at her arm, "something's there."

He brushed her shoulder. "Just a piece of Spanish moss."

"I thought it was a snake."

"A snake is not moving in water or air this cold."

He swung toward the sound of the engine, concerned they might have picked up on Dodee's cry. But the boat continued on, one of the big lights broken into many beams as it stabbed through the woods. Stands to reason. If they hadn't picked up on all their crashing about, they weren't going to hear Dodee's cry. Not with the outboard engine roaring in their ears. Which is something he should have realized. And they should have, too. If they were really smart, they'd cut the outboard.

He grabbed her hand. "C'mon. We got to keep going."

He positioned Polaris in relation to the moon, found all they had to do was follow its yellow brick road, and labored on, fighting to lift each foot from the suction of the mire only to have it sucked back in when he put it down again. But the full moon gave sight to the night, allowing him to see shapes and forms before bungling into them. Only the Spanish moss took him unawares, and he hoped his story to Dodee about the snakes was true.

But, God, he wearied.

Every muscle ached and cried out for rest. And Dodee's muscles must have as well, for she suddenly stopped.

"I can't go on. Why don't you go on without—no, don't leave me."

"I'm not leaving you," he said, glancing around. "We're in this together."

But where were they together?

The boat's light beams still played through the woods

down-channel. He would have to make a play soon or the
guys with the probing eyes would come searching back his
way. And if he tried hunkering down where they were, in
roots and mud and water, already freezing, they'd end up
with hypothermia by morning.

And those guys would still be out there.

Trouble was, how much strength did they have left?

He looked forward and saw a strange sight. Light from
above and below. The moon above, its reflection below.
Open water. With a diagonal bisecting it.

"Look," he said with a jolt of enthusiasm. "There's
Jody's leaning tree. It intersects the main channel with the
small one the group took. If we can make it we'll be able
to swim across to the other side."

"I don't think I can swim—"

"The PFDs will keep us afloat. All we've got to do is
doggy paddle. It's gotta be easier then stomping around in
this cesspool. Once we get across, we're on dry land."

He took her hand and they started out again, feeling a
new burst of energy, but fifteen minutes later it was only
the sight of the leaning tree, taking a long time getting near,
that kept him going.

Suddenly the muck was gone.

He took a step and landed in water up to his chest, still
thirty feet from the tree. A path of open water led off to
his right, all the way across the channel. But a big heat sink
gathered around to drain the warmth from his body.

Not going to be easy.

He turned to her, still on higher ground.

"Okay, Dodee, the water's cold. But we're gonna make
it. What we have to do is swim as hard as we can, both to
build up body warmth and to get across before it's all
sapped out of us. Can you do that?"

"You giving me a choice? Because if there's a bus coming by in fifteen minutes, I'm for catching it. Otherwise,
let's get on with it."

"First we need to take off our shoes or they'll weigh us

down and we won't be able to kick." He inched up onto a log and worked at the mud encrusting his laces, which smelled like rotten feet.

"Have you done this before? You haven't been a jungle fighter in the past you didn't tell me about?"

"Boy Scouts." He tugged off his shoes and tied the laces together, hanging them around his neck. "We had a little survival course at camp, and had to swim across a pond with our clothes on." He took her shoes, tied them together, and hung them around his neck with his own. "The ones who made it were the ones who were able to kick with their feet."

He eased back down into the water and helped her in.

"God, it's freezing."

"I told you it was cold. We've got to go like hell. Ready?"

"Don't lose me."

They started swimming and came out from beneath the tree-overhangs and into the open moonlight, the trees on the other side not that far away.

They could do this. Just keep at it. One arm after another. Feet kicking.

He glanced down the channel to see the lights still probing the woods, then glanced behind. Sonofabitch! She wasn't there. "Dodee!"

"What?"

He swirled in the water to find her ahead of him. "Oh. I didn't know you could swim that well."

"High school swim team," she said between breaths. "Never did it clothed in cold water though."

"You okay?"

"Keep up and shut up."

He smiled at the joke, yeah, keep up.

Not funny ten minutes later. His arms kept churning and his feet kept kicking, and she kept gaining. And the damn trees weren't getting any closer.

"You okay, sweetheart?" she called.

Oh great. Now she's concerned about him? He needed a new girlfriend. One who was mild and meek and helpless and minded her own damned business.

He heard the sound of an engine and swung toward the boat—it hadn't moved—then back to shore.

A car's headlights flashed high on the trees, rising and falling, rising and falling, as it bounced over the humps and bumps of the dirt road, then passed out of sight heading for the highway.

Farouk's minivan? It didn't sound like it.

They swam out of the moonlight and into the shadows under tree branches. He reached for the bottom and stood in only three feet of water.

Sonofabitch. They'd made it. Cold and freezing and shivering and weary as shit, but they'd made it.

THIRTY-EIGHT

HE CLIMBED ONTO THE SHORE, and helped Dodee up. She moved right into his chest, lips quivering, arms scrunched together. He held her close, trying to give her some of his body heat, but he didn't have a lot to pass over.

The beginning stages of hypothermia had probably already set in. Wet clothes weren't helping. They weren't going to get far in their condition. And nowhere at all if they didn't get moving. At least they were shivering. Had they passed that stage they wouldn't be thinking straight.

So who said he was?

He pushed her gently away. "We got to get going."

"You're always saying that. I can't go any farther."

"Hang in there with me, Dodee." He bent down and helped get her ice-cold feet into her shoes. "Hang with me and when we get out of this I'll take you someplace warm." He struggled into his own shoes, his toes so frozen they could snap off. "Hang in there and when we get out of this, we'll lie out in the hot sun until every goose bump feels like hot chicken soup."

He climbed to this feet and put his arm around her shoulders, guided her up to the road, and turned toward the parking lot.

"We need to be quiet when we get down here," he whispered, "just in case someone's still around."

She stopped. "Then why are we going?"

"Because a car just headed out the other way. Probably standing guard at the highway. It's too damn long to hike out anyway. Our best bet is Farouk's cell phone. With everyone out looking for us we should be okay.''

Oh, yeah, okay, right. Farouk's phone might not be their best bet, it might be their only bet.

They moved down the road, sticking to the shadows, and stopped in the shelter of the trees at the edge of the parking lot. The fickle full moon, their ally in getting through the swamp, would betray them now when they broke cover.

He gazed out on two cars. An SUV with a boat trailer hooked to it sat aligned with the opposite trees. And near the concrete ramp where he had last seen it—he gave a little sigh of relief—Farouk's minivan.

So where was Farouk? He searched for movement and listened for sounds, anything to reveal another presence, but picked up nothing, no smell of cigarette, no flame of a match, and the only thing that disturbed the silence was a call of a nearby owl, answered by a far-off friend, and the rustle of an animal in a tree on the other side of the clearing.

He took a deep breath and let it out. Truth time. ''You stay here—''

''No, we're together.''

''I'm just going to get the cell phone. I'll be right back.''

He gave one last look around, then stole straight across the moonlit clearing, trying to keep low and silent. He took hold of the minivan's door, said a little prayer it wasn't locked, and tried it.

The door opened. And a seven-zillion-watt dome light popped on. Enough to light up the whole fucking world.

He shoved across the seat, snapped open the console, and grabbed for the cell phone. Empty. He stared at it a moment, not believing his eyes, trying to will it into existence, then slipped off the seat and eased the door enough to cut off the light.

No phone. What now? He yanked open the door, searching the ignition, and shut it again. No phone. No key. What now?

The animal rustling in the tree drew his attention to the SUV with the boat trailer.

What were the chances it was unlocked? With a key? Or a phone? What other option did he have? He straightened up and headed for it. No need for stealth now. If the minivan's dome light hadn't alerted anyone, walking to the SUV—

"That's far enough."

Jim spun around as the voice cut through the darkness.

Farouk's tall, gaunt figure came toward him in the moonlight, with Dodee's much smaller figure in front of him.

"Nothing funny."

Except Farouk's figure didn't speak with Farouk's voice. Dodee came to him and he put his arm around her.

"Get over to the car."

"Leo? God, Leo, what are you doing here?"

"Around the trailer to the back door."

Oh, yeah, Leo.

Leo the Lion with a gun in his hand, which motioned him to get moving.

He held Dodee close and rounded the back of the trailer, the shadow of the tall trees not ten feet away. But could he make it?

"Stay close to the trailer."

With Dodee?

"No sudden movements."

What other option did he have?

"Or I'll shoot Dodee first."

Certainly not that one.

"Far enough. Hands on the trailer, both of you."

Jim leaned over and did as he was told. He felt Leo patting him down as his mind raced for some way out. But deep hypothermia must have set in because nothing bumbled down the pike.

"Okay, you can stand." Leo opened the back door of the SUV, took out a cell phone, and walked around to stand between Jim and the trees. He punched in a number and waited with the phone at his ear. "Yeah, Sarg, I got them. You can come in."

"The fishermen?" Jim asked. "You're in with them?" He held out his hands. "Why did you even come on the Elderhostel?"

"Because they're the only ones roaming the area this late in the year." Leo shook his head, raised his free hand and let it drop, and shook his head again. "It should have been so simple. Find out where the group was going and keep the boat somewhere else. But ohhhh noooo. No fucking luck." He kept shaking his head. "The story of my life. A chance to make four million bucks and one bad luck thing after another. First the weasel we hired for local grease double-crosses us and tries to get backing for his own permit. Which irritated the hell out of Sarg. So Sarg drowns him. Just knocks him in the water and holds his head under 'til the bubbles stop coming. Well, what are you going to do after that? Huh?"

Leo seemed to want an answer, so Jim shrugged, shoulders and hands.

"Then Davis comes looking for his fish-kill. Talk about bad fucking luck. He finds them as they're hiding that log in the swamp and pieces everything together. Well, in for a nickel, in for a dime, Sarg kills him, too." He shook his head again. "And talk about bad fucking luck, a dynamite box falls off the boat and who finds it? The sheriff. And who hears about it? Harold. Who expects a Harold to show up on an Elderhostel? A retired FBI asshole? Writing a book? Sees plots everywhere he turns? What are the odds? Huh? Talk about bad fucking luck. What are the odds?"

Jim shrugged again, staring at Leo the Lion slowly unraveling before his eyes.

"I kept trying to turn him off course but ohhhh noooo, not Mr. FBI." He threw out his hands and raised his head to the heavens, moonlight accentuating the furrows in his face. "I need a break. I need a fucking break."

Jim crouched, ready to rush him, but the gun came down before he could move.

"Want to know the killer?"

"The killer? You mean Sarg—"

"The cruncher? The killer cruncher?" His head shifted to Dodee and back. "Want to know the killer cruncher? Huh?"

Jim shrugged. "You going to let us go?"

"The cruncher is?" Leo said, voice fallen to a whisper, "it's worthless. Third- and fourth-cut trees. Yeah. Oh, right off we found three virgin growth specimens"—he drew himself upright—"and we're thinking millions." He giggled. "But that's it. The rest are worthless." He giggled again, shaking with it, mirth flirting with hysteria. "Talk about bad fucking luck."

"You *could* let us go," Jim said.

"We wouldn't tell anyone," Dodee added, voice quivering from either cold or fright.

The laughter fell away. Silence stretched. Leo shook his head. "I tried to dissuade you," he said in a flat voice. "Had Sarg plant the car at the hydro-plant. Told you how worthless Harold's theories were. Nothing worked. One more day. If you had laid off just one more day, it would have been all over. But when I saw you at the canoes I just knew you'd be out here." He shook his head again. "And here you are."

"Killing us will only make matters worse," Dodee said.

"Oh, I'm not going to kill you." He held his hand over his heart. "I am certainly not going to kill you. No, sir." Then he nodded. "Sarg is." And he laughed again, the strength of it shaking his body and dancing him around until it passed. "You almost got away, though. Gotta give you that. Thought you had. Give you credit for that. What I can't figure is why you came back to the car a second time."

Jim cocked his head. "A second time?"

"A second time. When I almost caught you the first—"

Leo turned to the Toyota minivan and back. "Whose car is that?"

Jim stared at him. Where was fucking Farouk? "It's mine. My car." And where was fucking Farouk's cell phone?

Leo shook his head. "No."

A beam of light bounced off the treetops behind him, like a vehicle coming down the humps and bumps in the road.

Leo stepped back, moon-glow glancing off his brow and deepening his eye sockets. "No, you have a Lincoln."

The lights again, someone coming.

Leo slipped under the shadow of the trees. "Whose car?"

A scream pierced the night, a frenzied, maniacal shriek. *"Allah Akbar!"*

And a Satanic-like figure fell from the sky like a bolt of yellow lightning, smashed into Leo, knocking them both to the ground. The gun fell from Leo's hand and a cell phone rolled onto the ground.

Jim took a step for the gun, but a hand snatched it up and a tall, gaunt figure jumped to his feet.

The bouncing lights were closer now, along with whirling flashes of blue and white, falling on and off a mad, mud-streaked face, giving the crazed eyes and wild grin a surreal incandescence.

Another scream split the air. "The falcon has destroyed the lion!"

And fucking Farouk threw both hands high in the air.

"I am a hero, yes!"

THIRTY-NINE

SUNLIGHT STREAMED through the window as he packed his bags. Morning had come too early. Even at ten o'clock.

Dodee came over to him as he zipped up the bag, turned him around, and crawled into his arms. "I'm still cold."

He held her and stared out their room window, through the trees to the lake.

"And tired," she added.

He knew about tired. They'd had to hang around while a sullen Sarg and dejected Bill were locked into cells.

The Leo the Lion, in between bouts of giggling spasms, had confessed to everything. And, finally, they took statements from him and Dodee and Farouk and let them go. By the time they got back to the Conference Center, the roosters were crowing.

It had been a hell of a week, and while he didn't want to go through it again, he wasn't ready for it to end either. Not before he had decided how he felt about her.

Well, that was dumb. He knew how he felt. But how would she take it if he told her?

He wasn't just blurting things out and taking a chance on getting blasted full of holes. Better to play it safe. Find out how she felt first. Tell her too soon and he could end up losing her.

"When do you need to be back?"

She pulled away and gazed up at him. "What have you got in mind?"

"Why don't we drive on down to the Keys and soak up the sun, like I promised you out in the swamp."

A smile spread across her face. "So I can pay you back big time for saving me?"

"That works, too."

He gave her a long kiss, interrupted by a knock on the door. He crossed over and opened it on Oxra and Farouk.

"We wanted to say goodbye," she said, and motioned to Farouk. "Thank you for bringing him back in one piece."

"Not me. He was the one who brought us back."

"Yes," Farouk said with a grin. "The jackrabbit and the falcon. We destroyed the lion."

"You destroyed the lion."

"Yes, I am a hero."

Oxra rolled the dark orbs of her eyes. "I shall have to live with this for the rest of my life. Come, we have to go."

Jim stepped out of the room and stuck out his hand. "Thanks for saving our lives."

Farouk shook his hand, and Dodee's, who had followed him out.

"Thank you for saving us, Farouk," she said.

A huge grin spread across the gaunt face and his wild eyes opened wide as he threw his hands in the air. "I am a hero, yes!"

Oxra shook her head. "Yes, darling, you are a hero, you have always been my hero, but if you keep saying that everyone will think you are crazy."

Farouk's arms fell, and his smile dropped, replaced by a crestfallen face.

"'Bye, Jim, Dodee," Oxra said. "Maybe we'll see you on another Elderhostel."

She headed for the parking lot with Farouk following behind, but he stopped after a few steps, turned to them, quickly glanced at the departing Oxra and back again, wild eyes and big grin, and silently pumped his arms into the air. Then he hurried to catch up.

Dodee's hand slipped into Jim's as they moved inside. "You never know about people, do you?"

"Nope. Unless they're named Barry and come from New York."

"I better go to the bathroom."

"Okay, I'm gonna start loading the car."

He gathered up their bags and carried them out, passing Elaine on the way back to her room, and met Topsy standing at the trunk of their car.

"How's the vacation going?" he asked.

She smiled. "Going to try it for another week. How about you? Come to a conclusion about your feelings yet?" He nodded and she nodded back. "Tell her?"

"As soon as I figure out how she feels."

"How she feels?"

"I'm not going to make a fool of myself, Topsy. I need to know it's safe to tell her without taking a chance on losing her."

Topsy shook her head. "Love is not about playing it safe, Jim. Love is about courage. It takes courage to open yourself up to let another in." She stuck out her hand. "Great meeting you, Jim. I'll say a prayer for you."

He shook her hand. "You too, Topsy. And I'll say one for you."

"Oh, no. I need a whole bunch."

He strode back into the room to find Dodee loaded up with her sketchbook, purse, and their hanging things.

"Here, I'll take those."

"No, I'll take them. In the meantime, sweetheart, if we're heading for the Keys, might I indelicately suggest you use the bathroom."

"Yes, Mommy."

And he did, washed his hands, and dried them as he walked around the room, looking in drawers and under the bed, making sure nothing was left behind. Then he hurried out to the car and checked the packing of the bags in the trunk.

A car horn sounded and he turned in time to see Topsy wave as she and Elaine drove by, leaving them the last ones in the lot.

Damn Topsy.

He shut the trunk of the car.

Easy for her to say.

He turned and stared toward the dining hall and the administration building.

Love isn't playing it safe.

He glanced over to the fishing pier.

Well, he was playing it safe.

And gazed out to the sun sparkling like diamonds on the lake.

Dodee came around the back corner of the car. "Are we camping out here, sweetheart?"

He looked down at the ground and shook his head.

Damn Topsy.

"You don't want to go down to the Keys?" she asked.

"Yes, I do."

"Then what's wrong?"

Sonofabitch.

He turned to her. "I love you," he said quickly, barely choking out the last word, suddenly emotional and almost sobbing. "I do."

"I know, sweetheart."

"You do?"

She came up and put her arms around his neck. "And I love you, too."

And she kissed him.

When she broke the kiss, he stared at her for a moment, then crossed his eyes, gave her a big crazy grin, and threw his arms into the air.

"I am a hero, yes!"

MEMORIES CAN BE MURDER

A Charlie Parker Mystery

CONNIE SHELTON

While stowing boxes away in her attic, Albuquerque CPA
Charlie Parker uncovers chilling information about her
father—and his work as a scientist during the Cold War
years. Worse, she now suspects the fatal plane crash that
killed both her parents was murder.

Determined to solve the fifteen-year-old crime, Charlie
quickly learns that asking questions is dangerous. Soon
dead ends—and dead bodies—have her worried she's
next on the hit list. But what secret is worth killing for
after all this time?

"Charlie is slick, appealing, and nobody's fool—just what
readers want in an amateur sleuth."
—*Booklist*

Available March 2002 at your favorite retail outlet.

WORLDWIDE LIBRARY®

WCS414

DEATH
OF THE
PARTY

A FAITH CASSIDY MYSTERY

Catherine Dain

Actress-turned-therapist Faith Cassidy knows that dreams are born and broken every day in Los Angeles, and only the strong survive. So when her bungalow is burglarized, and an impromptu block party gets an uninvited guest—a corpse wearing her stolen bomber jacket—she fights back.

The only eyewitness leads Faith back to a past she left behind: the world of hard partying and drugs. As a former lover tries to seduce her into returning to a dangerous lifestyle, she wonders if his reappearance in her life plus another dead body is more than a coincidence....

"A pleasant series addition of easy-to-read prose and intriguing characters."
—*Library Journal*

Available March 2002 at your favorite retail outlet.

WORLDWIDE LIBRARY ®

WCD415

Take 2 books and a surprise gift FREE!

SPECIAL LIMITED-TIME OFFER

Mail to: **The Mystery Library™**
3010 Walden Ave.
P.O. Box 1867
Buffalo, N.Y. 14240-1867

YES! Please send me **2 free books** from the Mystery Library™ and my free surprise gift. After receiving them, if I don't wish to receive anymore, I can return the shipping statement marked cancel. If I don't cancel, I will receive 3 brand-new novels every month, before they're available in stores! Bill me at the bargain price of $4.69 per book plus 25¢ shipping and handlng and applicable sales tax, if any*. That's the complete price and a savings of over 15% off the cover price—what a great deal! There is no minimum number of books I must purchase. I can always return a shipment at your expense and cancel my subscription. Even if I never buy another book from the Mystery Library™, **the 2 free books and surprise gift are mine to keep forever.**

415 WEN DFNF

Name	(PLEASE PRINT)	
Address		Apt. No.
City	State	Zip

* Terms and prices subject to change without notice. N.Y. residents add applicable sales tax. This offer is limited to one order per household and not valid to present Mystery Library™ subscribers. All orders subject to approval.
© 1990 Worldwide Library.
™ are registered trademarks of Harlequin Enterprises Limited

MYS01-R

CHANGELINGS

JO BANNISTER
A CASTLEMERE MYSTERY

It begins with contaminated yogurt in a
supermarket. Next, the tampering of
showers in a girls' locker room. Caustic
soda in baby powder. Cholera in cough
medicine. An anonymous note promises
much more—unless the town of
Castlemere pays a ransom of one
million pounds.

Superintendent Frank Shapiro, recovering from a bullet
wound, has been cleared for desk duty. But with Sergeant
Cal Donovan on holiday cruising the Castlemere Canal,
he must rely on Inspector Liz Graham as hysteria rises.

The situation worsens when the detectives learn Donovan's
abandoned boat has been found—and that the volatile
sergeant is believed dead by the hand of the blackmailer....

Available February 2002 at your favorite retail outlet.

 **WORLDWIDE LIBRARY**®

WJB410

A Great Day for Dying

Jonathan Harrington

A DANNY O'FLAHERTY MYSTERY

An assassin wearing a leprechaun mask shoots the grand marshal of New York's St. Patrick's Day parade, and Danny O'Flaherty is the only witness. But when police accuse Danny's friend and IRA activist Brendan Grady, Danny is determined to prove Grady's innocence.

While juggling teaching at an inner city high school, romance with a feisty Irish beauty, and threats that go beyond politics into the world of hard drugs and danger, Danny must reach back to his own past, to a woman he once loved, and the caprices of fate that can both bless and shatter lives.

Available March 2002 at your favorite retail outlet.

WORLDWIDE LIBRARY ®

WJH413